The Missing Room

Brian Jarman

for Julia and my family

One

Lloyd thought he'd woken up. It was hard to be sure because he'd been having dreams about waking up in strange places. They were feverish, vivid and surreal, the kind he often had since the illness.

He thought he knew where he was as well, although he would have been hard pressed to put it into words. Home, was the only word that came to him. Or a sort of memory of home. Because even though he was far from clear about his surroundings, there were certain things that were not as he would have expected. The silence, for example, which was more than the absence of noise – it was an almost audible stillness. But he couldn't have named the sounds that were missing.

And the light. It was unnatural somehow, too bright. It was coming through the curtains, but it wasn't sunshine. It was white rather than yellow. It was all familiar and strange at the same time. It was not an unpleasant feeling.

As he was puzzling over these things, Lloyd noticed a presence, sensed it before he saw it. He turned his head to his left, away from the window and the light. It was standing there looking down at him. It looked oddly cherubic, curly blond hair framing a serene face.

'You're not dead then?' it asked, and the questioner seemed sincere, curious. It was the voice of a boy, a teenager, and now that Lloyd was focussing a little better, the face was also familiar in an indefinable way.

'I was beginning to wonder myself,' said Lloyd, and his own mumbling sounded strange to him.

'Are you going to die?'

'Without a doubt.'

'I mean soon. Are you going to die soon?' the voice persisted. The face registered scorn at the feeble, obvious reply.

'I'm not planning on going just yet, no,' said Lloyd.

The boy stood there, scrutinising him closely as if trying to discern some visible sign of illness. Lloyd felt unnerved.

'They say you're not right,' said the boy. 'There's something wrong with you and nobody really knows what. Is that true?

'More or less.'

'They say there's something not quite right about me too, but in a different way.'

'What way?'

'Trouble at school.'

'You'll have to tell me about it later. I'm tired now.'

'You've only just woken up.'

'I know,' said Lloyd. 'That's just the trouble.'

As intrigued as Lloyd was by his visitor, he was glad when the boy left the room so he could give his undivided attention to his stupor. It was almost lunchtime when he woke up again a couple of hours later, feeling slightly more with it. But his arms and legs had what he thought of as that metallic feeling – not quite an itch, not quite pins and needles.

He was in the front bedroom at The Noddfa, the farmhouse where he'd spent his teen years with his Auntie Mona after his parents died. She was his father's sister. Mona by name, not moaner by nature. Mona the Martyr, more like. Marta, she should have been called, although there was a bit of the Tartar in her too. She was always taking someone in under her wing, as she had him, home to The Noddfa.

6

Even the name of the farm itself seemed suddenly significant to him, now for the first time: The Sanctuary, a strange marriage of the English and the Welsh, of home and away. He'd never thought about it this way before, but such ideas could bounce around his head now when he was bedbound. Despite his pain, his wooziness, it was a relief for him to be here.

He'd come home after many years away, not willingly, it had to be said. It was only when this damned illness got the better of him, and the doctors in Uruguay could do no more, that he had to face defeat as he saw it and come back. Not that the doctors in London could do much more for his strange jumble of symptoms.

And so here, he was, back at The Noddfa. For the first time in many weeks he was aware of a slight tingle of anticipation as he thought of the view of the rolling hills that lay the other side of the curtains. He pictured the house as if from an aerial shot, as indeed he had for so many years. There was a large photograph like this hanging up in the downstairs hall.

The house was an L-shape, the foot of the L a typical old black and white farmhouse, one storey with dormer windows in the roof. And added on to this, the larger, later stroke of the L, three storeys high if you counted the attics. It was also mostly half-timbered, but with some red-brick at the back of the house and at the front on the cellar level. He was in the front bedroom, on the first floor of the newer part. It was odd to think he was actually in the house. He could only picture it from the outside, as it were. The anticipation would have to do for now, though, as he certainly did not have the energy to get out of bed and open the curtains.

The brass doorknob rattled and the door creaked open. In bustled Mona, a pile of clean linen under her arm. The smell of it brought more memories of the place floating towards him like bubbles and bursting, releasing other clean smells like beeswax and bleach which he now realised for the first time made up the

7

distinctive smell of the place. Clearly he'd known it when he was a boy, because he could recognise it now, but was unaware of it then. This in turn triggered the buried image of the bluebags his grandmother, Gran The Noddfa as she was known to him, used inexplicably to put in the wash to make whites whiter. And then, the blue bags of salt you used to get in a packet of plain crisps. He rather thought though that then they would have been known simply as crisps, as plain was the only variety, if indeed variety was the appropriate term. Flavours came later.

'Well?' enquired Mona brusquely, so as not to show undue sentiment. 'Feeling any better?' It was almost a challenge.

'Not much,' he said, not feeling like talking.

'Think you can manage to come down for dinner?'

Dinner of course was the mid-day meal, on the table at half-past twelve sharp, a regime unaltered since the days when the farm had many workers who may have been anywhere on the hills, and so meals were served with military precision.

'Don't think so. Maybe I'll make it down in time for tea,' he said, slipping easily into the local language, although it was a long time since he'd used the word tea to mean an evening meal.

'I'll bring you something up on a tray,' said Mona, pressing the linen down into the bottom drawer of the clunky oak chest.

'I'm not all that hungry.'

'Oh, you have to have something to eat,' said Mona, as if to a sulky schoolboy. 'I've made some leek and potato soup. Your favourite. It'll do you the world of good.'

He knew it was useless to resist, although he didn't feel as if he had the strength to lift a spoon.

'Here, let's throw some light on the subject,' said Mona, and she swished open the curtains of the long casement window. The view came as something of a shock to Lloyd. He flinched.

'Heavy fall in the night,' said Mona.

The hills were blanketed with snow. That explained the stillness and the white light. Now he knew what had been

8

missing - the normal soundtrack of the farmyard: tractors, dogs, hens. All muted by the snow. It was probably twenty years since he'd seen snow like this, proper snow. Apart from the odd skiing trip. In the kind of flashes that were supposed to come just before death, he saw the childhood joys of snowballs, snowmen, sledging. He remembered the sledge his father had made him – big, chunky, unwieldy, but it had lasted and lasted. (And the go-kart! How he loved that go-kart, even if it did have pram wheels.) There was nothing quite like the magical transformation of its first fall, when in an instant life changed. Nothing was as it had been the day before. Routines changed. School was out. You could have fun, get out of doing things you didn't want to do. But the magic went as quickly as it had come. The snow got dirty. You couldn't do what you wanted to do, go where you wanted to go.

He wanted Mona to shut the curtains again, as the light troubled him, but he knew she wouldn't approve of him lying there with the curtains drawn all day. He sensed that she had some idea of what he was going through, but her understanding went only so far.

'Who was that boy?' he asked, for something to say.

'Alex? Didn't you know him? No, I don't suppose you would,' she said, answering herself. 'He'd have been a little twt of a thing when you last saw him, I daresay.'

The word twt – itself meaning little thing – conjured up a dim image of a little boy he knew a long time ago.

'Who is he?' Lloyd asked again.

'My niece Molly's boy. Up from Cardiff. Let's see – Molly's your cousin so he'd be your second cousin.' Mona was always keen to get family trees straightened out.

'Is he in some kind of trouble?' asked Lloyd.

'Aye, you could say that,' said Mona, thrusting her eyes upward. 'Something about putting a lighter to a girl's hair in school. No lasting damage, thank God. Excluded, as I think they

9

say now, for a couple of weeks after the holidays. I told Molly to send him up here and I'd sort him out. She's just about at her wits' end, poor thing.'

'What did he do that for?'

'No-one really knows. He doesn't talk much. Just grunts most of the time. Maybe you can get something out of him. He's shown more interest in you than in anything else since he got here.'

'And how're you going to do that? Sort him out?'

'Oh, I've got my ways and means,' said Mona with a mischievous smile. 'For you too, when it comes to that.'

Lloyd didn't want to hear just at that moment what ways and means Mona might have in mind for him.

'Anyone else under your wing?'

'Well, there's Great Uncle Stanley, of course. He's been here a couple of years now. Couldn't manage by himself any more.'

Great Uncle Stanley. Lloyd had forgotten he was still alive. He was Mona's Great Uncle, so he'd be Lloyd's Great-Great Uncle, his Great Grandfather's younger brother. He must be well into his nineties.

'Bloody hard work he is too,' Mona was saying. 'Keeps me waiting on him hand and foot. He's in the corner room overlooking the orchard. He's away with the fairies.'

That was Mona's way of saying he was gaga, or suffering from dementia, he supposed was the acceptable term these days.

'Rambles on about all sorts, half of it rubbish. You mustn't take any notice of anything he says,' she warned, looking at him with an odd frown, as if this were something very important he remember.

'Still, I don't suppose your paths will cross very much,' she said more cheerfully, getting up from the end of the bed where she'd perched and patting it smooth. 'And you mustn't keep me talking here all day. I've got things to do. Ooh, it's already eleven o'clock, look. Time's going on and I haven't even mopped out yet.'

Lloyd realised that time for Mona was very different from his own concept of it. For her there were fixed points, by when certain things should be done. For him, it was all a bit of a blur.

'There's one thing I'd like, Mona, if you could manage it,' said Lloyd.

'Oh aye, and what's that?'

'A radio.'

When he was in this state, even reading was too much trouble. His vision played nasty tricks. Lines of the print would curl up at the ends of the page, and sometimes the whole page would blur into something resembling Russian. At other times one or two words would grow bigger and dominate the page: usually words with lots of straight lines next to each other, like communication. These distortions disturbed him far more than the mere inconvenience of being unable to read. It was as if his world was disintegrating before his very eyes. At such time his only refuge, the only thing that could take him out of himself, was the radio.

'Oh, I expect we can find you one of those,' she said, and bustled back out of the room.

Lloyd had many more questions for Mona, but they would have to wait. Again he felt bathed in relief when he was alone, not least because he could pull the covers over his head to shut out the light, and look forward to the radio which would help shut out his thoughts, and the world. This was the only way he felt he could cope with his ordeal. The things he missed most were his wonderment at the world, his sense of adventure. He couldn't see that he would ever be able to rediscover them. He'd tried to tell himself that this was an adventure too. But a stronger voice, that of his old self, told him his days of adventure were over, and this was probably even harder to come to terms with than the pain and torpor. He realised he was increasingly turning in on himself, but he didn't know what else to do.

11

He looked around him, at the half-timbered walls, the old beams stained a nutty brown. Mona had stripped them. The walls had been plastered and papered when he was a boy. People used to like covering things up then. Now exposing original features was the order of the day.

Events started falling into place. He'd been dreading the train journey from London the day before, but he'd managed quite well. Mona had picked him up in the Land Rover from the tiny station the other side of the valley. The evening landscape had been majestic, and for the first time in a long time he had a sense of hope, however fleeting. Blue hills faded to grey, the sky a kaleidoscope of the palest of blues, and peach-tinted clouds giving way to gunmetal grey. The dying sun threw biblical shafts and swathes of light through the shade. On the hilltops jagged fringes of pine trees were speckled with its golden rays. The scene was punctuated in the distance by the odd church spire or chapel gable and – or was this his imagination taking over – a spiral or two of smoke completed the bucolic picture of a bygone age. The valley meadows were a golden green.

Now everything was monochrome again.

Mona, like everyone else, was puzzled by his condition. He found it nigh on impossible to put his symptoms succinctly into words. It could just be a numbness, a painful numbness. Then there was the tingling, twitching, itching, fluttering, the pins and needles. It could be a dull, throbbing ache, or pinpricks or sharp stabs. He often felt as if he were being gripped by some tightening device around the neck, chest or legs, or as if someone were sitting on him. The headaches could feel like migraines with flashing lights, or sinusitis when he thought his face would fall off. Then there was what he thought of as the tinny thing – as if his body were conducting an electrical charge. At any given time he could experience one of these things or many. He thought of it as a kaleidoscope – that word again – of pain. It was like a symphony, or rather a cacophony – starting with solos and building up in a series of deeply disturbing crescendos. But there was hardly ever silence.

Now he had a new one in his repertoire. His body felt it was being sprinkled with snowflakes. He looked awkwardly up at the ceiling to see if any were coming though. But of course there weren't. Maybe it was one more sign that he was going mad, for there was mental confusion too, as well as that fluey feeling.

He drifted off into an uneasy half-sleep. He dreamt that a group of old people had been made to strip off and run through the streets by jeering crowds brandishing sticks. One moment the tormentors seemed alarmingly real, the next like characters from the Beano, and then they were even more frightening.

14

Two

Lloyd had taken to Montevideo the moment he arrived. On that first drive into the city from the airport more than a year ago, he could barely keep himself from staring open-mouthed out of the cab window. He'd never seen anything quite like it. Its weird amalgam of styles spoke of a particularly variegated history. A mock Tudor semi might have a Norman villa as a neighbour and a hacienda on the other side. There were even a couple of thatched cottages here and there. The old town on the hilly peninsula in the harbour though was purely Hispanic. Cobbled streets lined with small white houses ran down to the azure sea in all directions.

There was an old-fashioned romance about the place, and it put him in mind of a South American republic as it might be portrayed in Tintin books: its Art Deco football stadium, its old bull-nosed lorries, its covered market, the Mercado del Puerto, down in the docks. It was said to have been designed by Gustave Eiffel of Tower fame, and was being shipped from France to Buenos Aires. But when it docked in Montevideo the Uruguayans took a shine to it and somehow managed to hang on to it for themselves, putting it up there and then on the dockside.

Inside, huge wooden ceiling fans battled with the alarming flames that leapt from the grills behind wood and brass counters. Here you could order an *asado* – practically the whole ribcage of a steer and, feeling a little like Desperate Dan, sit at one of the tables in the centre of the hall and wash it down with some *Media y Media* – half cider and half white wine.

The capital had a sun-drenched, sleepy feel to it where business was conducted at a local pace. The country as a whole struck him at times as a sunny Wales. The population was roughly the same and everybody seemed to know everybody else.

The Foreign Office had not yet seen fit to entrust him with a high-profile mission. He'd just spent three years in Trinidad and was in Belize for three years before that. While Montevideo's importance rocketed during the Falklands War and its aftermath, it had then waned just as abruptly. But his job as Head of Media and Public Affairs at the Embassy was not without its stresses – at times of a ministerial or even royal visit, say, when he had to ensure that things ran like clockwork. Uruguay was still regarded in certain circles as the Switzerland of South America, a haven of stability in the often turbulent world of Latin American politics.

It was stress that was diagnosed when Lloyd first went to the doctor after one of these high-profile visits. Nothing was prescribed, save a general enjoinder to take things easy, whatever that meant. Lloyd accepted it, even though deep down he feared that there was something seriously wrong. He seemed to have one flu-type bug after another. Worse, he began to fear he was going mad.

A lot of the time he felt dizzy, woozy, and had troubling, psychedelic, surreal dreams. And then there was the terrifying sensation he could not have put a name to, although he was later to discover it did have a name - dissociation. Sometimes when he was walking along he felt his feet were sinking into the pavement as if it were soft snow. When he went to put his hand on the banister to steady himself going downstairs, it would melt away, so he began to question reality, the existence of the solid world.

All this worried him greatly, far more than he'd admit to others or even to himself. Then the panic attacks started, mainly when he was in closed spaces like lifts or planes, when he often thought he would surely pass out or even die. That he never did hardly stopped him being sure he would the next time.

His doctor in Montevideo, something of an Anglophile who wore tweed suits even in hot weather, clung on to his theory of stress, and signed Lloyd off work for a few weeks.

'I see a lot of this type of thing in your sort of job. You may not feel stressed, but that's what I think it is,' said the doctor, puffing away on his pipe. He looked at Lloyd for a few moments.

'Have you suffered a bereavement recently?

'Not recently, no,' said Lloyd. He wondered whether he should mention the death of his parents.

'Well, you must allow yourself to get well.'

With this permission, Lloyd more or less collapsed into a catatonic state, hardly getting out of bed. The Embassy were very understanding, his girlfriend a little less so. He found that friends all had their own diagnoses which usually seemed more relevant to them than to him. Teetotallers would say he drank too much, non-smokers that he should quit smoking. Those who asserted that it was depression were, he suspected, depressives themselves, while some of his overworked colleagues favoured the stress theory. There was even a woman at the British Council who stated confidently that he was pining for the hills of his homeland – she was Scottish herself – like some latter-day Welsh Heidi.

After a month or so he went back to work but soon came down with more flu-like symptoms. He went back to the doctor who this time looked into it in more detail, had some blood tests done and found that Lloyd had had the Epstein Barr virus, commonly known as Glandular Fever, about three months back. He was now suffering from post-viral syndrome, explained the doctor while stuffing his pipe, and would need complete rest. He signed him off for another three months.

Again the Embassy were sympathetic and accommodating, and told him to take off as much time as he needed. This didn't stop him fretting about his career and his future though, as he fretted about many things now that all he did all day was to doze, listen to the radio, and read when he felt up to it. He had never been a worrier before.

Some of his friends stayed by him but others took offence when they rang the bell to his flat and he couldn't get out of bed to see them. They seemed to take it personally, as if he just couldn't be bothered to make the effort, or that he was to blame in the first place. This hurt. His girlfriend Laure, a Canadian writer he'd met in Port of Spain and who'd come with him to Montevideo, lost patience with him and went back to Vancouver, ostensibly for a long vacation to see her family. But somehow he knew she wouldn't be coming back. He was bereft.

The weeks dragged on and he felt no better. In fact he felt worse. The doctor seemed to have run out of things to say. Lloyd couldn't help feeling that he was seriously ill with some rare disease and no-one could be bothered to find out what. He couldn't believe that anyone could feel so abysmal without it being serious. It was his boss at the Embassy who suggested that he went back to London and saw a specialist there. They'd pay the airfare. He dreaded the journey but realised he couldn't go on like this. He rang his friends Jack and Jill – the joke had long ceased to be funny – who had a large flat in Dulwich. They said of course he could stay with them for as long as he wanted, and they'd pick him up at Heathrow.

The journey left him exhausted and he could barely move for several days. But mentally he felt better to be back in the UK, and to have some kind of a plan. It was always a good feeling to know that something was being done, or would be done when he could get out of bed.

Luckily enough, Jack and Jill's GP in Dulwich took a special interest in 'this type of thing', although Lloyd remained far from clear about what type of thing it was. After giving him a thorough examination and asking endless questions, she sent him up to the Hospital for Tropical Diseases in Store Street to see if they could find anything. They couldn't.

She then sent him for more blood tests – a full MOT was how she put it. The nice Jamaican nurse who filled tube after tube with his blood was clearly impressed by the sheer number of potential illnesses.

'Lor', they sure are giving you a good going over,' she said with a bubbly laugh. 'My my, I don't think I've ever filled this many tubes for one person before.'

Lloyd felt comforted. They'd surely find something now. But when he went back to the GP, whom by now he was calling Sally, for the results she told him nothing had shown up. She looked pretty fed up herself.

She looked at him in a frank manner and said, 'I think you've got post-viral fatigue syndrome: Chronic Fatigue Syndrome it's sometimes called. Or ME. Myalgic Encephalomyelitis. Myalgia means muscle pain and Encephalomyelitis means inflammation of the brain.'

He certainly suffered from a lot of pain, which could move round the body like some particularly nasty form of torture. But alarm bells were ringing.

'Isn't that what they used to call Yuppie flu?'

'Yes, but it's a somewhat misleading term. It certainly doesn't just affect Yuppies, although a high percentage of quite active people seem to be affected. And it's not flu, although symptoms can be similar.'

Lloyd gulped.

'But it can go on for years, can't it?'

'Yes it can. But many people get much better after a few months.'

19

'What causes it?'

'Often we don't know. But in some cases it follows a viral infection during a period of stress in people's lives. You had the Epstein Barr virus. You'd just moved to a new job in a new country. It fits. But there is a lot we don't know.'

'I thought it was a kind of made-up disease.'

'A lot of people think that. But we're learning more about it all the time. It's not contagious and rarely fatal,' – Lloyd flinched at the word rarely –'although it does often seem to break out in clusters of people. At first it was known as the Royal Free Disease after a group of nurses at the Royal Free Hospital went down with it in the nineteen fifties.'

'So what's the treatment?'

Sally paused for a moment.

She wasn't much older than him, and had a friendly, intelligent face which suggested she was often amused by life. Lloyd appreciated her no-nonsense approach.

'I'll be frank with you. There isn't much we can do at the moment. You must pace yourself and get plenty of rest. But we find that people get better more quickly if you can do some gentle exercise. We don't want you to seize up, as it were. There's also some evidence that ME patients are low in magnesium. Supplements may help. I can give you some codeine for the pain and something to help you sleep, at least for a short while to get you into a routine. Pills aren't the answer.'

She must have noticed Lloyd's crestfallen face, how quiet he'd gone.

'Look, I have to say that you're lucky in a way,' she said. 'You're fairly high-functioning. Some people are completely bedridden with it. I know you probably don't feel lucky. But you mustn't let go of your sense of well-being.'

Lloyd's heart sank. He certainly didn't feel lucky. And he had long ago lost his sense of well-being. It was because of his ill-being that he'd come to see her. He'd liked and trusted her and thought she understood. Now he felt let down.

'I can refer you to a specialist at St Mary's in Paddington if you like,' she was saying. 'He's the foremost CFS specialist in the country. I doubt he'll be able to tell you much more than I have, but at least you'll know that someone is keeping an eye on you.'

'So there's no question of me going back to work any time soon?'

'I wouldn't advise it. You need rest now. Otherwise it probably will take years.'

It was all pretty bleak. The consultant at St Mary's was very understanding. He was a Sikh who'd spent three years in Peru doing his masters in microbiology and so they talked a little at first about life in South America. Lloyd was overjoyed to find that he seemed to understand what he was going through, and took it seriously. But his hopes of a magic cure were soon dashed.

'How long does it take you to get up in the morning?' asked the doctor.

'Well, if I do get up in the morning, it's a couple of hours before I can get going.'

'And when you do, what's the first thing you do?'

'Go out and buy a paper.'

The doctor bent over a sheet of paper on his desk and seemed to cross something out.

'That's a good start,' he said. 'It's good to have some kind of routine. It's the first thing I suggest to people, to go out and buy a paper.'

Lloyd's heart sank again. Good God, was this all the top consultant in the country could say? Go out and buy a paper? Stick to a routine? Lloyd had always had a certain horror of routine. He had joined the Foreign Service for adventure, to go out and see the world. And while the job hadn't quite brought

21

him to the swashbuckling world of derring-do he'd naively imagined, at least it had taken him to many interesting parts of the globe. And now he was being told that the pinnacle of his aspiration was to totter to the corner shop for The Times.

'I read recently that they'd found the gene expression for the disease.'

'Well, it's one study,' said the doctor. 'I wouldn't set too much store by it. And even so, it'll probably be years before any treatment comes out of it.'

He must have noticed Lloyd's look of despair.

'But we are learning more and more about it all the time,' he said gently. 'Don't give up hope.'

He did have one new suggestion, though – Cognitive Behavioural Therapy or CBT.

'It's about managing symptoms.' he said. 'It's not for everyone, but you may as well give it a go. What have you got to lose?'

'No cure then?'

'No cure.'

'Doesn't this therapy imply it's all in the mind?'

'Not at all. It's about dealing with it in a more informed way.'

Lloyd wasn't sure about the CBT. He talked it over with Jill, an NHS psychotherapist.

'It's the panacea for all ills at the moment,' she said. 'It's cheap for the NHS and you do all the work. Personally I think it's vastly over-rated, and unsuitable for half the cases it's prescribed for. But he's right – why not try it? You never know.'

No, you never know, thought Lloyd, not without some bitterness. On the appointed day he plucked up the courage and got the train and the tube up to the clinic in Paddington. The panic attacks now came on practically as soon as he saw a train. His mouth would dry up, his heart start pounding, and he would feel dizzy and slightly sick. He found the only way he could go through with staying on the train was to concentrate on taking deep breaths and stare at the floor.

He didn't take to Keith, the CBT man, whose office was in a Portakabin behind Paddington Station.

'So, you've got ME?' he said, and it sounded like a challenge.

'So they say,' said Lloyd.

Keith raised his eyebrows and smiled, as if to say 'You're not as stupid as you look.' He asked Lloyd all the questions that everyone else had asked him. Lloyd answered them as patiently as he could. At the end of the session, Keith said that Lloyd wasn't 'owning' his symptoms, and put quotations around the word with his fingers.

'No you're right,' said Lloyd. 'I don't own them. I don't want anything to do with them. I try to ignore them as much as possible.'

Keith smiled his rather supercilious smile.

'You're going to be quite a challenge,' he said.

For some reason, Lloyd felt pleased. He wondered where Keith was from. He was tall and dark, probably mixed race, and had a slight accent which sounded vaguely familiar but which he couldn't for the moment place. Must be a Commonwealth country, he thought, with a name like Keith.

Keith asked him to fill in an activity diary, charting everything he did throughout the day, how he felt physically at each stage, and what his moods and thoughts were, particularly negative ones. It was all about negative thinking, and challenging it with positive thoughts.

Lloyd found all this very tedious, until he discovered he could, if not exactly make things up, at least embellish it a little and have some fun with it, to make his day more interesting than it actually was. 'Eleven to eleven-thirty – did the Times crossword,' he wrote, whereas it had taken him a good hour and a half and even then he failed to find four clues.

Keith was pleased when he went back a week later, and Lloyd felt like a schoolboy being praised for his homework.

'This looks pretty good,' he said, tapping the paper with his index finger.

Lloyd opened up a little more to him this time, hinting at how useless and worthless he felt not being able to work. His next homework was to write down any negative thoughts he had, and alongside write ways of counteracting them with something positive.

He told Keith he had trouble sleeping because of the muscle pain, which seemed to favour his neck and back when he was lying down. He would spend half the night trying to get to sleep and half the next day making up for it. He was changing day for night.

Keith tossed a booklet at him called 'Sleeping with terminal cancer,' and when Lloyd raised an enquiring eyebrow, Keith said, 'Same rules apply.'

Lloyd wasn't exactly sure what was required in the positive column, so when he was feeling particularly useless he tried to think of the great and good whose achievements during their own lifetime were limited in some way.

'Van Gogh sold only one painting in his entire life,' he wrote at one point, and later, 'Emily Bronte wrote only one novel (but what a novel, and there was some great poetry).'

'I like this,' said Keith at the next appointment, and Lloyd couldn't help smiling.

By the end of his allotted twelve sessions, they were quite good mates. Keith had even shared his own problems sleeping whenever he had to travel for work. The sense of irony was not lost on Lloyd – why didn't Keith read or re-read 'Sleeping with Terminal Cancer' (Same Rules Apply)? – but he had the satisfaction of feeling that some balance between them had been redressed.

It had come to Lloyd that Keith must be Trinidadian, where the sing-song accent was oddly similar to that of the Welsh Valleys. But he couldn't think of how to ask him. Keith himself provided an opportunity at this last session, a cold November morning. He watched Lloyd peel off several layers of clothing before he sat down in the rather stuffy office.

'You know, for all my years in this country, I've never mastered that knack,' said Keith.

'What knack?'

'The knack of putting on different layers of clothing so you can take off what you need to as and when. You English are very good at that.'

'I'm Welsh, for the record,' said Lloyd. 'Where are you from?'

'Trinidad,' said Keith.

'I thought as much', said Lloyd, and went on to tell him a little about the three years he spent there.

'There's not much more I can do for you,' said Keith eventually. 'You're in a pretty good place mentally. What I can tell you is that the patients I see who are doing the best are those who regularly get up early, stick to a routine.'

Lloyd was confused. So far everyone had told him to rest as much as possible.

'Resting and lying in bed all day are not the same thing,' said Keith. 'You're at a stage now when gentle exercise and measured activity will help you.'

It was all very well for Keith to say that, but it was always in the mornings that Lloyd felt at his worst. He'd read somewhere that ME felt as if you'd run a marathon with flu and a hangover. He'd never run a marathon and doubted he'd ever had flu and a hangover at the same time, but this seemed to describe his morning sickness perfectly. He would wake up unrefreshed and his natural inclination was to turn over and doze with the radio on in the background.

But he took Keith's words on trust and tried his level best to obey. No sooner had he got into some kind of stride, though, than he would spend a painful, sleepless night and then become nocturnal again until he could, by the greatest effort, get back into whack.

He tried other things. He went to a Taiwanese acupuncturist on Wigmore Street. He felt a surge of hope when he rattled off question after question – things no-one else had asked – and then catalogued the myriad of symptoms Lloyd had experienced at one time or another. It seemed that at last someone understood completely. The acupuncturist, a quiet, sour-faced man, explained what was wrong with his energy flows, and how he would restore the balance in his body. And he did feel wonderfully well after the first session.

But the relief was only temporary, and wore off in a couple of days. After six sessions he gave up. It cost a lot of money. Same thing with reflexology. And colonic irrigation. He wouldn't repeat that in a hurry. Even though the South African nurse was as nice as she could be, and confessed her own tendency to binge drink, he didn't want to spend £50 a session for the several more she told him he needed.

'You're not relaxing,' she admonished as she endeavoured to flush out his insides. 'You're holding something back. I've got most of the cling-ons out but there are some really stubborn black hard bits in your upper intestine that you're not letting go of. There's no telling how long they've been there.'

How could he relax with a metal appliance the size of a vibrator up his ass?

In desperation he turned to the Central London ME Clinic off Harley Street, where after a couple of perfunctory questions the quite elderly doctor with huge bouffant grey hair and a large red artificial flower pinned to her chest prescribed a series of expensive vitamin injections, steroids, and some pills to help him sleep. These certainly did the trick and knocked him out on the spot. But when he went back to see Sally, she was furious.

'These pills are for epileptics,' she said. 'No wonder they knock you out. But they're going to do you no good in the long run. Same with the steroids. You're bound to feel better at first. But if you keep on taking them, they'll do you harm. Why did you go there?'

'Sheer desperation,' said Lloyd.

He felt worse than ever, as if hope was disappearing beyond his grasp. He heard of various supplements that would do him good – Tyrosine, Selenium, garlic. He thought they did help a little, but it was hard to tell, and there were days when he felt close to despair.

It was Mona who suggested he go to The Noddfa for a few weeks.

'Some good country air and plain home cooking will soon get you back on your feet,' she said over the phone.

He dithered about this for some time. True, she would take good care of him, but Mona didn't hold with people lying around in bed half the time. If nature abhorred a vacuum, Mona abhorred an inert body.

As it turned out, there had been an outbreak of ME in the local young farmers' club. Previously energetic young men were hardly able to leave the house any more. In Mona's eyes, reasoned Lloyd to himself, this would give the illness some degree of legitimacy. And as welcoming and sympathetic as Jack and Jill were, it couldn't be much fun for them to have him moping about the flat all the time. So in the end he gave in. Jack drove him to Euston, and he managed to get a train with only one change. Mona brought him to The Noddfa, and he promptly took to bed for several days.

Mona had indeed been more understanding than he'd first given her credit for, although she made it clear that she thought he ought to get out of bed. It wasn't so much that he wouldn't, but he couldn't. It was if someone had pulled his plug out. It was hard to convey this to people who said, 'Well, we all get tired from time to time,' as if it were something he could snap out of. Thoughts of Van Gogh or Bronte did not help, and he'd given up trying to explain.

Mona came into his room with a basket of dirty washing under her arm. It was late afternoon, three or four days after his return.

'Are you going to grace us with your presence downstairs today?' she asked.

'I don't think so Mona. I'm not too clever. Maybe tomorrow.'

'Aye, let's hope so,' she said, looking at him carefully through slightly narrowed eyes. 'Ah well, I'll bring you up some sandwiches for your tea. I've boiled a ham. What do you want with it?'

Lloyd was still not hungry but knew better than to say so.

'Ham will be fine,' he said. 'With a bit of mustard.'

'Good boy, speak up,' said Mona, who liked nothing better than a healthy appetite and a willingness to express it.

It was soothing to be cared for like this – not that Jack and Jill had not cared for him, but they'd been out working all day. It was still a relief when she closed the door behind her, so he could turn over and go back to sleep. But no sooner had the door closed than it opened again. In sauntered Alex, his thumbs twitching frenetically on some device in his hands.

He sat down in a chair by the window, as if Lloyd wasn't there and he hadn't come to see him.

'Are you ever going to get out of bed?' he asked eventually, still pounding away at his game.

'I think there's a fair chance,' said Lloyd.

'When?'

'Maybe tomorrow. I'll have to see how I am.'

'Well it's very boring of you.'

'Why did you set fire to that girl's hair?' asked Lloyd, who was increasingly finding the subject of his own health tedious in the extreme. Alex took the question in his stride, but looked at Lloyd for the first time since he entered the room. It was rather a disdainful look.

'I was bored,' he said. 'It was an experiment.'

'What kind of experiment?'

'To see if her hair would burn, of course.'

'What stopped you?'

'She turned around and screamed before I had the chance.'

'Would you have gone through with it?'

Alex looked through the window, pondering what he seemed to think was an interesting question.

'Probably.'

'But she could have been terribly hurt. Scarred for life. Or even killed.'

'Oh no, we'd thought of that. It was in the chem lab and we had a canister of water ready to throw over her.'

They lapsed into silence and Lloyd began to drift off again. Alex went to stand by the window, looking out into the valley below.

'I'm bored now,' he said, with something of a challenge in his voice.

'Some people would find it interesting to be on a farm,' said Lloyd. 'Why don't you go out and help Gareth?' Gareth had worked on the farm since he was young, and now farmed it with his son.

'Boring,' said Alex.

'Don't you think it's somewhat ironic that you can go outside and don't want to, and I want to go outside but can't?' asked Lloyd.

Alex gave it some thought.

'What's ironic?'

'The contrast of unexpected opposites with humorous effect', said Lloyd wearily. 'Look, you have to find your own point in doing things. Find your own interest in life.'

'There is no point. There's no point in anything. You can't do anything by yourself anyway.'

'Of course you can. Think of Rosa Parks. She changed the course of history by refusing to move in the bus. So in a way she achieved something by doing nothing.'

She'd been in the news for receiving some award or other, and Lloyd was gratified to find that Alex knew something about her.

'Well, if she hadn't have made a stand, someone else would have.'

'You can't know that. And anyway it mightn't have been for a long time. She changed the life of millions of black people for the better.'

Alex seemed to find this intriguing.

'But that was a one-off. She didn't mean to change anything. You can't change anything if you really want to.'

'Have you heard of the Enigma machine?' asked Lloyd.

'Something to do with the war, wasn't it?'

'That's right. It was a machine the Germans used to encrypt all their top secret plans so they could send them to each other without us knowing. It was a sort of typewriter which changed the letter you typed into another letter. Then another. Then another. It had 158 million million million permutations. They thought no-one could ever crack the code.'

'Well? Did they?'

'Churchill set up a team of mathematicians in wooden huts in the grounds of a country house north of London called Bletchley Park. The odds against them cracking the code were thousands to one. But eventually they built their own machine with dozens of cogs which whirred around fast enough to detect patterns in the German messages. That machine was called the Colossus. It was the forerunner of the computer.'

Lloyd was exhausted now and lay back on his pillow.

'Well? Did they crack the code?' asked Alex, jumping up and down on the bottom of the bed where he'd perched. Lloyd thought he'd already explained that.

'Yes, they did. And they reckon it shortened the war by two years. They saved millions of lives. There was a point to that, wasn't there?'

'Are you a spy?' asked Alex after reflecting on all of this for a moment. Lloyd couldn't help giving a little smile, albeit a week one.

'No. Not really.'

'They said you worked abroad. In an embassy or something.'

'Well, OK, I did. I worked for the Foreign Office. We did have to gather intelligence, as the phrase goes. But it wasn't spying as you think of it, like James Bond or something.'

'So how do you know all this?'

'Before I went abroad they showed us around Bletchley Park.'

'Will you take me there some day?'

'Yes, I will.'

'Promise?'

'Promise.'

'Perhaps when you get out of bed we can do an experiment.'

'I think you've done enough experiments for a while,' said Lloyd.

'Or solve a mystery,' said Alex. 'I could be the sleuth, going round doing all the detecting, and report back to you in bed. Do you know of any mysteries that need solving? Do you think this place might be haunted?'

Lloyd was impressed that Alex had grasped the situation so quickly and risen to the challenge.

'As a matter of fact we did used to think there was a ghost in the house,' he said. 'It was supposed to be the ghost of Aunty Maisie. You could hear footsteps in the room where she died, and in the corridor outside.'

'Which room is that?'

'The room Great Uncle Stanley's in.'

Alex seemed to lose interest.

'I'm not going in there. He's scary.'

But something Alex had said stirred within Lloyd some buried memory. Since he'd come back to The Noddfa all kinds of blurry images of his childhood, or rather teen years, in the farmhouse had began to resurface. He hadn't been conscious exactly of this one that came to him now, but it was suddenly vivid, as if it had been always at the back of his mind.

'Well, there is The Case of The Missing Room,' said Lloyd.

Alex was alert now again, engaged. He dropped his game and came back to kneel on the bed.

'What missing room?'

'That's for you to find out,' said Lloyd. 'Somewhere in this house is a missing room.'

'If it's missing, how do you know where it is?' asked Alex. Lloyd couldn't help admire his logic.

'Go and have a look,' he Lloyd. 'Work it out. You know what the best cure for boredom is?'

'What?' said Alex.

'Curiosity.'

Alex's face brightened and he bounced out of the room, forgetting to be cool and cynical. At least it had got him out of his room, thought Lloyd. Now he could get some sleep. But he found he couldn't. He was feeling a twinge of something he hadn't felt for ages: excitement. It might well do him good to have something to keep his mind off things. When he first came to The Noddfa when he was twelve, he'd tried to find out what was in the missing room, but had never succeeded. Maybe Alex would have more luck.

Three

'You survived the crash then?' asked Great Uncle Stanley.

Lloyd didn't know what he meant exactly, but his mind turned to the car accident that killed his mother and father. He wondered whether to go along with him, or try to reason with him. Mona had warned him that Great Uncle Stanley would be lucid at times but talk gibberish in the next sentence. He was sitting in a straight-backed chair by the window. Before he could answer, Great Uncle Stanley asked another question, a surprisingly pertinent one.

'So how was Uruguay?'

'Oh, very good. I liked it a lot.'

'And now you've got this mystery illness. Well, I expect Mona will sort you out.'

'And how are you?' asked Lloyd.

'Oh, much better since I had this bionic eye fitted,' said Great Uncle Stanley. 'But reading's still difficult. Mona got me some special books but they turned out to be in Old Norse. Welsh I could have got on with, but Old Norse is a bit of a stretch.'

There was a silence, when neither seemed to know what to say.

'Still, it's nice to see the church spire is back in its place.'

They both looked out of the window at the church spire poking up behind the brow of the hill. They were sitting in Great Uncle Stanley's room a few days after the snow. Lloyd was feeling a little better and had got up and dressed the day before for the first time, which seemed to cause some excitement in the household.

It was a good-sized room with two windows overlooking the orchard. Mona had brought some of the old man's things in to make him feel at home, so it had an old-fashioned feel to it, as if it were a stage set; a huge mahogany chest of drawers, a fringed cloth on a round table, an old radio. Over his knees was a blanket made up of multicoloured crocheted squares.

The snow had gone as quickly as it came. Maybe that's what he meant – he couldn't see the spire because of the snow. Now it was one of those dull days, slightly misty, but everything appeared unaccountably clearer and closer. The trees seemed stitched like black lace onto the hilly horizon and the hedgerows outlined the fields as if they'd been painted by Gaugin. By the side of the barn on the farm opposite Lloyd noticed a small pine he'd never been aware of before. Sounds seemed sharper too: an electric saw the other side of the hill, and when it was quiet, the whistle of the wind in the woods and the sinister caw of the watchful crows. A storytelling of crows, he'd read somewhere, was an alternative collective noun to a murder of crows. Lloyd thought storytelling was better than murder, the way they gathered and chattered. He couldn't help feeling it was a macabre story they had to tell.

'Why, did the spire go away?'

'Oh yes, they took it away for cleaning,' said Great Uncle Stanley, happy to inform. 'It was half way up the hill. Well, most of it was. The rest was somewhere else. Look, there's eight of them now.'

'Eight of what?' asked Lloyd, looking out of the window again.

'Those black things. Sometimes there are twelve of them and sometimes only three. Mostly three. Or three and a half.'

Lloyd wondered if he meant the crows. But he couldn't see any. And how could there be half a crow?

34

'Still, it's very good to see you again after all this time,' said Great Uncle Stanley. 'I've always wondered why she wasn't crying.'

'Who wasn't crying?'

'Mmm?' said the old man, lost in his thoughts.

There was a knock on the door, and a curly head popped around it.

'Lloyd, can I have a word with you please?'

'Excuse me,' said Lloyd to Great Uncle Stanley.

'Certainly, boy.' He pronounced it 'booy.' 'Very nice to have a chat with you. Pop in again sometime.'

'Yes, I will. Very soon.'

'I'll show you some photographs. If my eye's working.'

Outside, Alex was fairly dancing in the corridor.

'I think I've got it,' he said.

'Got what?'

'The missing room. Look, come into my room.'

He took Lloyd into the small bedroom at the back of the house that used to be his. It had all changed now, new paper and paint and furniture. Carpet had replaced the old lino, and there was even a wash basin in the corner. It was the same room and yet it wasn't, as if his was in a parallel universe where all the clocks were very slow.

'This used to be my room,' said Lloyd, looking around. But Alex wasn't interested.

'There's this wall here, you see,' he said, slapping the wall opposite the window. 'It must be about twelve foot long.' This room was in fact in the eaves of the smaller part of the house, with a dormer window.

'Ye-es......,' said Lloyd.

'And then come out here, and along the corridor towards the front bedroom where you are. Hurry up.'

The corridor ran along the length of the larger part of the house, where it abutted to the smaller part.

35

'I'm coming,' said Lloyd, unable to walk very fast.

'This wall here,' said Alex, tapping it as he went, 'is also about twelve foot and so...,' throwing open the door of a small washroom, which was the mirror image of what was now Alex's room at the back, '.....is this. So these three walls are the three sides of a square. The window of my room looks out to the back, the window of this room looks onto the front, and in between there's a missing twelve feet. It must be the missing room because it's in the middle of the house and there's no windows. I'm right, aren't I?'

'Yes, you're right.'

'What's on the fourth side?'

'It's Mona's room. It stretches from the back to the front of the house, under the eaves.'

'Can we go and see it? We can tap it to see if there's a secret door. I've done these three walls.'

'Well, we'd have to ask Mona of course. But I'm pretty sure there's no door. I looked for one when I was your age, and on the three other walls as well.'

'So how d'you get to her room?'

'It's up the backstairs, which goes up from the kitchen. You see, the house is an L-shape. The foot of the L is the smaller bit, which originally was a cottage. That's where Mona's room is. Then somebody came along and added this bit, the bit we're in now, which is much bigger. It's got an extra floor, the attics, up those stairs, look. The space is where the two bits join.'

'What's beneath the missing room?' asked Alex.

'Well there's a sort of space too, but less of one, I think. It's between two fire places which are back to back, one in the dining room and the other in the living room.'

'So isn't it just a chimney?'

'It's a bit big for a chimney. And anyway, the space below is smaller. Chimneys get smaller as they go up, not bigger.'

'What d'you think's in it?' asked Alex. 'Buried treasure? Or maybe it's the start of a secret passage.'

'I don't know,' said Lloyd. 'That's the mystery.'

'Can we go and see the downstairs now?'

The stairs led down to the back passage, as it had always been called, and that led into the living room in the smaller part of the house. As they went along it, Lloyd in his turn slapped the wall.

'That's where the downstairs space is,' he said.

In the living room, they inspected the fireplace, an inglenook with two small settles either side. Mona came in from the kitchen with a duster in her hand.

'What on earth are you two looking for in the fireplace?' she asked.

'I'm telling Alex here about the missing room,' said Lloyd.

'Ooh yes. You always used to call it that didn't you? I haven't thought about it for ages.'

'We're trying to find out if the downstairs space is smaller than the upstairs one,' said Alex.

'Ah, well there's been a development there,' said Mona, putting down her duster on the sideboard. 'Come with me.'

She led them down the front hall as it was called, a passage which ran parallel to the back one, past the front door, and into the dining room. When Lloyd had first seen it, it was unused, its walls a bare, yellowish crumbling plaster lined with wooden shelves. It was known then as the Cheese Room, presumably because cheese was made or stored there. Over the years Mona had turned it into a rather swish dining room, had the old plaster stripped away to reveal the half-timbered walls underneath. But when Mona raised her hand to direct his gaze at the fireplace, he was completely taken aback.

'Wow,' he said.

The old Victorian fireplace had been ripped away and behind where it had been, in a much deeper alcove, was an even older one, and on its left an ancient oven, its roof a brick dome. Mona had done a great restoration job, fixing an old iron arm and chain so it could swing over the fire. All it needed was a cauldron.

'That's fantastic,' said Lloyd. Mona looked pleased. Alex looked bored.

'Did you expect this to be there behind the old one?' asked Lloyd.

'Well people did say that in these old houses there often was something like this. I had a couple of historians staying here one time and they were most interested in it. So I got Wyn – you know, Cousin Cath's boy – built his own house – to come and have a look. It was only a thin partition wall and once we knocked through that a bit, all of this was here, more or less intact. We just had to do up the brick a bit, polish up the grate, and put these tiles on the floor. I did look around for the oven door until someone told me they didn't have them then – they'd heat up the bricks with a fire and then seal it with stones and that would bake the bread. And look, we made another discovery.'

In the corner to the right of the fire, half-hidden behind the end of the fireplace which jutted out slightly, were three brick ledges or steps which curved around and upwards towards the back wall.

'Don't you think that looks like the start of a spiral staircase?' asked Mona.

Lloyd did, although it would be a very narrow and rather precarious one. Mona thought it might be one of those priest's holes. Lloyd thought about it. There was a date on the front of the house, over a dormer window above the front door: 1664. His history at this period was sketchy to say the least, and he wasn't sure how much religion persecution there was at this time, how much priests would need holes. And if they did, what would bring them here, up a Welsh hill in the middle of nowhere?

It did strike him though, that the opening up of the fireplace made the space above more mysterious, not less. He'd always been fascinated by it, but at the back of his mind there was always the niggling doubt that it was just a matter of architecture, of fireplaces and chimneys, where one part of the house was added to the other.

This put a different light on things. There was now much less space between this grate and the one in the living room. He bent down and looked up the chimney. It did indeed get narrower as it went up, and he could see a tiny square of light at the top. This could not account for the space of about a hundred and forty four square feet above. Elsewhere in the house use was made of every nook and cranny. Alex followed suit and stuck his head up.

'Weren't you curious about the steps when you found them?' Lloyd asked Mona.

'Well, yes, I was,' said Mona. 'But what could we do? Knocking down an old partition wall is one thing, but I thought if we started messing around with brick walls we could bring the whole house crashing down.'

'Can we go up and see your room, Auntie Mona?' asked Alex.

'Whatever do you want to do that for?'

'To see if there's a secret door into The Missing Room.'

'I told you,' said Lloyd, 'I've already done that and there's nothing there.'

'I might find something you didn't,' said Alex.

'Well, aye, alright, there's nothing to stop you,' said Mona. 'But there is another secret way in.'

'Is there?' said both Alex and Lloyd.

'Yes, from the attics,'

'Of course. The attics,' said Lloyd, remembering.

'What? Can you get in from the attics?' asked Alex, looking from one to the other.

'There's a place where the small part of the house joins the bigger part,' said Mona. 'From the attics, you can look into roof of the smaller part, and if you peer down, you can just about make out a dark space. But you can't see much.'

'We could take a torch,' said Alex.

'Not even with a torch.'

'I could wriggle down.'

'It's too small.'

'But you must be able to see something?'

'Well, I think there's a kind of ledge there,' said Mona. 'That could have been the place for the priest's bed, couldn't it?'

'Oh, so you have been peering down yourself?' said Lloyd with a teasing smile.

'That was a long time ago,' said Mona. I put some boards against the hole when there were young kids running around. It looked quite dangerous.'

'Can we go and have a look?' said Alex, looking from one to the other. 'Please!'

'Well, not now at any rate. I've got to take Lloyd down to the doctor.'

'Why, is he going to make you better?' said Alex.

'Doubt it,' said Lloyd.

Despite his protests, Mona had made an appointment with Old Doctor Thomas, who was known as Old Doctor Thomas when Lloyd was Alex's age, so God knew what he must be like now. Lloyd was astounded that he was still alive, let alone in practice. But Mona insisted that he'd been seeing the Young Farmers with 'this fatigue thing' and was bound to know something about it.

'And don't you try to go sprwting around in the attics while we're gone,' said Mona, wagging her finger at Alex. 'They're locked, and I've got the key. As Mona turned to leave the room, Alex gave Lloyd a wink. Lloyd frowned and shook his head, warning Alex not to try anything.

'So what did Great Uncle Stanley have to say to you?' asked Mona as she raced her Land Rover down the hill towards Llanfair.

'Well, he seemed to think the church had gone missing, and he was counting things,' said Lloyd.

'Yes, he does that,' said Mona. 'Threes and eights usually. You never know what it is.'

'And he seemed to think I'd survived a crash, and something strange about someone not crying.'

Mona frowned.

'He relives the war a lot,' she said.

'Is it best to go along with him, pretend you know what he's on about?'

'Oh, ignore him. You never get anywhere otherwise.'

As they approached the little town, they passed the house where Lloyd had lived with his parents before the crash that killed them. It was a 1930s semi with bay windows. Lloyd gave it the merest of glances, conscious that Mona was registering his look. He thought he should be feeling some emotion, some nostalgia, but he didn't. It was a different house now. It had been pebble-dashed and the woodwork painted white rather than the old sage green. There was a new red front door, and the small front garden had been paved over for the car. It wasn't their house anymore, his and his parents'. That had vanished a long time ago.

Old Doctor Thomas, who looked exactly the same as Lloyd remembered him, covered the same ground as everyone else had. After he'd asked all the questions, he told Lloyd he'd have to pace himself, get some gentle exercise every day, sleep regular hours, eat healthily, limit himself to one or two drinks in any day, and quit smoking. Lloyd was sick to death of hearing this, as if he and his lifestyle were to blame. He didn't believe it.

'Don't you think I haven't tried all those things by now?' he said. 'Of course you feel a bit better, but you still have all the underlying symptoms and keel over now and again, and you don't even have the things to help you through like a cigarette and a pint now and again.'

'But you will feel better in the long run.'

'But it's such a long long run. To get through it, I need more than fine words and a guilt trip. I need hope.'

'Well, that's put me in my place,' said Old Doctor Thomas.

Lloyd softened a little, embarrassed by his outburst. He smiled.

'It wasn't meant to,' he said. 'It was meant to put you in mine.'

'Look,' said the doctor, 'this is all about you getting well. It's not about a battle between the two of us.'

''No,' said Lloyd as gently as he could, although that was exactly what it felt like.

He came away with some more codeine to help with the pain. The doctor had also offered him some sleeping pills but Lloyd was wary of them after that episode with the clinic in London, so he declined.

Mona was waiting for him outside in the Land Rover.

'Guess who I saw?' she asked after he'd told her how he'd got on.

'Who?'

'Joan.'

'Who?'

'Joan Hamer. Pantycelyn.'

Pantycelyn was the next farm down the hill from The Noddfa.

'You were sweethearts at one time, weren't you?'

'No, not really' said Lloyd. 'She's four or five years older than me. We might have held hands a couple of times when we were waiting for the school bus.'

Mona's matchmaking was as legendary as her skills in organisation and delegation. But romance was the last thing on Lloyd's mind, let alone sex.

'Well her son – Rhys his name is – has this fatigue thing. He hardly ever leaves the house. She's very worried. I thought maybe you could have a chat with her.'

Lloyd was already worn out by the day's events, and did not want to think about making plans.

'Well, sometime maybe......,' he said vaguely.

'So I've invited her up to tea tomorrow.'

Four

Lloyd was clutching onto a balloon. It was yellow. It wanted to float up away from him. As light as it was, the effort to hold onto it was almost too much for him. It wasn't a balloon exactly – more like a speech bubble from a cartoon, coloured with a highlighter. He was dimly aware that it represented reality, or maybe even existence itself. If he let go, he would lose his reason or his life.

He didn't want to let go of either, but it was hard to keep holding on, because apart from the burden of the bubble, he was aware only of pain. Not agonising pain, but a dull, confusing pain. He didn't know how much longer he could hang on, but he knew he had to figure it out.

Sometimes, when he drifted into consciousness, he was aware that this was just another bad episode of his condition, but a few minutes later, it seemed, he was back in the conundrum, where death seemed a real possibility. How could he feel this bad and survive?

Often there seemed to be some sort of puzzle to solve in these half-dreams. There was a recurring one where he had to make sense out of patterns in different panels. Each panel had a time limit, and he had to crack the code before moving on to the next. He never seemed to get beyond the first one. Sometimes this didn't matter, and he sort of knew it was a dream. But other times it was vital, and his career, relationships and whole future depended on solving it.

As he gradually emerged from this nightmare, towards lunchtime, he felt exhausted, as if he'd come through a long ordeal. Even though he'd been through this kind of thing more times than he could count, he never seemed to build up any understanding of it. Each time was as bad as the first. Sometimes worse.

He stretched himself from the foetal position and turned over to look towards the window. It seemed to be a sunny day outside. He began to think he might after all survive it. He switched on the radio that Mona had brought up for him. It was a comfort to have Radio 4 on, even if the reception was lousy.

He knew he'd be more or less bedbound again for two or three days, maybe managing to get up in the evening for a few hours. While he felt calm and a part of him somewhere realised this too would pass, he couldn't help worrying that he was never going to get better, that his life would now be like this, that he was worthless, useless. And that as kind and as well-meaning as people were, no-one really understood it. The fact that some still thought of it as a made-up illness, or that he had only himself to blame for it, depressed him profoundly. But how could they understand it when he didn't understand it himself?

He could only lie there trying to keep cheerful. Outside he could hear Misery's mournful, piercing screech, which didn't help matters. Misery had been born before he left the farm, one of the tribe of a dozen or so feral cats who lived in the woods above The Noddfa. Everyone hated Misery, but she was an excellent ratter. The best they'd ever had. So they wanted to keep her sweet.

Mona threw scraps of leftover food for her and her brood over the back wall, just enough to keep them near the farmyard but never enough to fill their bellies and make them neglect their ratting duties around the barns and sheds.

It was not the done thing to name the cats, but Misery's wailing – you couldn't call it a miaow – was so unlike the sound of any other cat that the name came naturally and stuck. Now there were only two or three cats, and Misery was still there. She must be quite an old lady by now.

By lunchtime Lloyd was feeling worn out but a little less woozy, as he put it. The door opened and in trotted Turk, followed by Mona bearing a tray. Turk padded round to the side of the bed where Lloyd's face was lying in the crook of his arm and nudged his wrist up quite forcibly with a cold, moist nose, wanting to be petted. Lloyd couldn't help give a little snort of mirth. At least he could stroke him without making the effort of sitting up, which at that moment was beyond him. Turk sat on the mat and thumped his tail, a look of superiority spreading over his face.

'I thought he might cheer you up a bit,' said Mona. 'I popped my head round the door earlier on and you seemed dead to the world.

'I've bought you up a sandwich,' she said, putting the tray down on the unoccupied side of the bed. She'd even been down to buy him a copy of The Times. 'You can eat it later if you don't feel up to it.'

Lloyd knew this was a kind of special dispensation from Mona, the stickler that she was for meal times. There was something to be said for her strict routine, Lloyd reflected. It gave her a framework, an agenda of what had to be done when. One of the most frustrating effects of his illness was that his days had become formless and this gave him a sense of empty time. Whereas he once hated routine and ritual, he had more respect for it now that his illness prevented him from joining in.

He grunted thanks, and hoped she'd go away, but she'd whipped out a duster and was giving the dressing table a good seeing to.

47

'Do you think it's because you had a busy day yesterday that you're feeling like this today?'

'Who can tell?' said Lloyd. 'Maybe, but it seems to come and go with a will of its own.'

'Don't forget Joan's coming up for tea.'

Lloyd groaned out loud.

'I'm not sure I can face it today, Mona,' he said into the pillow. When he was like this Lloyd was plagued by the feeling that he was letting people down. He couldn't cope with any pressure to see people or do things. He just wanted to stew in his own juice, as Mona would probably have put it.

'Let's see how you're feeling when the time comes,' she said. 'I won't put her off. And Alex is itching to come up to see you. He wants to go up in the attic to look at that space by the chimneys but I've said he's not to go up there without you.'

'Oh, thanks.'

'Well, I'm not having someone falling down there without anyone knowing. Anyway, I've told him you're not feeling well and he can't see you just yet. I don't know what's got into him. He's dancing around like a mad thing.'

'He wants to solve The Mystery of The Missing Room,' said Lloyd.

'Well, he can wait until you're up and about again. How long do you think that might be?'

'Two or three days, maybe. I don't know.'

By mid-afternoon Lloyd was feeling more human, managing to sit up and even beginning to feel a little bored. He'd listened to the Afternoon Play, a rather feeble comedy set in a Belfast youth club where all the kids seemed ridiculously middle-class. He'd done as much of the crossword as he could.

Mona came in to fetch the tray, and Turk bounded up to greet her from his vigil on the mat. Lloyd had managed a couple of lamb sandwiches, and Turk had managed the other two. They were delicious. Mona clung to her tradition of doing a roast or something similar for dinner.

'What's Alex up to?' asked Lloyd.

'Playing those computer games of his,' said Mona. 'Why he can't go outside and look for mischief like normal boys I don't know. What do they see in them, all these youngsters? Do you know?'

'Not really. Tell him he can come up for a bit if he likes.'

'Oh, that's all he's been waiting to hear,' said Mona, and bustled out.

Sure enough Alex sauntered in shortly and came straight to the point.

'Auntie Mona says I can't go up into the attic until you're better. When that's going to be?'

'A day or two,' said Lloyd.

'It must be very boring.'

'You're right. It is.'

'I've had an idea about that room.'

'Shoot!'

'Have you got a laptop here?'

'Yeah.'

'Has it got a webcam?'

'I think so.'

Alex sat on the end of the bed and leaned forward eagerly.

'We'll we could get a long cable with a camera and light on it, and lower it down into the room and explore it that way.' He sat up, arching his back in triumph.

It wasn't a bad idea. Lloyd would never have thought of it himself.

'It could be possible, I suppose,' said Lloyd. He screwed up his eyes and tried to imagine it. He didn't want to give Alex any false hope. 'Where would we get the cable from?'

'There'll be a computer shop in Llanfair, won't there?'

'Hmm, wouldn't bank on it.'

'There must be,' said Alex.

Lloyd reflected that Alex was probably more up on these things than he was.

'And if there isn't, I could get my Mum to send it up from Cardiff,' Alex was saying. 'When does Mona go to town next?'

'She usually goes into Llanfair on Tuesdays and Fridays.' It was Wednesday.

'Will she be going this Friday?'

'How should I know? Ask her.'

'You ask her,' said Alex.

'Why, are you scared of her?'

Alex snorted. ' 'Course not. It's just.........'

'Just what?'

'Well you might have to lend me the money,' said Alex.

'Haven't you got any?'

'Well it's like... it's like I'm not supposed to really have any. As a punishment for what I tried to do to that girl's hair. That's why I'm here really. So I won't get into any more trouble. Isolated. Penniless.'

That didn't stop him asking Mona about going into town, thought Lloyd. He must resent being here, away from all his mates, and maybe he saw Mona as his jailer. But at least he seemed to think that he and Lloyd were now partners in..... what? Not crime, surely. Adventure, maybe.

'Ok,' said Lloyd. 'I'll ask her.'

'What can we do till then?' asked Alex.

In fact Lloyd had been giving this some thought himself. How could he keep Alex occupied while he was in bed? He hadn't come up with much.

'What's that writing on the front of the house?' asked Alex. 'Could that be some clue to The Missing Room?'

Another part of Lloyd's boyhood came floating back. There was indeed an inscription below the dormer window on the low part of the house, above the front door. He couldn't remember

50

the words exactly. Something about redeeming our souls. Not particularly inspiring, Lloyd had always thought, and a bit odd.

It was not uncommon for farmhouses in the district to have some kind of inscription on the front. His favourite, on one of the neighbouring farms, was, '*Not We From Kings But Kings From Us.*' It showed a good old rebellious Welsh spirit. For Lloyd was still proud of his homeland, despite the fact that he'd left it many years before.

'I suppose it could be a clue,' he said to Alex, even though he very much doubted it.

'Why don't you go and write it down and we'll have a look?'

'OK,' said Alex, and bounced out of the room.

It was one way of getting rid of him. If he was to see Joan briefly he'd have to get some rest. He still didn't quite feel up to it, but he didn't want to put it off either. It would be good to see her again after all this time. He did have a schoolboy crush on her as they waited for the school bus, although he wouldn't admit it to Mona. He wouldn't have been much more than twelve, just after he first came to The Noddfa. She would have been about sixteen, but she was nice to him. She could have treated him as a snotty school kid, as he was.

That Christmas she gave him a tie. He must have mentioned that he liked ties with square ends – they must have been the latest thing – because she'd sown the pointy end up flat. But their relationship never went much further than a bit of horseplay in the back of the bus.

A year later she was pregnant. She never revealed who the father was, but she had the baby and brought him up at Pantycelyn. He didn't see much of her after that.

A single mother was a rarity in rural Wales back then. They usually left the area, or passed the baby off as a brother or sister. It wasn't exactly common now. But Joan had always held her head high, taken no notice of the wagging tongues, and had been a wonderful mother.

51

Her son must be, what, eighteen or nineteen? And now this. This illness. Lloyd could just imagine how worried she must be, how much it would mean to her to have someone to talk to who understood. He remembered how liberating it was when he first met fellow-sufferers. In London he'd joined an ME Action group, whose meetings were not very regular or full because of course the membership was not exactly active. But he made a couple of contacts and met two or three for a drink a couple of times. Just to be able to discuss the bizarre farrago of symptoms was a fillip in itself. They ranged from aching lymph nodes to zoning out. This last phrase, he discovered, described the feeling he often had that the solid, real world was dissolving, similar to the clinical term of dissociation. It was a huge relief to find it had a name. The people he met had most if not all of the symptoms he had, even the ones that made him secretly feel as if he were losing it.

He heard Mona walking down the corridor to his room. He'd learned to tell the treads of the various occupants of the house, which was just as well, as no-one ever seemed to knock.

'Joan's here,' she said, hovering at the door. 'Are you up for a bit of tea then?'

Lloyd had made up his mind.

'No, I'm not well enough. But she can come up here for a while if she likes.

Mona's face lit up, and she immediately went down to send Joan up.

Joan did knock, softly, and crept into the room with her shoulders hunched, as if she were expecting to find something unpleasant. Her face brightened up when she saw him.

It was extraordinarily good to see her again. She hadn't changed one bit, and he told her so, as hackneyed as it sounded. Her brown shoulder-length hair was, he was fairly sure, the same style. It suited her. She looked shorter, probably because Lloyd was taller. But even though she was smiling now, she looked care-worn, exhausted.

They made small talk, catching up on the last eighteen years or so. They remembered times when, headlined their lives since and all the time Lloyd knew that she was desperate to talk about her son. She seemed unable to broach the subject, so Lloyd did.

'I hear Rhys has got something similar to what I've got,' he said. 'How's he doing?'

'Not so good', she said, looking down at a ring she was twiddling. Once she started it all came tumbling out.

'He's like a different person. Hardly comes out of his room. He used to be so outgoing. About six months ago he had a bad bout of flu and even after the worst symptoms were over it went on and on, or rather it went and came back again. Two or three other people in the Young Farmers had it as well. At first Old Doctor Thomas thought it might be depression, but the pills he gave made no difference so eventually he sent him to a consultant in Aberystwyth, and he diagnosed ME. He was meant to go to agricultural college in September but he couldn't make it. '

She paused. 'How long have you had it?'

'About nine months.'

'And how long can it go on?'

Lloyd remembered the first time he'd ever heard of ME, on a doc spot on Radio Wales years ago. They were talking to a GP whose wife had had this flu-like illness for twenty years. This struck Lloyd at the time. What a complete nightmare, he'd thought. How can anyone live for twenty years with flu? Of course, he didn't want to tell Joan that.

'It can last for months and months – even years sometime,' he said.

Joan looked crestfallen.

'That's what I was afraid of,' she said.

'But look, he's young,' said Lloyd, 'so he's far more likely to make a recovery sooner'.

She brightened a little.

'Is that true? You're not just saying that?'

'It's true. According to what I've read.'

'Isn't there anything to be done?' she asked. 'I was hoping you'd have a few tips.'

Lloyd wished he had a magic remedy. He could only trot out the standard prescription of plenty of rest, light exercise and a healthy diet, the very advice he himself had thought woefully inadequate.

'There are things you can try,' he said, wanting to say something positive, concrete. 'Supplements and so on. Some people swear by garlic, and there's a school of thought that ME sufferers lack magnesium. Try it.'

'And do they know what causes it?'

'Not really. But they're making progress all the time. They've found the gene expression for it, which means it's definitely not all in the mind as some people used to think. The latest theory is that it's caused by too much bad bacteria in your stomach, which produce a gas called hydrogen sulphate. This is what causes animals to hibernate. That makes sense to me. I have a lot of stomach problems too. But that was only one study. Doctors warn you not to take too much notice of a single study.'

Joan looked as if she was concentrating, trying to commit all this to memory. She didn't look very comforted.

'Don't lose hope, Joan. I know it's very hard to get through for all concerned, but you will get through it.'

He also knew that even with all these developments, any effective treatment was probably still years away. The best thing for the moment, in his experience, was to talk to people. But he hadn't found this easy himself, and he doubted Rhys would.

'You know, I should be up again in a day or two. I'll gladly come down and have a chat with him. A problem shared is a problem halved and all that. Sometimes the worry of it is worse than the thing itself.'

'That would be great,' said Joan, 'but it may take a little while. He just lies on his bed and doesn't even seem to want to see us, let alone any outsiders.'

'Well, just tell him I understand what he's going through. I'll come when he's ready.'

'Thank you,' she said, getting up from her chair.

'I'm sorry I couldn't be more help.'

'Oh, you've made the world of difference,' she said.

'Come again soon,' said Lloyd.

'Yes I will.' She bent down and gave him a peck on the cheek.

Lloyd had a doze after she left. When he woke up he felt drained, but at least he was no longer feverish.

He heard footsteps along the corridor. It was Alex this time, and he came in bearing a supper tray, which he held high on one hand like a waiter in an old film. Lloyd could see the whole lot falling on top, but Alex managed somehow to guide in smoothly down onto the bed. Mona's methods may be beginning to pay off, thought Lloyd.

Alex sat down on the bed, produced a crumpled piece of paper from his jeans pocket, and held it out to Lloyd who was tucking into his steak and kidney pudding.

'I've written down that writing on the front of the house,' said Alex.

Lloyd put down his fork and took the paper.

'*Deliver, Redeemer, Our Souls This Awful Night,*' he read out.

'Where do they want their souls delivered to?' enquired Alex.

'Deliver in the religious sense means save,' said Lloyd.

'It's still weird. Do you think it's one of those word thingies?'

'What word thingies?'

'You know, when you jumble all the letters to make other words.'

'Oh, an anagram,' said Lloyd. 'Could be. Lots of letters. Hundreds of possibilities. Why don't you see what you can come up with? I'll do the same, and we can compare notes tomorrow.'

Alex seemed satisfied with this suggestion. He waited for Lloyd to finish his supper. He jabbered away, asking questions about which films Lloyd had seen and what music he liked. He didn't seem deterred by the fact that they seemed to have very little in common in this regard, and gave detailed accounts of his own likes and dislikes. Eventually Lloyd asked him to take down the tray.

When he'd gone, Lloyd fell back against his piled-up pillows. He was so weary, but he knew he wouldn't sleep for a long time because he'd been in bed all day. At least he felt a little better now, as he usually did in the evening, so he could read or listen to the radio. He could, as he termed it inwardly, fester. He felt free at last from any fresh challenge, whereas once he would have relished any that came his way. And one way or another, it had been quite an interesting day.

Five

'We'd be alright if it wasn't for this bloody war,' said Great Uncle Stanley. He was staring out of the window, looking quite anxious. 'Still, the snowdrops are out in force. It'll be daffodils before we know it.'

For the first time in three days, Lloyd had managed to surface before lunchtime, shower and dress. He'd been sitting in Great Uncle Stanley's room, having quite a decent conversation until he suddenly went off on this war thing. There were Japanese tripods in the orchard, first three of them, then eight. They'd moved inside the trenches, but the most worrying aspect seemed to be that the people in the house could not defend themselves because their ammunition was in the garden shed.

'Of course our shed is still half-way up that hill. And the rest is somewhere else.'

Great Uncle Stanley was often given to repeating himself. Most of the time, he was quite cheerful. He would even laugh helplessly sometimes. Occasionally though he seemed aware of his condition, would ask what was wrong with him. At times the laughter would turn into weeping. Or at least it seemed so to Lloyd. It was hard to tell.

Great Uncle Stanley pondered a moment.

'Of course, the real mystery is why she wasn't crying,' he said. 'What do you think? Hmm?'

Lloyd was thinking about Alex, and paying little heed to what Great Uncle Stanley was saying. He was wondering if Alex would come out of his sulk today. He'd become impatient yesterday because Lloyd was still in bed, and not exploring the attics with him or going to town to try to find a webcam. In the end, he'd been downright rude.

'You're just lying there because you're lazy,' he'd said. 'There's nothing really wrong with you.'

Lloyd told him to go away until he was in a better mood. Alex had stormed out of the room, shouting, 'Don't blame me for your crappy life,' and slammed the door.

Lloyd had been hurt by this. He hadn't seen him since then. So he was thinking that maybe he should go and make it up with him, be the adult, although he didn't feel like it. He was feeling much better today though, better than he had for quite a while. These periods of well-being could come on as unexpectedly as the bad times.

'Well, I think I'll be going for a little walk,' he said.

'Good on you boy,' said Great Uncle Stanley. 'I wish I could come with you, but me pins aren't up to it anymore. Come again soon. I enjoy our little chats. You can tell me more about your travels.'

Lloyd assured him he would, although so far he hadn't had the chance to say anything much about them. Mona came in to fetch his breakfast tray.

'Ooh, hello,' said Mona she said to Lloyd. 'You're looking perky.'

'Yes, I'm feeling almost back to normal today.'

'Well, that is good news. Long may it last.'

To Great Uncle Stanley, she said, 'Was that OK?'

'Yes I will have some thanks,' he said.

'What will you have?'

'I don't know. I'll think about it.'

She caught Lloyd's eye and winked. He followed her downstairs, delighting in his normalcy. They passed through the living room, which was empty and looked as if it had just been giving a thorough cleaning. He could smell beeswax and Brasso. The brass candlesticks gleamed on the mantelpiece, as did the copper kettle and its stand underneath. From the kitchen came the smell of something very familiar. Cawl – lamb stew. Of course. It was Saturday. There was always cawl for dinner on Saturday. He went through to the kitchen.

Turk flopped off his chair in front of the cream, cast-iron kitchen range and padded towards him to greet him, nosing up his arm with a gentle yet insistent nudge. He was an old man now, and it was surprising how moist his nose still was. It was as if he was saying, 'I know how you feel. It'll be alright.'

Lloyd bent down and cupped his jaw in one hand, massaging his ear with the other as he remembered he loved.

'Yes, I know,' he said to Turk, 'I *know*,' without knowing what he knew.

He straightened up.

'Where's young Alex?'

'The last time I saw him he was down in the dining room, playing Scrabble,' said Mona, frowning slightly at Lloyd's antics with Turk. She loved animals, but was quick to disapprove of soppy behaviour towards them. 'God knows what he's doing down there. It's bitterly cold. I don't keep the radiators on.'

The Noddfa was indeed a very cold house, apart from the kitchen, and the central heating was used sparingly. Before it was installed, Lloyd remembered waking up to frost on the inside of his bedroom window, and finding the facecloth as stiff as a board in the washroom.

'Who's he playing Scrabble with?'

'Himself. He was sort of arranging the tiles on the board to make words or something.'

'I'll go and see what he's up to.'

59

'Don't be too long. Dinner's in half an hour.'

Lloyd made his way down the front hall, eyeing the left-hand wall carefully in an effort to gauge how much space there was between the walls of the living and dining rooms, now that Mona had opened up the grate and oven in the dining room. As he went into the dining room and peered around the door into the fireplace, he decided that there was very little. Maybe just enough for a couple of chimneys. That made the uncharted space above even harder to explain.

Alex was sitting at the table moving Scrabble tiles around on the green back of the board. Lloyd rubbed his hands together. It was like an ice-box.

'Aren't you cold?' he asked.

'No,' said Alex. He showed no surprise or even pleasure in seeing Lloyd up and about. 'I think I've cracked it.'

He sounded excited, and seemed to have forgotten all about their little set-to. Youth may have its moods, thought Lloyd, but he almost envied how easily its bad ones were forgotten.

'Cracked what?'

'That anagram thing on the front of the house,' said Alex. 'Look.'

Lloyd went over to the table and peered over Alex's shoulder at the board. On it the tiles were arranged to form the words:

TREASURE
IS
HIDDEN
OVER
THE
FIRE

Alex looked up expectantly.

'What are those letters then?' Lloyd pointed to a string of tiles below which spelt out:

SMUUGLLLOW

'Those are the ones left over,' said Alex.

'I'm afraid it doesn't quite work like that,' said Lloyd. 'For it to be a proper anagram you have to use all the letters. If you just picked random letters you could make it spell almost anything.'

'Like what?' asked Alex, his face wrinkling in disagreement.

Lloyd considered for a few moments. He moved the tiles around, and formed the words:

THESE
FURTIVE
WALLS
HIDE
NO
GOLD
SIRE

The letters he had over were:

EMUURR

Alex looked at it.

'The SIRE is a bit random,' he said.

'Exactly. It's all random,' said Lloyd. 'At least I used up more letters than you.'

'So what?'

'So neither of us can form a meaningful phrase out of the letters. So it can't be an anagram.'

Alex's face fell. Lloyd was himself surprised. With so many letters he thought there would be lots of phrases to be made. He moved the tiles around, but he couldn't come up with anything that made any sense. For something to do, he started arranging the tiles back to the original inscription, putting one word under another:

DELIVER
REDEEMER
OUR
SOULS
THIS
AWFUL
NIGHT

He looked at it idly, wondering what to do next, when something struck him. He gave Alex a sidelong glance to see if he'd noticed it too. But Alex now seemed bored and was moving his chair back and making as if to go.

'I've just noticed something,' said Lloyd.

'What?' said Alex, stopping in his tracks.

'Look.'

'Look at what?' demanded Alex, sitting back down.

'Look at the letters. Don't you see anything?'

Alex looked at them for three seconds.

'No.'

'Look at the first letter of each word going down. What do they spell?'

'D-R-O-S-T-A-N,' spelled out Alex.

Lloyd waited.

'So?' said Alex. 'There's no such word.'

'Don't you do Welsh at school?'

'Yes. We have to.'

'You still have to?'

'Yes, up to GCSE.'

'Well, that's better than in my day,' said Lloyd. 'Then you could drop it before you started O Levels, as they were called then.'

There was a pause.

'Don't you like Welsh?' asked Lloyd

'It's alright. It's a bit pointless.'

'Oh let's not start on that again. There may be a point to it now. DROSTAN. Does that mean anything to you?'

'No,' said Alex, bored again.

'Try splitting it up into two words.'

'Well, *tan* is fire.'

'Yes, and *dros*?'

'That means over or above.'

'So put them together and what do you get?'

'Over fire.'

'Exactly,' exclaimed Lloyd, in what he thought was a Eureka moment. Alex remained unimpressed.

'I think that's a pretty weak clue,' he said, 'and not very likely.'

'Dinner's ready,' shouted Mona from the end of the hall.

They trooped up into the kitchen, both lost in their thoughts. Lloyd had always wondered about the inscription. *Deliver Redeemer Our Souls This Awful Night*. What awful night? It did seem an odd phrase. Could that be because the initials did indicate a safe place for Welsh speakers in a way that their English persecutors could not fathom? Could Mona's theory about a priest's hole be right? But wouldn't that mean that it would have been a Catholic priest who was being pursued into hiding? And didn't the persecution of Catholics come to an end after the reign of Elizabeth I, or possibly James II, early in the seventeenth century?

Lloyd's knowledge of English history was sketchy to say the least. He was taught Welsh history in school. But this didn't help him much either, because he didn't know anything about Catholicism in this part of the world then – how strong it was or even if it existed. And even if the room were a hiding place for Catholics, why advertise the fact in the inscription on the front of

63

the house? He'd have to find a way of looking this up. There was no broadband at The Noddfa, and it would take ages to google it. Lloyd looked over at Alex, and he seemed to be mulling things over too.

'What's up with you two?' asked Mona. 'Cat got your tongues?'

'We were wondering........,' began Alex.

Lloyd wondered what they were wondering.

'Yes?' said Mona.

'Well we were wondering,' said Alex again, glancing at Lloyd, 'if we could go up in the attic to have a look at The Missing Room?'

Mona thought for a moment or two.

'Well, alright, if the two of you go up together. But be careful. You'll have to move that board I put against the gap. In fact, I'll come up with you'

Alex bolted down the rest of his cawl and almost choked. He knew he'd have to stay in his place at the table until the others had finished and kept frowning impatiently at Lloyd as he savoured his cawl. It was a simple dish, just scrag end of neck, onions, carrots and potatoes slowly stewed. There were more complicated version involving leeks and bacon and God Knows What, but Lloyd had never tasted anything better than Mona's basic recipe. It summoned up a rush of memories of the happier, more care-free times of his youth.

'Doesn't Great Uncle Stanley ever come downstairs?' asked Lloyd.

Alex folded his arms in a study of impatience.

'He'll come down for a couple of hours in the afternoon sometimes,' said Mona. 'I've offered to put a bed for him in the front room but he seems happy enough up in his own room. He likes his view over the orchard. And he can keep an eye on all those things advancing on the house.'

Lloyd put down his knife and fork and lapped up the soup with a spoon.

'That was wonderful, Mona,' he said.

Alex jumped up, pushing back his chair with a screech on the flagstones.

'Hang on a minute,' said Mona. 'I've got to get the key first.'

She opened the door in the corner and climbed up the narrow stairs to her room.

'I've been thinking about *Dros Tan*,' said Alex. 'It could be a clue to The Missing Room after all. Then only Welsh speakers could understand it, if they knew how to read it. And the inscription sounds funny, doesn't it, as if they had to make it fit?'

'I've been thinking along those lines myself,' said Lloyd.

They smiled at each other like comrades in arms, in on a secret.

Mona came down brandishing a rather Gothic looking key.

'We'll need a torch as well,' said Lloyd, and Mona told him where it was on the shelf above the Aga.

Mona led the way along the back passage, with Alex following and Lloyd bringing up the rear. When they reached the top of the stairs, Mona took them up the half flight which led to the attic door on the right. She produced the huge key from her pocket and opened it with a rattle. The other side was another half flight going up in the other direction, leading them to the first of the attic rooms, which Mona had converted into a bedroom. It was freezing, and they all shivered. Its window in the gable end looked out onto the woods at the back of the house.

A door in the opposite wall led into the middle of the three attics, where the top triangle of the roof of the smaller part of the house joined on – the place where they could look down into the space below. The door was small, and set above a large wooden beam, so that even Alex had to bend down to get through it.

The middle and far attics were junk rooms. A similar door opened out into the far attic, which had a small window in the front gable end of the house. The middle attic had always been dark and creepy to Lloyd.

They looked around for a moment. There was a dusty old wash-stand, iron bedstead, trunks and leather suitcases, a wind-up gramophone, a wicker wheelchair, a dressmaker's dummy and so on. On the right hand was where the gable end of the smaller part of the house, or at least the top part of it, joined the bottom part of the attic roof. A sort of triangle of beams came about half way up.

Against it was a large piece of plasterboard, held in place by a bookcase one end and a large trunk the other. First the three of them slid the bookcase along. It held a few books and was very heavy, and they could only move it an inch or so at a time. Then Lloyd and Alex moved the trunk while Mona held the plasterboard in place. They all stood there for a moment wondering what to do with it.

'There's more room in the far attic,' said Mona. 'Let's put it in there.'

Despite their mounting excitement, or maybe because of it, it was an awkward process manoeuvring the board through the small door frame. It was heavy and difficult to get a good hold of. They finally managed it, resting it against the inner wall, and fairly scuttled back to the middle attic to see what their endeavours had revealed. When it came to it, Lloyd could not recall exactly what you could see from up here.

Where the roofs joined, they could now see all the top of the end section of the smaller part. There were two beams forming the top of the triangle. Another large beam bisected the gable vertically from its apex, and both halves were bisected in turn by smaller beams running from the roof towards the bottom of the middle beam. To the right of one of these smaller beams was a hole, where the plaster was missing from a triangular section.

'That's where you can peer down into the space below', said Lloyd. 'This end section is flush with the corridor wall which runs from your room, Alex, to the washroom, so that's the start of the missing space.'

Lloyd lay flat on the floorboards, inched forward a little through the hole, and shone his torch below. Alex immediately lay down beside him, wriggling his way through. It was a tight squeeze, and Mona hovered above them, asking what they could see.

Their view was partly obscured by more beams under the smaller roof, and the floorboards that covered most of the space between the wall and the large brick chimneystack. But they didn't quite reach to the bottom edge of the roof. There was a gap where parts of the floorboards were missing – about six inches wide and a foot long. When Lloyd shone the torch downwards through the gap, its beam couldn't find the floor: they were too high up.

To the left, he could make out the corner of the chimneystack, which suggested that there was indeed a large space around it.

'Look!' shouted Alex so suddenly that Lloyd gave a start and almost dropped the torch. 'There *is* a sort of ledge down there.'

Lloyd peered down into the gloom and tried to train the torch where Alex was pointing. Yes, there was something, but he couldn't quite get the angle of the torch right.

'Give it here,' said Alex, grabbing the torch.

There was a yell, a flash of light, a second's pause, a crash, and then darkness. Alex had dropped the torch. It fell down the hole.

'Oops, sorry,' he said.

'Well that's that,' said Lloyd, squirming back from under the eaves.

Mona was sitting on a trunk.

'Well?' she said.

'Alex dropped the torch,' said Lloyd. 'I heard it smash on a hard surface, it sounded like, at the first floor level, so I would say there is some kind of space down there.'

Alex had crawled back too, and sat on his heels, looking fairly sheepish.

'And we think we did get a glimpse of a sort of brick ledge down there, certainly wide enough for someone to sleep on,' continued Lloyd. He couldn't remember seeing that before. 'But then it all went black.'

Alex had plonked himself down in the wicker wheelchair.

'Have you got another torch Auntie Mona?' he said.

'Well, I don't think I've got another in the house,' said Mona, who looked annoyed at the loss of the torch but faintly amused by his cheek. 'Gareth would have one in the barn somewhere, no doubt.

'Can we go and ask him?'

'He's not here this afternoon. Anyway, that's enough for now.'

'But I could crawl through the hole, and you could tie a rope around me and lower me down, and I could see what's really there.'

'Look,' said Lloyd, 'even if you could get through the hole in the wall, and then down between the floorboards, there's no guaranteeing we could get you back. Mind you.........'

'But you could pull me back up.'

'Oh no you don't,' said Mona. 'I'm not having anyone stuck in the bowels of my house.'

'But........'

'No buts. I forbid it.'

'Well can we try to get a webcam on a long lead?' he asked Lloyd.

'What the hell's a webcam when it's at home?' asked Mona.

'It's just a small camera you can attach to a laptop,' said Lloyd. 'Did you hear about that woman in America who had a webcam fitted in her home so anyone could go on the internet and see what she was up to?'

'But you couldn't see everything, could you?'

'Everything,' said Lloyd, with emphasis.

'Oh, my God. Well, I'd rather her than me.'

'What, even when she was on the loo?' asked Alex.

'Yes, thank you Alex,' said Lloyd. 'There's no need to go into all the details.'

'Well? Can we get one?'

'I suppose it's not a bad idea,' said Lloyd. 'We could lower it down with a torch and watch on the laptop.'

'Where can we get one from?' asked Alex.

'Do you know if there's a shop in Llanfair that sells computers and stuff?' Lloyd asked Mona.

'No, there isn't. That I can tell you for a fact.'

'Maybe they'd have them in Aberystwyth,' said Lloyd, feeling the thrill of the chase. 'It's a university town. There must be a call for such things.'

'Will you take us there, Auntie Mona?' asked Alex, charm itself.

'Well, I suppose we could go for a drive one afternoon,' said Mona, heaving herself off the trunk. But come on down now. It's perishing up here and I've got my jobs to do.'

Before he followed the others down the stairs, Lloyd went over to the bookcase they'd moved. On the bottom shelf, he'd spotted an old set of history books Mona must have bought him at some jumble sale or one of the house clearance sales she liked going to: eight volumes of Harmsworth's History of the World, with green covers embossed in gold. He'd dipped into them a couple of times as a kid, but couldn't remember any of it. He looked out the volume that covered the seventeenth century in England and Wales.

'What's that for?' asked Alex, as he brought it down the attic stairs and waited for Mona to lock up.

'It's a history book. We can look up priests' holes and religious persecution at the time the house was built.'

'Oh aye, that'll be interesting,' said Mona. 'I never thought of looking in them books. But you can do the washing up first.'

69

Lloyd looked back at Alex. He looked appalled and was scowling at Mona's back.

'I've been giving you two far too easy a time of it,' Mona was saying. 'Now that Lloyd's back on his feet, he's going to have to muck in, and so are you, Alex.'

Lloyd washed and Alex dried. Once he'd got over his initial reluctance, Alex put his back into it and almost seemed to be enjoying himself. One of Mona's methods no doubt, thought Lloyd. Get people involved, make them feel useful. Deep down people, even teenagers, liked to be asked to do things. Lloyd was finding it quite therapeutic himself, as if it were helping with his feeling of worthlessness. Often it's the small things in life that make it worthwhile, he told himself, not for the first time.

When they finished that, Mona asked Alex to bring down his dirty washing and put a load on. She was making him work for his trip to Aberystwyth.

'I don't know how,' said Alex.

'Oh, I'll show thee how,' said Mona, who tended to revert to the archaic pronoun when asserting her authority on a family member.

Alex stayed leaning against the sink, not knowing how serious Mona was. Lloyd knew she was very serious, even though she had a slight mischievous smile on her face that she was trying to hide.

She took a step towards Alex.

'Go on,' she said. 'Now. I've got a system for washing and you've got to take your slot or miss it.'

'Alright, alright, I'm going,' said Alex, and slunk off upstairs.

'Well, I've got to start getting him doing things,' said Mona. 'I can't be doing with him moping about the place all day kicking his heels.'

'Oh no,' said Lloyd, trying to suppress his own grin.

When Mona had shown Alex how to programme a load on the washing machine, Alex and Lloyd sat at the table while Lloyd leafed though the Harmsworth's and found a section entitled *'The Spacious Days of Elizabeth'*.

He was amazed to find that Elizabeth I died in 1603: he thought she had reigned further into the century. But persecution of Catholics continued under her successor James I, especially after the Gunpowder Plot of 1605. He thumbed through to find out who was monarch at the time The Noddfa was built in 1664, and again was surprised to learn that it was Charles II, after the restoration of the monarchy in 1660. He knew even less than he thought.

'He came to power saying he'd continue the Commonwealth's policy of religious toleration,' Lloyd informed the others. 'But in 1662 he passed the Act of Uniformity, which made acts of Puritan worship illegal. Large numbers of Puritans, or Nonconformists as they became known, were sent to prison.'

'What are Puritans?' asked Alex.

It was one of those words you thought you knew until you were asked to define it.

'Er, people who want religion to be simple – no fancy churches or priests or........whatever,' said Lloyd, not entirely sure of himself and glancing at Mona to see if she thought he was right. She merely raised an eyebrow as if to say, 'How should I know?'

'They're the ones who went to America in the Mayflower,' continued Lloyd, more confidently than the felt. 'For freedom.'

'So are they Christians?' persisted Alex.

'Oh yes, Puritans, Protestants, Catholics – they're all Christians.'

'So they all believe in the same God?'

'Of course.'

'So why are they always fighting?'

'Well, because they all believe that their way of worshipping is the right way. And then it becomes a power thing. It's the same thing with Christians, Jews and Muslims. They all believe in the same God. It's the prophets and messiahs they fight about.'

'It's always religion, isn't it?' said Mona.

'So that would make sense in a way,' said Lloyd, trying to get the conversation back on track. 'If the Act was passed in 1662, and the house, or at least the main part of it, was built two years later, they may well have incorporated a place to hide Nonconformists. God knows there are enough of them in Wales. Presumably there were then too. Probably more. So it wouldn't be a priest's hole, but a Puritan's hole.'

Lloyd was pleased with the way it was working out, even if Puritan's hole didn't quite sound right. He thought about the phrase *'this awful night'*. It would make sense if written by a Puritan, unable to practice his religion without fear of imprisonment. Or worse, presumably.

Alex seemed bored and unimpressed by all of this, and Mona didn't look as engaged as Lloyd felt. They sat in silence for a moment or two, lost in thought. The phone rang, and the three of them gave a little start. It had a loud bell on the barn in case everybody was outside the house. Mona went into the living room to answer it.

'It's Joan,' said Mona, coming back after a couple of minutes. 'For you,' and she looked at Lloyd.

He went through and picked up the receiver from the desk.

'Hello?'

'Hello Lloyd. How are you today?'

'Not so bad today. A lot better in fact.'

'That's great,' said Joan.

She sounded upbeat herself, much more so than the other day.

'I've been talking to Rhys about you,' she said. 'He'd like to meet you.'

'Oh,' said Lloyd. 'I wasn't expecting that so soon.'

'Well, neither was I. But I didn't put any pressure on him. He suggested it himself.'

'Suggested what?'

72

'Oh, that you come down for tea tomorrow. We'd both love you to.'

Lloyd promised he would. But after he put the phone down, he wondered what on earth he could say to Rhys that wouldn't let him down, as he himself had felt let down by all the people he had so far seen.

Six

There was a spring in Lloyd's step as he set off down the lane the next afternoon – something he hadn't experienced for many long months. His sense of well-being was lasting, and although he was careful not to count any chickens, he couldn't help but feel a renewed surge of hope.

It was the kind of winter's day he loved: bitterly cold and crisp, with the palest of blue skies. There was a stillness about the countryside which carried with it............what? An undercurrent of expectancy? No, surely it was just his own mood.

The lane swept gently down past the meadow until it came to the woods below, where there was an abrupt, steep drop down to the bottom level. There it skirted a little hollow before joining the main road. He thought of his teen years when he used to walk down to the school bus, Turk trotting in front of him. He was just a puppy then. He was too old now to make the journey. As Lloyd had left through the kitchen door, Turk had plopped off his chair and made a half-hearted attempt to follow him, as if he too remembered. But he'd just made it out into the yard, sniffed the air, gave an almost apologetic look up at Lloyd, and turned on his heels, tail between his legs. He knew he couldn't do it.

As he wound his way down the hill through the woods, past the little lane up the cottage known as The Holding, Lloyd wondered what had become of Ifor. He'd be two or three years younger than Lloyd and they used to play in the woods together, building dens and rudimentary tree houses, and smoke the odd cigarette. Ifor's father was a Welsh Nationalist councillor who had married a nurse from Dominica, so Ifor had the distinction of being the only black Welsh-speaker that anyone knew. But of course at that age you spared very little thought for such uniqueness. Punished them for it, even. When Mona told him to be extra nice to Ifor, he'd asked her why. He thought for the first time that he may not have been very nice to Ifor.

They did sometimes sit together on the school bus. Although he wouldn't have put it into words, or even concrete thoughts, he felt a duty to look out for him. Sometimes he'd call for Ifor at The Holding. His mother would answer his knock but would only ever open the door an inch or two, so he could only see one eye and half a mouth. She always spoke very quietly and slowly in her accent that enchanted him. More often than not it was, 'No, I'm afraid he can't come out. He's got work to do.'

But sometimes he would be allowed out, and they'd go roaming the woods, climbing trees or damming streams.

He thought Ifor had done very well at school and gone on to....Oxford, was it? He'd have to ask Mona. They'd lost touch, and Lloyd had always regretted it. He wondered what Ifor was doing now. He even thought for a second or two of going up The Holding to see if his parents still lived there.

But he passed on by. Up till now he had had little interest in looking up any of his old pals, or cousins even. Maybe now he was feeling better he would be up for it.

As he emerged from the woods he looked down at Pantycelyn on the opposite side of the valley. It nestled in its own little hollow below a rocky outcrop (the name meant Holly Hollow). On the farther side of the yard was the old half-timbered farmhouse, now in ruin, the skeleton of its roof sagging dangerously in the middle. Opposite was the new house, or at least Lloyd still thought of it as new: a boxy red-brick affair from the 1960s which was now looking decidedly dated. It served to underline the fact that Lloyd's boyhood was from a different era, that what had once seemed modern to him now belonged to a bygone age.

Joan greeted him at the back door. The front door, he recalled, was never used, as so often was the case in farmhouses. The feeling of old modernity continued as she showed him into the kitchen. It was exactly how he remembered it: frosted glass cabinets and pale blue and cream paint. He was struck too by the distinctive smell. Polish of some kind. Maybe wax on the red floor tiles. And then there was the same kind of baking smell. It was comforting, homely.

Joan herself was looking like a different woman from two or three days before, as if a weight had been lifted from her shoulders. She gave him a warm hug.

'I'm so glad he's agreed to see you,' she said. 'I think he's been having a particularly hard time recently. He's getting a bit desperate.'

She smiled at how it sounded.

'Well, you know what I mean. It'll be great for him to have someone to talk to.'

'Where's he now?'

'Up in his room, where he usually is. You can take cups of tea up and then we can have our tea down here afterwards.'

The kitchen table was laid for Sunday tea. Three places, Lloyd noted. Joan was hoping Lloyd could coax Rhys down.

Lloyd made his way carefully upstairs carrying two mugs of tea even though he was not much of a tea drinker. He'd never been upstairs at Pantycelyn before, and it had that feeling of forbidden territory that children have when they go somewhere they're not allowed. He knocked with his elbow on the door indicated at the top of the stairs.

A barely audible voice said, 'Come in.'

Rhys was lying on the bed watching football on a TV on top of a chest of drawers at the foot of his bed. He sat up as Lloyd came in the room. He was a good-looking lad, with a strong resemblance to his mother. But he looked exhausted, drained.

There was another look on his face. Fear. People often remarked how well ME sufferers looked, and despite himself Lloyd had taken this as another sign that they didn't fully accept there was anything really wrong. But worry had clearly taken its toll on Rhys.

They shook hands and introduced themselves. Rhys stayed sitting on the bed, in quite a stiff, awkward position, and Lloyd sat down in an old leather armchair by the window.

'So how're you feeling at the moment?' said Lloyd, wishing he could say something more meaningful, nervous about what he would say. Rhys was not forthcoming at first.

'Well, you know, not too good,' he said quietly, with a weak smile.

'What are your symptoms?'

Rhys trotted out a familiar litany of symptoms, adding that they changed all the time.

'Yes, they do,' said Lloyd. He felt Rhys was holding something back.

'You know there's probably nothing you're feeling that I haven't felt at some time or another,' he said.

'Well, there's a lot of weird stuff,' said Rhys.

'What, like you think you're going mad, or going to die, and no-one can help?' said Lloyd.

Rhys brightened a little.

'Yes, it is like that sometimes,' he said. 'But then, just as you think you're getting used to it, something new comes along.'

'What new thing came along last?'

'Well, it sounds a small thing, but it sends me nuts.'

'Well, what?'

'Itchy ears.'

'Ah, yes. Itchy ears. Mine itch so badly sometimes that I think I'm going to poke my finger right through into the brain. It's a sign that there's something wrong with your immune system, apparently.'

Rhys opened up a little more after that. Lloyd told him about all the doctors he'd seen, the specialists, the therapists, and what they'd said.

'Who are you seeing in Llanfair?' he asked.

'Old Doctor Thomas.'

'What's he like?'

'Alright, I suppose, but he can't tell you much,' said Rhys.

'He's probably no worse than a lot I've seen. Do you know anyone else who's got it?'

'There's a couple in Young Farmers. But they seem to be getting over it.'

'So will you. It'll just take time. You've got to accept that.'

'My friends think I'm turning my back on them. They don't understand.'

'Well you can't really blame them,' said Lloyd. 'You don't understand yourself, do you?'

'That's true,' said Rhys.

'You'll find your true friends will stick by you.'

'And I feel I'm letting Mum down. She's worried about my future, and the farm.'

'You're not letting anyone down. Your Mum's just frustrated because she can't help you. But you must try not to worry about others for a while. You've got to concentrate on getting better. Worrying won't help. Try to do just one thing every day, no matter how small.'

'Like what?'

'Anything. Go for a walk. Write a letter. When I'm feeling really ill I do nothing, when I'm feeling better I try to do too much. That's not really the best thing.'

'But it's so hard,' said Rhys.

'Yes, it is. But it's the only thing we can do. The important thing is not to shut down, even though that's all you want to do. You mustn't give up hope.'

By the end of their talk, Lloyd was convinced that Rhys did indeed have ME. They were speaking the same language, a language that non-sufferers could not understand. He was surprised to find that he'd been up there for more than an hour. He gave Rhys a couple of ME Action booklets he'd brought with him, and their website address. Ultimately he himself hadn't found them to be of much use in his quest for health, but at least they'd reassure Rhys that he was not alone, and not in fact too badly off.

'Are you coming down for tea?' said Lloyd.

'Aye, alright then.'

When Joan saw them coming into the kitchen she raised her eyebrows and smiled at Lloyd.

'Well?' she said.

'We do have a lot of the same symptoms, and for what it's worth I think he's got the same as me.'

'What about you, Rhys?' she asked. 'Was that useful?'

'Suppose so,' said Rhys, reverting to his more taciturn state. But Joan seemed to think that progress had been made.

They sat around the kitchen table eating the fine tea that Joan had laid out: home-made pork pie and chutney, cheese and bread and butter, Welsh cakes and bara brudd.

'I haven't had bara brudd for years,' said Lloyd, tucking into the fruit loaf.

When they'd finished, he said, 'Well, I'd better get doing. Rhys, do you want to walk part of the way with me?'

'Aye, alright then.'

It was a long shot that paid off. Lloyd was surprised.

As he was getting his coat from the hall, Joan came out and gave him another hug, then kissed him on the cheek, but near the lips.

'I can't thank you enough,' she whispered.

Rhys walked with him as far as the wooded bank on The Noddfa lane.

'So what do I do now?' he asked.

'Well, as for that, you've just got find your own way through, tread your own path,' said Lloyd. He had to look away before he saw Rhys's face fall.

'But you know what Churchill said,' he shouted over his shoulder.

'What?'

'When you're going through hell, keep going.'

Rhys managed his second weak smile of the afternoon, and held up his hand in a wave.

As Lloyd trudged up the hill, he couldn't help but feel a bit of a fraud, prescribing hope when all too often he himself felt close to despair.

Seven

Lloyd finally made it down to breakfast the next morning for the first time. Alex had only one topic of conversation: the proposed trip to Aberystwyth. Lloyd had almost forgotten about it. Mona wasn't too sure.

'Snow's forecast again,' she said, ramming toast into the rack. 'It might be hard going over Plynlimon.'

'What's that?'

'The mountains between here and there.'

'Oh, come on, Auntie Mona, you promised.'

Mona and Lloyd looked at each other over their mug rims.

'We did really,' said Lloyd, putting his mug down first.

'It'll be alright in the Land Rover, won't it? And if it's forecast the gritters will be out.'

Mona narrowed her eyes in annoyance.

'Let's see what it's doing after dinner,' she said.

That strange reluctance again, that blowing hot and cold. But Lloyd himself had got the bit between the teeth. He'd been afraid that he might suffer after yesterday's walk but as it turned out he felt almost as fit as a fiddle and intended to make the most of it while it lasted.

'But if snow's coming in, wouldn't it be better to start off now while it's clear?' he said. 'We could have fish and chips for dinner. My treat. Save you cooking. And you could do a spot of shopping while me and Alex look for that webcam.'

Alex stared at Mona.

'Oh, alright then, if it'll stop you two moithering me. But first you clear up and I'll do out.'

'What's she doing out?' Alex asked Lloyd as Mona went to take something in the pantry.

'It means sweeping and mopping the kitchen floor,' said Lloyd.

When they'd finished, Mona said she'd go and get ready.

'What's she getting ready for?' asked Alex after she'd gone up the backstairs.

'She means she's putting on her town clothes,' said Lloyd.

'It's weird here, man,' said Alex, rolling his head and affecting a kind of American hippy accent.

When she came back down, Mona looked round with a nod of approval.

'I'll just take some soup up to Great Uncle Stanley,' she said. She found a thermos in the pantry, filled it with soup from a jug she'd put in the microwave, put it on a tray with some bread and butter and a bottle of water, and carried it towards the door. Alex was so anxious to speed things up that he rushed to open the doors for her.

'Wrap up warm,' she said when she came back down. 'It's going to be a bit nippy in the Land Rover.'

It was an old one, and the heater didn't seem to make much difference. So they all found scarves and gloves and set off.

As they were going down the lower part of the lane towards the main road, Mona suddenly said, 'Why don't we see if Joan and Rhys want to come along?'

Lloyd would never himself have thought of asking them and didn't think for a moment Rhys would want to come. Mona pulled in at Pantycelyn gate and Lloyd hopped out. He found Joan in the kitchen. She said she was sorry – she seemed genuinely so – she'd promised to visit her grandmother in the old folks home in Llanfair, but she was keen for Lloyd to go up and ask Rhys.

He was lying in bed reading. To Lloyd's great surprise, he said, 'Aye, alright then,' without any further prompting. The surprise must have registered on Lloyd's face, for Rhys added, 'I've been thinking about what you said about doing things.'

They'd got him kitted out properly, then Rhys and Lloyd said their goodbyes and went out to the Land Rover. Alex had jumped into the front seat with Mona, so they got into the back.

'Hello Rhys,' said Mona cheerfully. 'Very good to see you.'

'Hello,' said Rhys.

'Mam not coming?'

'She's going to see Gran.'

Lloyd introduced Rhys to Alex. They glowered at each other and grunted something. As they got further away, Lloyd noticed that Rhys was looking pale and worried. He was fidgeting and distracted, unable to concentrate. Lloyd knew what an ordeal this must be for him. He tried to keep asking him things, telling him things, making small talk. But Alex seemed to be vying for his attention and would interrupt, talking about the webcam they would need, whether he thought they could get one with a built-in light and so on. Lloyd filled Rhys in on The Missing Room. Rhys seemed politely interested but hardly riveted.

They passed through the little village of Llangurig, the last one before the mountains. Just beyond it was a rare piece of straight road which ran alongside the river, before it suddenly veered off to the right up around a crag that jutted out into the water's course.

An old image came to Lloyd. It was a car wreck – a mangled white car at the side of the road opposite a house surrounded by pine trees. He couldn't be sure now where they image had come from. Was it a picture he'd seen in the local newspaper? Or was it one that he'd formed after his parents' death, before he knew the details, imagining that this is where it would have been?

But no, he surely had that image in his mind long before his parents were killed. Somehow, he now remembered, he had thought it was a premonition of his own death. He believed as a child that this is where he would die. When they used to pass it in the car, his mouth would dry up and his heart start pounding. And even though it no longer held the same terror for him, he was surprised to feel a little panicky as the Land Rover approached the spot.

Here, sure enough, was the house. It was almost exactly how he remembered it – the image must have been firmly embedded in his mind. It looked like the gatehouse or lodge of some grand manor, but there was no drive sweeping past it. It was bang on the side of the road, a kind of Edwardian mock-Tudor built of stone on the ground floor and half-timbered on the storey above with many gables. It was only when they'd passed it, turned the corner up the hill and left the river behind that he started breathing more easily, and joining in the conversation again. It startled him how vulnerable he was to such childish fears.

They wound their way up Plynlimon, the road snaking round its contours. They could be very bleak, dismal in drizzle, but the pale winter sunshine showed their stark beauty off to their best. The colours of the brush below the snowcaps were as stunning as they were unexpected; blues, purples, browns, yellows. Not much green at all. No wonder in Welsh you'd often describe a hill as blue, or some other colour.

There was no sign of the threatened snow clouds. Lloyd took in a deep breath of mountain air and felt a surge of well-being, happiness. He glanced over at Rhys. Even he seemed to have relaxed a little. He was sitting still, looking out of the window at the view.

It was then that he caught sight of a sign saying Devil's Elbow. He noticed that it now had a Welsh translation underneath: Penelin Y Diawl. It didn't used to. He was glad that Welsh was making some kind of comeback. When he was young, even

86

though he learned a little at home and at school, it was still regarded by many as an old, worthless language, spoken mainly by farmers in the hills.

Yet his heart sank a little, as it had always done on seeing the sign. Devil's Elbow was a long sweep of the road into the crook of a steep valley towards a plummeting mountain stream, before turning back on itself and climbing up the other side to the highest point of the road. As a child he would feel a thrill of terror during the ascent. At the top, if he remembered rightly, just after the road took a sharp bend to the right, was a small lay-by with a small wooden shack which sold teas and snacks. It had stunning views of the valley stretching out over the sheer drop below.

He had a memory – one of those we carry with us of a seemingly trivial, meaningless moment – of his Dad buying a plastic plant from the shack. 'This will last forever,' said his Dad, holding it up and examining it as if it were a newly-discovered species. Maybe he was struck with the phrase, as he had learnt by then that nothing did last forever. God knows what his Dad wanted to buy a plastic plant for, but people did in those days.

It was at this bend, a year or two later, that his parents' car left the road, plunged down on to the rocks below, burst into flames, and burnt them to a frazzle.

He could see Mona's eyes in the rear-view mirror, appraising him and frowning slightly. The Land Rover had gone quiet, as if the others could sense the tension. Lloyd felt giddy. Mona had to slow down considerably as they reached the crook of the elbow, where a little stone bridge crossed the rushing stream engorged by melted snow. The climb to the summit was steep and when they reached it the Land Rover almost came to a stop as they turned the sharp corner before the lay-by. Lloyd couldn't help looking down. Directly below was an outcrop of rock with a single, gnarled spruce struggling for survival. It was on to this that he'd always imagined his parents' car had crashed, although he wasn't sure that anyone had ever told him this.

Lloyd wondered if Rhys knew about the crash. Probably. He was looking down too, as was Alex, but that was hardly surprising. It was a stunning view. They rounded the bend, and sure enough the little shack was still there in the lay-by, but it had been spruced up considerably. Mona asked if anyone wanted anything, but nobody did. This seemed to break the tension though and Alex started chatting away again.

Soon they were approaching Aberystwyth on what Lloyd as a child had called a sea road. He would have been hard pushed to define exactly what a sea road was, and indeed had been stumped when his parents asked him to. Something to do with the sweep of the road towards a wide horizon. And the sound of seagulls, of course, although they had nothing to do with the road itself. All he could say, was he knew when he was on one.

Mona parked in a small car park off a back street behind the prom. They walked through the Victorian shelter with a glass roof to the sea front. Aber hadn't changed much over the years, reflected Lloyd. There were small differences of course; new shops, cosmopolitan cafes, a new office block here and there. But it had the same distinctive character of a seaside resort rolled in with a Welsh market town finished off with a whiff of university cool.

Mona took them to a cafe on the front, where the King's Hall used to be. It used to have an amusement arcade and bumper cars in the basement and was Lloyd's Mecca when he came here with his Mum and Dad. Everywhere he looked, there was a memory of those days; the cliff railway climbing Constitution Hill (he could never see the point of going up a hill for a view), the pebbly beach, the bandstand on a little platform jutting out over the beach. It was near here the Punch and Judy man would pitch his tent. He wondered if there was still the crazy golf near the castle. He'd like to go and see, if they had the time. He could almost taste the memories, seasoned with the salt air.

They sat in a booth by the window and all ordered fish, chips and mushy peas, except Alex who wanted pizza. Lloyd asked Mona a few questions about the place – did the Punch and Judy man come, what was it like when she came as a girl – but otherwise they ate without much conversation.

'Ooh Look!' said Mona when they'd finished. 'The clouds are rolling in.'

They all followed Mona's finger out to the Irish Sea, where heavy charcoal-grey clouds were moving rapidly towards them from the North West.

'We'd better not be too long about this. I've just got a bit of shopping to do. You go and get your bits and pieces and we'll meet back at the Land Rover,' and she looked at her watch, 'at let's say half past three. Rhys, what are you going to do?'

'Is it alright if I just go and sit in the Land Rover?'

'Yes, of course,' said Mona. 'Can you find your own way?'

He nodded and she handed him the keys. He was bearing up quite well, thought Lloyd, silent but calm. He and Alex set off down Fordd Y Mor in search of a computer shop. It meant Sea Road, oddly enough. He was sure it had an English name the last time he was here. But it wasn't Sea Road.

'Why's he gone back to the Land Rover?' demanded Alex.

'He hasn't been very well. He's got the same thing as me. He's not been getting out much and it's probably very tiring for him.'

'The big wuss,' said Alex.

'Look,' said Lloyd. 'It's an illness, like chronic flu. Why can't you try to be a bit more understanding, rather than just blaming him?'

Alex didn't respond, and fell silent. They rounded a corner and leant into the biting wind that had come in. They found a computer shop easily enough. They were approached by a salesman who looked as if he were a student doing a holiday job.

His badge bore the name Alun. Luckily, he was quite interested in what they wanted a webcam for and seemed to know what he was talking about. He showed them one about the size of a golf ball. A ten foot cable was a bit more of a problem, but after a few minutes out the back, he produced one he thought would do the trick.

'Have you got a webcam with a built-in light?' asked Alex.

'No, I've never heard of those,' said Alun. 'It captures what it sees, so there has to be light.'

They bought the webcam and cable, and went in search of a cheap shop to buy a couple of small torches and some tape to fix them to the cable. This wasn't so easy to find and by now the sky was grey and the first flakes were beginning to fall. Time was going on. Lloyd said they should be heading back to the Land Rover and could get the torches and cable from Llanfair in the morning, but Alex was bent on looking around a bit more. They stopped and asked a couple of people but they didn't seem to know. The snow was coming down thick and fast.

'I'm going back to the Land Rover,' said Lloyd. 'You can do what you want.'

Lloyd turned on his heels and started walking towards the car park. The crazy golf would have to wait. He could sense Alex trudging sulkily a few steps behind him. They got to the Land Rover five or ten minutes late. Mona and Rhys were already sitting inside, Rhys in the back.

'Come on, be quick about it,' said Mona, as Alex dawdled at the door. 'Let's just hope the gritters have been over Plynlimon.'

Alex was totally silent.

'Did you get what you wanted?' asked Mona as they reached the main road out of town.

Lloyd waited for Alex to respond but he didn't.

'We got the camera and cable,' said Lloyd, 'but we still need torches and tape. Could we get those in Llanfair tomorrow?'

'Oh, I'm sure you could get them in Davies's.' Davies's was the ironmongers.

The snow was already like a white curtain in front of them. The old wipers could barely keep the windscreen clear, and were groaning with the effort. As they left Aberystwyth behind and headed for the mountains, traffic became thinner and thinner. The gritter must be ahead of them, thought Lloyd, for their lane was brown and slushy but the oncoming lane was white.

At first the travellers faced the snowstorm with a spirit of adventure. Even Rhys seemed quite excited, and joined in the banter. But by the time they had passed through Ponterwyd and began the climb it was dark and the road was more treacherous. They must be catching up with the gritter, as the grit couldn't have been very long on the road. Lloyd knew that Mona was a good driver and was used to such conditions, but he could see her worried frown in the rear view mirror. A couple of times, when the road took an upward turn, the Land Rover slithered slightly and the wheels spun. Mona proceeded slowly. The travellers were now silent and tense: the groan of the wipers, the swoosh of the sludge and the drone of the motor were the only sounds that filled the vehicle.

A mile or so before they reached Devil's Elbow, they saw flashing orange lights ahead. It was the gritter. Mona settled down behind it, and the tension eased palpably. When it came to the lay-by at the top, it indicated and stopped. Mona pulled in behind him.

'Get out and see what he's doing,' she said to Lloyd.

Lloyd jumped out, pulled up his hood and leant forward into the driving snow. He shouted up at the driver, who seemed to be just sitting there. There was no reaction. He shouted more loudly through cupped hands. The window was wound down slowly.

'Are you going any further?' he shouted.

'Nah,' said the driver. 'Turning round. Got to do the other side. Another's coming up from Llangurig. He's got a plough on his front.'

'How long will that be?'

'Couldn't really say. He's supposed to be here in about half an hour. But who can tell in this weather?'

He made it sound as if gritters rarely went out in the snow.

'We're in the Land Rover behind,' said Lloyd. 'Is it safe to go on?'

'I wouldn't if I were you.'

Lloyd went back and reported this to Mona. She kept the engine running. It was bitterly cold inside. They watched the gritter turn around and chug slowly away back towards Aberystwyth. It was strange sitting there all alone, the headlights creating a pool of light which emphasised the darkness outside and the thickness of the snow. Lloyd could just about make out the outline of the mountain-tops surrounding them. They were menacing somehow. He could sense that Rhys was nervous now. His head seemed to be darting around, unable to focus on anything for very long. Lloyd tried to keep him talking, but it was difficult to keep conversation up.

'Oh my God,' said Mona suddenly.

'What?' the others all said at once.

'I've just noticed I'm low on diesel. It's almost in the red. Sod's law, isn't it? I'm usually quite good.'

'You'll still get twenty miles out of her, at least,' said Lloyd.

'But how much will I use if I keep the engine running?'

No-one really knew. Mona switched the engine and the lights off, and this only increased the sense of isolation. Traffic petered out altogether. And as ineffective as the heater was, it was much worse when it was off. Lloyd could hear Rhys's teeth chattering. Mona had soon had as much as she could take, and switched the engine back on. The wipers had now given up the ghost completely and moved only about an inch into the thick blanket of snow. Mona produced a scraper from the shelf under the dashboard, and Lloyd got out and cleared it as best he could.

'At least it seems to be slackening off,' he said when he got back in.

Mona tried the wipers again, and they made it over to the other side and back again.

'Thank God for that,' she said.

They'd been there for about three quarters of an hour, when Mona said, 'God knows where this other gritter is. We can't stay here all night. I'm going to try it. It should be OK if I take it slowly. We've got enough weight on board.'

She sounded as if she were trying to convince herself. And as soon as they crept around the corner, it was obvious that it was a mistake. Even though there was in fact only two or three inches of snow, and Mona was in first gear, squeezing the brakes as gently as she could, they started sliding down the road as if in slow motion. The Land Rover was pointing towards the crash barrier on the right hand side beyond which, as all except Alex knew only too well, was a sheer drop.

Mona said she didn't want to accelerate the slide by turning the steering wheel back towards their side of the road. Fortunately, the Land Rover was sliding at an angle further down the road rather than towards the edge. No-one uttered a word as they slid with agonising sluggishness down the slope. After what seemed minutes, but was probably seconds, the back of the Land Rover hit the rock face on the left hand side of the road. It stood still for a moment or two, then, with a strange creaking noise, the front swung slowly around and came to a rest against the cliff, leaning slightly as its nearside wheels settled into the shallow furrow between the rock and the road. They breathed a collective sigh of relief.

Well, I guess that's that,' said Mona. 'Nothing for it but to wait until the other gritter comes up. Do your coats up and put your hoods up. We've got to keep warm.'

Alex gave a rather stagey 'Tsk,' but obeyed.

Below them, just their side of the Elbow, they could see the stationary tail lights of another vehicle, and just after it, round the bend, the rear and front lights of another. Others had clearly had to give up too.

Rhys was now lying with his head against the seat, his teeth still chattering, probably as much from fear as from the cold. Lloyd just hoped this wouldn't bring on a total relapse. Joan must be getting worried, he thought. There was no way of letting her know. Lloyd was the only one with a mobile, but there was virtually no coverage on the hills.

Only Alex seemed unaffected by the travails of the journey.

'So if it *were* a priest's hole, or Puritan's hole or whatever,' he was saying, 'do you think it'll be empty, or do you think there might be a priest's or puritan's skeleton or something?'

No-one answered.

'What do you think, Auntie Mona?'

'Oh, I wouldn't think so for a moment,' she said distractedly.

'Well do you think there'll be something in it, like a trunk?'

'It's pointless to speculate,' said Lloyd. 'We'll soon see.'

'If we ever get there,' said Alex, or at least that's what Lloyd thought he said. His low voice was muffled by the fur on his parka hood.

Time passed extraordinarily slowly. Alex suggested they play I Spy, and said, 'something beginning with S'. No-one took him up on it.

'It was speedometer,' he said after a couple of minutes.

It started snowing again. Mona would switch the engine and heater on until the worst of the chill was taken off, then switch them off for as long as she could stand it.

'There's no telling how long we'll be here,' she said.

Just when Lloyd was beginning to think they might well have to spend the night here, he saw the beams of headlights swing around the lower corner, followed by a flashing orange light.

'That must be the gritter,' he said.

'What else could it be?' said Mona.

They followed its progress past the furthest vehicle, and Lloyd's heart leapt when the lights started moving off. The gritter rounded the Elbow and after it passed the lights of the other vehicle, it too moved off. Half way up, the gritter stopped. Their eyes were all fixed on it. They heard its engine roar, and then it started up towards them, clearing the other side of the road.

'I'll get out and see if it's going to turn round and do our side,' said Lloyd.

He flagged the gritter down, waving his arm, but it was moving so slowly that the driver wound his window down and kept going.

'Are you turning around at the top?'

'Aye.'

'And going back to Llangurig?'

'Aye.'

'So we might as well wait for you to come back?'

'Aye.'

Lloyd waved his thanks.

'We might as well wait for him,' he told Mona. 'We can keep behind him, at least until we're lower down and the road is clearer.'

She needed no convincing. She was taking no more chances, no matter how slow it would be behind the gritter. They soon saw its lights turning the corner and heard it bearing down upon them. As it passed, the plough piled a ridge of dirty snow alongside them. Mona started up, waited for the gritter to get ahead a little way and eased out the clutch.

The Land Rover revved, surged forward a little then fell back, unable to breach the ridge. Mona took a deep breath and tried again. This time it climbed out easily and broke through the ridge. Everyone breathed out audibly.

They followed the gritter almost until they'd got to Llangurig where the road became wider, straighter, flatter and clearer. Mona overtook it.

The rest of the journey was slow but uneventful. When they turned into Pantycelyn yard it was almost eight o'clock.

'I'll come with you,' Lloyd said to Rhys, wanting to see that he was alright and explain to Joan.

'No,' said Rhys. It was the most assertive Lloyd had yet heard him. He must have realised himself how he sounded, because he added more softly, 'I'll be alright. Thank you for a nice day.'

They watched him walk slowly towards the back door. An outside light had come on, and Joan appeared. She gave them a smile and a wave.

'I hope this hasn't knocked him back,' said Lloyd. 'I thought a day out would get him out of himself, boost his confidence.'

'You can give them a ring tomorrow morning,' said Mona.

'We've got something else to do tomorrow morning,' said Alex. 'Buy some torches and explore The Missing Room. '

Eight

Lloyd was back in Montevideo. He was standing in front of the ambassador's desk. The ambassador was shuffling papers.

'It's no good, Lloyd,' he was saying. 'You've been off almost a year now. And where has it got you? Or us? Or me?'

Lloyd tried to open his mouth to speak, but he couldn't.

'I'll tell you where. Nowhere. It can't go on like this. What are you going to do about it?'

Lloyd had no idea what he was going to do about it.

'You're letting everyone down,' said the ambassador.

Lloyd finally managed to speak.

'I know,' he said.

'Well there's no need to be defeatist about it. It's only a matter of hours before we go to war. And then what will you do? Have a Ferrero Rocher.'

The ambassador snapped his fingers and a liveried flunky came forward bearing a silver salver with a pyramid of gold orbs. He knew if he ate one it would make him sick. But he knew, too, he couldn't refuse. His only option was to roll over and go back to sleep.

When he woke up, he felt he was still in front of the ambassador's desk. He had a sense of déjà vu. Well not seen exactly, but sensed. He'd already sensed this. A teenage presence, waiting. Before he emerged from under the covers, he knew Alex would be there. He expected him to speak, or prod him any minute. But he didn't. To give him his due, he must have been itching to, but he restrained himself. Maybe he was under Mona's orders.

In due course, Lloyd poked his head above the duvet. Alex was sitting on a chair he'd pulled square to the side of the bed like a policeman waiting to interview someone in hospital. Turk was lying at his feet. Alex must have worked out that Lloyd responded to Turk, he thought as he reached out to stroke him.

'How are you feeling?' asked Alex.

'Too early to tell,' said Lloyd.

He looked at his watch. Just after nine. In fact he was not feeling too bad, considering yesterday's trials. He wondered about Rhys. It was probably a bit early to ring.

'Mona says she'll take us down to get some torches,' said Alex.

Lloyd considered a moment.

'Why don't you go?' he said. 'That'll give me a chance to come round.'

Alex opened his mouth as if to protest, then seemed to conclude it wasn't such a bad idea.

'Alright.'

'Get the lightest torches you can. Small ones. You may as well get a few.'

'Alright.'

'And some duct tape.'

'Duck tape?'

'Duct-t. It's strong tape for fixing pipes. The ironmonger will know what it is.'

'Alright.'

'And some string.'

Lloyd told him to bring over his trousers which were over the back of the chair by the window. He got his wallet from his pocket, took out two tenners and handed them to Alex.

It wasn't long before he heard the Land Rover roaring down the lane, and in no time at all he heard it roar back up again. He must have dozed off.

Alex burst in and emptied his spoils from a Davies's plastic bag onto the bed. There were five very thin silver torches, a roll of brown duct tape and a ball of string. Alex was looking at him expectantly.

'Very good,' said Lloyd. 'Just the job.'

Alex grinned, then frowned.

'What's the string for?'

'I thought we could lower a couple of torches down on string, independently of the webcam, so we can move the light around as we need to.'

Alex nodded.

'Well come on then. What are we waiting for?'

Lloyd told him he'd get up if he left him, so Alex gathered up the lighting equipment into the plastic bag, made a deep bow and backed out of the room making circular motions with his hand, in the manner of an old-style servant being dismissed by a monarch.

Lloyd braced himself to get up. He had aches and pains in his forehead, neck, armpits and hands, and he felt dizzy, but it could have been worse. And he was aware that once he did manage to get up, he would very gradually start to feel better.

He went over and drew back the curtains. The snow had already thinned quite considerably. He dressed and found his laptop at the bottom of his suitcase, patted his knee for Turk and made his way to the kitchen with Turk at his heels.

Mona was finishing up the breakfast things.

'Any trouble getting into town?' he said.

'No, it had started to thaw and the roads were clear.'

Alex was sitting at the table, arranging the webcam, cable, tape and string in front of him as if for some military operation. On seeing the laptop, he jumped up and said, 'Let me see if I can plug in the webcam. I've read the instructions.'

Lloyd saw no reason why he shouldn't, so he handed it over. Alex would probably be better at it anyway. He got himself some juice and toast and sat down next to Alex as he fiddled. He plugged in the laptop, switched it on, and looked for the USB port for the webcam cable.

'It fits!' he shouted, and Lloyd was hugely relieved, as if it needed an extraordinary stroke of luck to bring this about. Alex pressed keys rapidly, and just as Lloyd was thinking there was bound to be a hiccup or two, a picture of Lloyd's plate appeared on the screen.

'It works, it works!' sang Alex, and the three of them bent over the screen as Alex trained the camera on various objects around the table, then around the room.

'Well, I never,' said Mona. 'Whatever will they think of next?'

The images were quite sharp once the camera focussed. They played around with it for a while, showing each other on the screen.

'Come on then,' said Alex presently. 'Let's go up to the attic.'

'Hang on a minute,' said Lloyd. 'We have to get the other things ready first.'

He taped one of the torches to the cable just above the camera.

'Ooh, those are nice little torches,' said Mona. 'I've never seen such a slim one before. Very handy.'

Lloyd then tied pieces of string about ten feet long to two of the other torches and made loops the other end.

'What are those for?' asked Alex, pointing at the loops.

'We can put them round our wrists,' said Lloyd with a rather pointed look at Alex, 'so we can't drop them.'

Alex seemed to approve.

'Right, I think we're about ready,' said Lloyd.

Mona went up to get the key from her room, and they all went up to the attic. Lloyd asked if there was a socket in the middle attic.

'No, I don't think there is,' she said, biting her fingernail. But I had a couple put in the first attic when I was doing it out as a bedroom.'

Lloyd found one at the top of the stairs and plugged in the laptop. It wouldn't stretch into the middle attic.

'We can still see the pictures from here,' said Alex.

'But I'm not sure the webcam's cable is long enough,' said Lloyd, 'and we want to be able to manoeuvre it according to the images we're seeing.'

'Can't it just run off the battery?'

'It might not last long enough. We wouldn't want it to go blank just as we were on the point of discovering something. We'll have to find an extension cable.'

Mona thought there may be one in the Glory Hole. This was a kind of out house by the back door, built under the roof of the smaller part of the house. It was where all kinds of jumble made its home. Alex followed Lloyd downstairs and when they opened the door it seemed doubtful they'd be able to find anything in the mess of old furniture and obsolete electrical appliances. But there were shelves high up around the walls, and from one of these Lloyd spotted a length of white cable hanging down. He stood gingerly on a kitchen chair and reached for it. It was indeed an extension cable and they took it back up to the attic, Alex running on ahead with it.

They plugged it in, and ran it into the middle attic where it reached just nicely to the spot by the hole in the gable end. They plugged the laptop into it. There were a few whirrs and clicks and an image appeared, a rather dark one of the dusty floor on which the webcam lay.

'Right,' said Lloyd, 'lights, camera, action.'

He switched on the torch attached to the webcam cable. He played it around a little, and checked the images on the screen. There was a circle of light around the torch, but just darkness beyond. They would need the two other torches.

'Put this on your wrist,' said Lloyd, passing Alex a torch on a string, and he did the same.

The two wriggled towards the hole in the eaves, pushing the laptop ahead of them. They kept it between them, so that Mona, kneeling down behind them, could see it too.

'You lower your torch down first,' said Lloyd to Alex, 'then we'll have some light as I lower the webcam down. The Secret of The Missing Room is about to be revealed.'

Lloyd's heart was pounding. Up till now the whole thing had been a bit of a game, a sort of Boy's Own adventure. But in a minute or two they could actually make a discovery, find something remarkable.

Alex inched forward, put the torch through the hole in the gable end and threaded it down the gap in the floorboards beyond. Lloyd followed with the webcam, but the torch attached to it got stuck on the edge of one of the boards, preventing him from lowering it. It was frustrating when they were so near and Lloyd's impatience was probably not helping. He jerked the cable gently. He didn't want to break the webcam or dislodge the torch from the cable. It didn't move. He gave it a sharper tug, and this time the torch jumped loose and fell into the space. Lloyd started lowering it slowly and then he and Alex wriggled back a little so they could see the screen. The first torch shone a cone of light into the well of the space, but had not yet found the floor. The torch on the webcam now jutted at a sideways angle – something they hadn't bargained for. It caught the dusty corner of the chimneystack. It was clear that there was indeed some kind of chamber down there.

'Here, take the other torch and lower it above the webcam,' Lloyd said, and Alex did so carefully.

'Now lower the first one.'

Lloyd gave the cable another jerk, and its torch shifted slightly in a downwards direction. There were now three interlocking circles of light. They gave a fairly good picture of an L-shaped vault built around the chimneystack. On the right-hand side opposite the chimney Lloyd thought he could just about discern a sort of brick ledge.

'Look!' shouted Alex. 'What's that?'

'It's the torch you dropped the other day,' said Lloyd.

In the far corner of the floor there seemed to be a quarter circle of bricks which were laid in a different direction from the others, with a rim of smaller bricks around it.

'Can you see, Mona?' asked Lloyd.

'Yes, yes,' said Mona, kneeling at their feet.

'So there is a room, after all,' said Lloyd. 'And look, there does seem to be a bit that was bricked up later – that circular part in the corner. That would fit in with those steps you can see starting up from the fireplace in the dining room. It looks as if the staircase to the room was bricked up at some point.'

'And there's a ledge there too,' said Alex. 'That would be for the bed for the priest or the thingy.'

'Puritan,' said Lloyd.

They lay there for a few minutes taking in their discovery. It was awesome to think that they were witnessing a part of history, something that had not been seen for maybe hundreds of years. Alex alone seemed disappointed that there was not anything in the room.

'We can't quite see the floor by the wall nearest to us,' he said. 'Maybe there's something else there.'

It was true. The way the cable and strings drooped over the floorboards, they could see most of the little chamber except that angle between the floor and the nearest wall.

'Why don't we try to swing the strings and cable towards it so we can see?' asked Alex.

'Hmm,' said Lloyd. 'It's a risky strategy. The camera or the torches might hit the wall and break.'

'Well, we've got spare torches,' said Alex. 'And the lens is surrounded with plastic and it's quite light so it wouldn't hit the wall very hard.'

Lloyd looked back at Mona. She raised her eyebrows and puckered her lips as if to say, 'He's got a point.'

'We may as well try to see everything now we're here,' said Alex, sensing he was on the verge of winning the argument.

'Alright then,' said Lloyd. 'But be careful.'

They found they could not easily swing the cable and strings towards them because of the way they drooped over the ends of the floorboards, but they could achieve a similar effect by tugging them up a little.

They watched as the three beams of light swung around like mini searchlights. It was weirdly eerie. Lloyd lowered the webcam a little.

'Look!' they all exclaimed at once.

As one of the beams swung into the corner, they all caught sight of something, like a bundle.

'Swing it back,' shouted Lloyd. It seemed that the revealing beam came from one of the torches Alex was tugging.

'It's not as easy as it looks,' said Alex, manoeuvring his strings as if trying to control some demented puppet.

They could hear the torches crash against the wall. They seemed to be made of sturdy stuff. But they couldn't see the bundle. Lloyd had a re-think: the light might have come from the webcam torch. He jerked the cable over to the corner. This time they saw it more clearly – a packet wrapped up in brown paper and string. It was about the size of an A4 envelope, and hardly looked as if it had been there since the seventeenth century.

'What do you think it is?' asked Alex.

'No idea,' said Lloyd. 'It doesn't look very old. Mona – any ideas?'

'No,' said Mona with a frown.

'How're we going to get it up?' pondered Lloyd.

'You could lower me down on a rope,' said Alex.

'No,' said Mona. 'I've told you we're not doing that.'

'Well, we could put a hook on the end of the string.'

'I don't think that would work,' said Lloyd. 'We couldn't get the string in the right position.

'Well, I've got the dinner to get on. You can work it out over shepherd's pie. Come on. Downstairs!'

Throughout the meal, Alex kept coming up with theories about the contents of the package: 'A treasure map!' and then a few seconds later, 'A missing will!'

No-one seemed to be able to come up with a solution for the retrieval of the package, until suddenly Lloyd had a brainwave, or he thought it might be. He couldn't be sure.

'I've got it,' he said.

'Got what?' asked the other two.

'How to get the package.'

'How?'

'With a fishing rod.'

'How is that different from my string and hook suggestion that you rejected?' demanded Alex.

'You've got much more control over a fishing line, so it's much more flexible. We could get the rod out over the gap in the floorboards, so we can flick the line into the right place.' He'd convinced himself by now.

'Hmm, it might just work,' said Alex, stroking his chin like a cartoon boffin.

'Who do we know with a fishing rod?' asked Lloyd, turning to Mona.

'Now you're asking,' she said. 'I'll have to have a think.'

When they'd all finished, Lloyd said he was going to ring Pantycelyn to see how Rhys was. He was apprehensive, dreading to hear that he was in a bad way.

'Hello,' said Joan.

'Hello, it's Lloyd. I was just wondering how Rhys was after yesterday.'

'Well he's a bit tired and fluey. He told me what happened and I think it was a bit of an ordeal for him. But in an odd kind of way I think it did him good, got him out of himself. We're both glad he went.'

'Oh, thank God for that,' said Lloyd. 'I was worried it might have knocked him back a bit.'

Then on the spur of the moment he asked, 'He doesn't happen to have a fishing rod, does he?'

'Well, yes he does, but surely you don't want to go out fishing in this weather?'

Lloyd explained what it was for, and Joan gave a little laugh.

'Do you think I could come down and get it now?'

'Just a minute, I'll ask him.'

He could hear her shouting up the stairs.

'Yes, that'll be fine.'

Lloyd went back into the kitchen and told the others about his plan.

'Can I come with you?' asked Alex.

'Suppose so,' said Lloyd.

After they'd done the washing up, they found some wellingtons in the Glory Hole.

'Can Turk come with us?' asked Alex.

'I doubt he'll want to.'

Turk was standing in the doorway watching them, his tongue hanging out of the side of his mouth.

'Come on Turk. Come on', said Lloyd, patting his thigh and walking into the yard.

Turk seemed undecided, as if he wanted to come but didn't feel up to it. He went through the same ritual as last time, sniffing air, before turning around and trotting back into the kitchen.

'Has he got ME too?' asked Alex. Lloyd couldn't decide whether this was funny, or just merely facetious.

When they got to Pantycelyn Joan and Rhys were waiting for them in the kitchen. Alex and Rhys exchanged sullen glances. The rod was on the table. It looked a very good one.

'Are you a good fisherman?' Lloyd asked him.

'I didn't used to be bad,' said Rhys, 'but haven't done any in a while.'

'Do you want to come back up with us and give us a hand?'

Rhys gave his mother a quick look.

'Aye, alright then,' he said, and seemed to surprise even himself.

Joan popped them up in her car, but wouldn't come inside. Mona was also pleased to see Rhys up and about, and she said he seemed to have a bit more colour in his cheeks than yesterday. She took them straight up to the attic.

There was only enough space for two of them to lie in front of the hole in the gable end and put their arms through. So Lloyd wriggled in first. They'd left the webcam down there, as close as possible to the package. He jerked it up a little to give Rhys an idea of the space. Then Rhys lay down alongside him. Mona and Alex watched.

It was an extremely frustrating process. As adept as Rhys was with the rod, it was one thing to get the hook near the string of the package, quite another to get it underneath. Time and time again the hook brushed above it. Then Rhys would get the hook to lie flat on the brown paper next to it and jerk it sideways, but it simply slithered back over the string. There was nothing to do but to keep on trying. Eventually it took. All four of them held their breath. With great caution and expertise Rhys reeled the line up slightly. The hook slid along underneath the string until it came to the short end of the package. He reeled it in a bit more. It lifted the package until it was standing on its end. Then he raised it slowly.

'Does it feel heavy?' asked Lloyd.

'No, quite light,' said Rhys.

The package came to the top of the chamber, up to the gap in the floorboards. This was the crucial part – whether he could get it through. Lloyd could see the rod shaking slightly in Rhys's hands. The tension was almost tangible. Very slowly, he eased up the package over the ends of the floorboards. It scraped against them, seemed to get caught for an instant, and then sprang free. Rhys reeled it in quickly and it came swinging towards them. Alex made a grab for it.

'Got it!' he shouted.

They scrambled to their feet.

'Who's going to open it?' he asked.

'I am,' said Mona. 'My house, my bundle,' and she virtually snatched it from him.

Nine

Mona looked at the bundle lying in her lap, and then up at three expectant faces. They were sitting on their heels in a semicircle around her. She seemed reluctant to open it. She was biting her bottom lip, holding her fingers above the string. Then with a sudden swoop she pulled apart the bow of the string. The brown paper opened up. Inside was a brown Manila envelope with a metal fastener. She undid it, peered inside, and poked around a little with her index finger.

'Well? What is it?' asked Alex when he could stand it no longer.

Mona was frowning, and it struck Lloyd that, even in this gloom, he could see she'd turned a little pale.

'Letters,' she said eventually. 'It's letters.'

'What do they say?' asked Alex.

'I don't know. I'm going to go and read them. Somewhere quiet.'

'Can't we all read them?'

'No,' said Mona firmly.

She ushered them all out, locked the attic door, led them downstairs, and went up the backstairs to her room.

Lloyd walked with Rhys down the lane.

'Thank you for your help,' he said. 'We probably couldn't have done it without you.'

'That's alright,' said Rhys, and smiled. It was the first time Lloyd had seen him smile properly.

'How're you holding up?'

'OK. I haven't even noticed the aches and pains for the last couple of hours. That's the first time in ages.'

'It does help to have something to occupy the brain,' said Lloyd. He'd experienced the same thing. Although it was an elusive remedy. Keeping your mind busy didn't necessarily mean that the body would feel better.

When they got to Pantycelyn, Rhys went upstairs for a nap. Joan made some tea and they sat at the kitchen table, drinking it out of her blue and white striped mugs, talking over old times.

'So what was in that package?' she asked.

'Nothing very exciting,' said Lloyd. 'Some old letters. Mona's looking through them now.' For some reason which Lloyd didn't fully understand, he felt the need to downplay their discovery, even to Joan whom he would have trusted with his life.

'Rhys was a great help,' he said.

'Thank you for all you're doing for him,' said Joan.

'I wish I could do more,' he said.

'You're doing more than you know. For both of us.'

When he came to leave, Joan gave him a hug and kept hold of him longer than he would have expected.

'If you're up to it sometime,' she said when she let go, 'we could go out for a drink or something one night. I don't get out much.'

'Yeah, that would be great,' said Lloyd, taken a little by surprise.

They settled on the Saturday after next, and kissed. Just a quick one on the lips.

On the way back up, Lloyd thought about the letters. Even though he'd told Joan they were not very exciting, he was consumed with curiosity, and was already beginning to feel a little awkward about his mild deception. He wondered about

110

Mona's reaction. It was natural in a way, he supposed, that she'd want to peruse their contents before anyone else. It was probably a piece of family history after all. Yet he couldn't help feeling her behaviour was slightly odd, secretive even. Why didn't she just take one or two out there and then in the attic and look them over? That's what he would have wanted to do. Why did she want to wait until she was alone before she read a word? What was she afraid of?

She was getting tea ready when he got back. She looked strange – preoccupied, worried – and barely mumbled a greeting to him. Alex was sitting at the table playing his game.

'Well?,' said Lloyd. 'What did you find in the letters?'

She gave a nervous glance at Alex.

'It's just boring family stuff,' he chipped in, not looking up. He already seemed to have lost interest in the whole thing.

'I'll fill you in later,' said Mona quietly, as she turned from the table to the worktop, and started sawing furiously at the loaf.

The meal was consumed in a rather strained silence for the most part. Nobody seemed to know what to say. Lloyd asked Mona what she was going to do about The Missing Room.

'I think I'll ring that historian who stayed here once,' she said. 'He was a nice chap. I've got his number somewhere, I'm sure. Maybe we should let CADW know or something. He'd know about that.'

'Who's Cadoo?' asked Alex.

'It's the group that looks after historical sites in Wales,' said Mona. 'They might want to interfere too much, tell me what I can and cannot do.' She was speaking as much to herself as to the others. 'On the other hand, there might be some grants or whatnot.'

Later that evening, after Mona had fetched down Great Uncle Stanley's tea tray and they'd cleared up, Mona and Lloyd found themselves alone. Alex was up in his room.

'Well?' said Lloyd. 'Are you going to tell me about those letters or not?'

Mona got out a bottle of Glenfiddich from the kitchen cupboard and poured them each a stiff one. This was by no means a daily occurrence, but it wasn't exactly unusual either. Mona liked one when they were talking something over.

'I've been dundering about it all afternoon,' she said, using a word Lloyd hadn't heard since he was last here all those years ago. It was one of Mona's favourites and used quite often in the family. Lloyd wasn't sure where it came from – whether it was a local word or something adapted from Welsh. It could mean to go on about something, and by extension to fret about something in your own mind. He noticed that Mona wasn't looking him in the eye.

'I just don't know what to do for the best,' she said, 'but I think there's nothing for it but to tell you, now they've been found.'

Lloyd was feeling pretty nervous himself.

'You're not going to thank me for it,' said Mona, 'but I can't see another way.'

'Well you'd better spit it out then. What on earth are those letters?'

'They're letters to your mother,' she said, after a large draught of whisky.

'To my mother?'

'Yes,' she said. 'Love letters.'

'Love letters?' He couldn't make sense of what he was hearing, and was reduced to repeating what Mona said. He took a large slug of whisky too.

'From my father?'

'No,' said Mona, who seemed to be examining something in her glass.

Lloyd let this sink in for a moment or two. When it did, it made his head spin.

'Did my father know?'

'He found out the night before the crash.'

'From the letters?'

'No, he never knew about those. There were other things that had made him suspicious. He confronted your mother. She told him all about it.'

'How do you know all this?' said Lloyd. His voice was as low as Mona's.

Mona stared down at her glass, which she was twirling back and fore.

'I think you'd better tell me all about it.'

Mona sighed.

'Apparently, your mother had been seeing this man for about a year,' she said sadly. 'I didn't know him. Your parents' marriage had been going through its difficulties for a while, but they held it together for your sake. But just before the crash it had been getting worse. Your Mam told me she had an old friend she was writing to, who was helping her through it all. She asked if the letters could come here. She said your father would get suspicious if they came to your house. I thought it a bit odd, and had suspicions of my own, but I was close to your mother and I suppose in the end I just took her at her word. I thought the world of your father too, mind. It broke my heart to see them ruining each other's life. So the letters would come here now and again, and I would keep them in the desk in the living room in a locked drawer and she had a spare key. In those days remember there was no email or mobile phones.'

'But you were helping my mother deceive my father.' Lloyd was getting angry.

'I didn't know that. In my own mind I was trying to help them both. And you.'

'So did you suspect that the letters were down there in The Missing Room?'

'Not suspect, exactly,' said Mona. 'But it had crossed my mind in a vague kind of way. You see, I'd always wondered what had happened to them. I went to look for them in the drawer after the crash and they weren't there. When you think if it, it's not easy to get rid of letters without anyone knowing. In those days we didn't have bin bags and anyone could have spotted them if she put them in the dustbin. She could have burnt them I suppose but that would have looked suspicious if anyone had happened to have been watching. And there are usually some scraps of paper left over. Maybe she didn't want to get rid of them. Maybe she couldn't bring herself to.'

'You've clearly given this a lot of thought,' said Lloyd, not quite kindly. 'But how did you know Dad had found out?' he asked again. 'They were going away on holiday to the coast that day, weren't they? I was going to stay here. Didn't they go? But they must have done. That's when they crashed. I remember you coming to school and bringing me back here and telling me they were dead.'

Lloyd was confused, asking questions then answering them in a rush, trying to sort out his thoughts.

'That was the plan,' said Mona. 'They were going to go away for a few days, just the two of them, to have one final go at patching things up. Or at least that's what your Mam told your Dad. Looking back, it must have been part of her own plan.'

'What plan?'

Another long pause.

'She was going to leave him. She told him the night before the crash. She probably foresaw the whole thing. She'd packed her bags and was ready to go. They had a row. He accused her of various things, and she came clean about the affair. She told him she wasn't going to Aberdovey with him after all. That was just a cover. She was going away with that man. Early the next morning, your father rang me. He told me all about it. He said she had the keys to the car and was getting ready to go. He asked me if I could take the Land Rover down to your house so he could follow them. There was no time to think about it. He was my brother and I just did what he asked. So that's what I did, and walked back up here and waited.'

Mona was now looking at him intently.

'So when did Mum put the letters down there?'

'Well, it could have been a few days before. She often popped up here. Didn't need to have a reason. She could have said she was going up to the loo and done it then. I remember when she was leaving here that last time. She hugged me very hard and said, 'Goodbye,' and I said, 'You're only going away for a few days,' and she said, 'Ye-es,' in a funny kind of way.'

'Hang on a minute,' said Lloyd. 'If Dad was following them, that means...., that means............' Lloyd was struggling to grasp exactly what it did mean.

Mona looked up from her glass. Her eyes were glistening.

'That means it wasn't your Dad in the car that crashed. It was the man she was running off with.'

'But.....but....what happened to Dad?'

'He'd been following her in my Land Rover. She picked the man up at the station. When they got past Devil's Elbow she must have spotted it coming round the bottom corner. She drove like a bat out of hell at the best of times, but she must have put her foot down and went straight off the road at the top bend. When your Dad got there the car was well ablaze. It had hit a rock below. He scrambled down as close as he could, but there was nothing he could do. The flames kept him back. He immediately started blaming himself for chasing her off the road, for her death. He came back here, and told me it would be better for everyone concerned if he went away. He thought I'd be called to identify the bodies. He made me promise to say it was him in the car with your mother. He'd thrown his own watch in the car. It had a leather strap which would have burnt off, so it wouldn't have been on his wrist. He'd worked it all out on the way back. It had an inscription on the back. It was from your mother.'

'Wouldn't the other man have had his own watch?'

'I never thought about that. Maybe your father didn't. Maybe he thought it was just a risk he had to take.'

'So did you identify them? Did you lie?'

'No, I didn't have to. I'm afraid the bodies were... were burnt beyond all recognition. I identified the watch and said I was pretty sure he was wearing it when he left here. And the locket your mother always wore. That seemed to be enough in the circumstances.

'But what about the other man? Surely he was reported missing?'

'I don't know about that. He wasn't from around here. Shrewsbury or somewhere I think. He'd met your Mam at some teachers' conference or something. Maybe he'd told his wife he was leaving her, and that's what she told everyone.'

There was another pause, during which Lloyd finally grasped the greatest significance of Mona's story.

He said in a very low voice, barely more than a whisper, 'So Dad's still alive?'

'Yes,' said Mona just as quietly.

They sat there for a moment. Mona couldn't look at him. She just sat there staring into her glass.

'Where is he?' said Lloyd eventually.

Mona took a deep breath and finished her story.

'In London somewhere. I don't know where exactly. I haven't got his address or phone number. That was another part of the promise. He said then if anything did ever come out, I wouldn't be implicated, like an accessory. He phones me once in a while to tell me he's OK, and to ask about you. But he won't tell me anything about his new life.'

There was another silence, broken only by the ticking of the kitchen clock.

'I'm sorry Lloyd,' said Mona. 'All this must come as a terrible shock.'

That didn't come near it. It was almost as bad as the news of his parents' death. Worse, in some ways. His parents and Mona were the three people he had loved and trusted most in his life. All three had deceived him. Anger, confusion and distress all swirled around his head and stomach. He told Mona as much.

'If there's one thing you must understand in all of this, it's that your father has always loved you very much. It was because he loved you that he wanted to protect you. Maybe he wasn't thinking too clearly exactly, but he said it would be bad enough if people knew your mother was running off with another man. It would have been a big scandal back then, round here. It would be even worse if he was implicated in her death in some way, however small a way. He thought he'd be charged with something, sent to prison even. I begged him not to go, to stay and face whatever had to be faced, but he kept going back to the effect it would have on you. In a way I could see he had a point. In the end I didn't have much choice. I wanted to protect him, and you too.'

'But in later years didn't he ever want to get in touch with me, see me again?'

'Oh yes, many times. But then he knew he'd be putting you through what you're going through now. Once he'd made the decision he had to abide by it.'

By now Lloyd was feeling decidedly ill, aching in every limb and feeling faint. But he had one more question.

'What about the letters? Can't I see them?'

'I suppose you've every right. But why upset yourself even more? In fact a lot of them are just about arrangements, where to meet and so on.'

'No,' said Lloyd. I don't want to see them. Not yet anyway. '

'Alright then. Believe me, I'm so sorry it had to come out like this. I didn't feel I had a choice. We were just trying to do what we thought was best for you.'

117

There was a tear running down her cheek. Up till now Lloyd had managed to keep calm, waiting for the next revelation. But he suddenly lost it.

'How could you, Mona. How could you fucking do this to me?'

'Lloyd, I......'

'You who I've loved and trusted all my life. It's all one big fucking lie isn't it?'

Mona put her head into her hands and started to sob.

'Isn't it?' he shouted at her.

She didn't respond. Just sat there sobbing. He threw his glass against the wall above the Aga.

'I'm going to bed,' he said, and left her there.

He felt exhausted and sick as his head hit the pillow. He knew he wouldn't sleep, and would feel awful tomorrow. But he'd already made up his mind to leave The Noddfa as soon as possible and go back to London.

Ten

Lloyd didn't sleep a wink until seven in the morning, and then only fitfully. It was as if a heavy weight was bearing down on his chest, sending ripples of pain through his body, as when a stone is thrown into a pond. He felt sick and dizzy, and every time he was just on the point of nodding off, it was as if a jolt of electricity jerked him, so he felt exhausted and wide awake at the same time. And he knew that when he finally did drop off, he'd be plagued by those disturbing dreams in which he had to solve some weird conundrum over and over again, sometimes knowing it was a dream, sometimes not.

He drifted off after dawn, when he could see the light outside and felt a little safer, protected to some extent from the nightmares. He dreamt his father was still alive. He woke with a start. He had that sick, sinking feeling in the pit of his stomach. For a while he still thought it was a dream, but almost imperceptibly fragments of yesterday's revelations appeared as if through a mist: the fishing rod, the letters, the stories. He remembered too his decision to leave The Noddfa, to go back to London. He was determined to go through with this, although he knew he wouldn't be going anywhere today, nor probably for a day or two.

He thought about his father, about whether he wanted to see him. Some part of him deep down knew that he did, but he didn't know when, or indeed how. Something was in the way. He couldn't picture it. He drifted off again.

At dinnertime Mona came in with some soup and a bottle of water. In a tone that he would not have adopted a day ago, he told her he was not hungry. He wanted her to go away. She said she'd leave it there, and poured him some water. He lifted his head off the pillow and drank greedily. He lay back down on the pillow. Mona hovered. He didn't say anything.

'How are you feeling?' she asked.

'I'm all in,' he said.

'Please don't be angry with me, Lloyd.'

'Of course I'm angry,' he mumbled. 'I'm angry with the whole thing. Can you blame me?'

'No,' she said quietly. 'No, I don't suppose I can.'

He wanted to ignore her, not to engage with her. But more questions had been running round his head all night, and he couldn't help himself.

'When did my father last ring here?'

He noticed he said my father, and not Dad.

'About a couple of months ago. I'd been telling him about your illness. It was him who suggested you came here.'

'So when do you think he'll phone again?'

'In a month or two, I should think. I'm sure he'll want to see you now that everything's.... well..... out in the open.'

'Well, I'm not sure I want to see him,' said Lloyd flatly. He was aware that he was punishing Mona in some way, but he couldn't help himself. He told her of his decision to leave The Noddfa as soon as he was up and about again. She was clearly upset. He didn't care. She sat down on the chair by the window.

'But you've been getting better here. You'll go on getting better. And you never know when your father will ring.'

'My mind is made up,' said Lloyd.

'Please don't go, Lloyd,' said Mona. 'I'm begging you now as I begged your father then.'

'I'm sorry Mona. I need to put some distance between me and here for a while.'

'But who'll look after you?'

He told her he could look after himself. Both of them knew this wasn't completely true. Mona looked at him, and seemed to accept that it was useless trying to dissuade him. She heaved a deep sigh and left him.

Lloyd didn't get up that day, nor the next. Mona brought him invalid meals on a tray. She spoke no more of Lloyd's planned departure. She seemed to have given up trying to change his mind. She was subdued, and Lloyd began to feel a little sorry that he was upsetting her. He tried to be more conciliatory, speak to her more kindly, but he was determined not to be diverted from his course.

That second afternoon, Alex came up to see him with Turk. For once he knocked on the door and came in quietly.

'Same old trouble?' he asked.

'Same old trouble,' said Lloyd.

'Mona says you're going back to London.'

'As soon as I'm up again, yes.'

'Have I offended you in some way?'

'Well, sometimes your tongue gets the better of you,' said Lloyd. 'You probably mean to be funny, but sometimes it comes out nasty. But that's not why I'm going.'

'I'm going back to Cardiff in a few days too,' said Alex.

'How d'you feel about that?'

'OK, I suppose.'

'Haven't you missed your Mum and Dad?'

'Sometimes.'

'Do you get on with them?'

'Sometimes.'

Lloyd wanted to tell him to cherish his parents, to respect them and be kind to them. But he knew such a sermon would cut no ice with Alex.

'Well, make the most of them,' he said. 'You'll probably be going away to university, won't you?'

'Maybe. I haven't decided yet.'

'It'll happen before you know it. I know you think it seems an eternity but once your youth has gone, it's gone. There's no going back.'

Alex looked annoyed that Lloyd was giving him this lecture when there were more practical matters to sort out in the short time they had left together.

'I'm sorry the holiday is over,' he said.

'Is that how you think of it, as a holiday?' asked Lloyd.

'Well, it was a bit of an adventure with The Missing Room, wasn't it? It's a pity that there was nothing in it but letters, isn't it?'

'I suppose so.'

'Were you disappointed?'

'Yes. In a way, I was disappointed.

'Maybe there's still something there that we didn't find,' said Alex. 'Once we found the letters we stopped looking. I don't think we looked properly into the other corner.'

'Maybe not.'

'Maybe next time we're both here we can have another look. What d'you think?'

'Maybe.'

'I was thinking,' said Alex solemnly, 'now that we've met, it would be a good idea if we stayed in touch. I mean I know we're sort of relations, but that doesn't stop us being friends, does it?'

Lloyd agreed it was no impediment.

'We could have more adventures together.'

Lloyd couldn't help giving a little smile. Their roles had reversed somewhat since the start of their time together.

Alex found pen and paper, wrote down his address and phone number and handed it to Lloyd. He asked for Lloyd's mobile number and, folded the paper up carefully and put it in his pocket.

'I want a mobile for my birthday,' he said. 'You can be the first person I ring. Well, I hope you're feeling better soon.'

He went out as quietly as he came in, leaving Turk on the mat. Quite a change from when he first saw him, thought Lloyd. He could hear Misery wailing somewhere out in the orchard. He was sorry the holiday was over too.

On the third morning Lloyd managed to get up at about eleven o'clock. He was still exhausted but the fevers had gone and the aches and pains had eased. The house seemed quiet. He went down to the kitchen. Turk was lying on the mat in front of the range, and thumped his tail in weary greeting, not lifting his head from his paws. There was no-one around, and the Land Rover had gone from its place in the yard. It was Friday. Mona would have gone to town. Alex must have gone with her. There was not a trace of snow left. It was a grey, overcast day and everything seemed washed out, vapid.

He got himself a bowl of cereal, not feeling up to much else. After he'd washed the bowl, he wandered up to see Great Uncle Stanley. Something he'd said when Lloyd first went in to see him had been troubling him ever since he found out about his father.

He found him in his usual place in the chair by the window, the rug over his legs. He was lost in his thoughts, and Lloyd wasn't sure he recognised him.

'The trenches are coming closer,' he said without any preamble.

'Which trenches, Uncle Stanley?'

'Well, the German ones. They used to be German, any road. I think they might be French now.'

Even Great Uncle Stanley wasn't old enough to have fought in the First World War, although Lloyd worked out he would have been a boy. Among the objects decorating his room were two brass shells mounted on a wooden plinth. They had pride of place on the mahogany chest of drawers. Lloyd knew they'd been awarded to Great Uncle Stanley's father, who had fought in the First World War, for some undisclosed act of bravery. If Great Uncle Stanley was back in those days, Lloyd doubted very much that he'd be able to get any sense out of him about more recent times. He decided coming straight to the point was the best plan. He had nothing to lose.

'You said the other day that she wasn't crying. Who wasn't crying?'

'Mona of course,' said Great Uncle Stanley without missing a beat and registering no surprise at the question.

'When wasn't she crying?' asked Lloyd, realising as he said it what a ridiculous question it was, but Great Uncle Stanley knew exactly what he meant.

'At your parents' funeral. Thought it was odd at the time. She adored your father. Always had. They were very close.'

Lloyd tried to think back to the day when his parents, or his mother and her lover as he must now get used to thinking of it, were buried. It had all gone by in a blur. And he was too busy fighting back his own tears to notice anyone else's, let alone the lack of them.

'Why do you think that was?' asked Lloyd. He sensed that he was being scrutinised very carefully.

'I don't know,' said Great Uncle Stanley slowly through narrow eyes.

'Did you ever ask?'

'No,' said Great Uncle Stanley. 'I used to think about it at the time, but could never work out how to broach the subject, if you know what I mean.'

Lloyd suspected that he knew more than he was letting on, or at least had his own suspicions. For some reason it was important for him to find out if anyone else knew about his father, if anyone else was in on the secret, or at least part of it. In this neck of the woods it was hard to keep something a total secret: there was usually some talk, even if it was inaccurate. But of course he couldn't ask anyone outright, because if they didn't know he'd be letting them know. He still wanted to protect his mother's name, despite her deceit, despite the fact that she had not just been running away from his father, but running away from Lloyd himself, deserting him without so much as a backward glance. He tried to recall if she'd given him a special hug goodbye, as she'd given Mona, but he could remember no such thing. But then, he would have no reason to.

He decided to have one more go at Great Uncle Stanley.

'If you didn't know for certain why she wasn't crying at the funeral, you must have had your suspicions. It's preyed on your mind all these years.'

But Great Uncle Stanley was now staring out of the window.

'I think the trenches have moved a little nearer,' he said. 'But I don't think there's anything to worry about. It'll be alright in the end.'

Lloyd gave up. He told him he was leaving for London.

'I'm sorry to hear that boy. I've enjoyed our little chats. Will you come and see me sometime?'

Lloyd promised he would. He asked the old man if he wanted anything. Great Uncle Stanley looked down at the little table next to his chair.

'No, indeed. Mona's left me a thermos of tea and some sandwiches. She keeps that biscuit barrel full, and a bowl of those boiled sweets I like. No, she looks after me very well, I must say. She's a good 'un.'

Before last night Lloyd would readily have agreed with him. Now he couldn't bring himself to. He felt she had betrayed his trust, that she wasn't the kindly Mother Hen people thought. He felt utterly alone.

He went downstairs, put on a coat and wellies, and set off down the lane. He had thought about ringing Joan beforehand, but decided against it. He'd chance it. It was just coming up to two o'clock. She'd probably be finishing up the dinner things.

Sure enough, when the back door opened, she was at the sink, washing up. Rhys had opened the door.

'How're you doing?' he asked Rhys.

'Not so bad,' he said. 'Quite good in fact. I've been to town this morning with Mam.'

He did look much better in an indefinable way. He had more colour, but more importantly a lot of the worry had disappeared from his face – not all of it, but enough to make a considerable difference.

'We bumped into Mona and Alex,' said Joan, drying her hands and coming towards him with a smile. 'She said you'd had a bit of a bad turn.'

'Yes,' said Lloyd. 'But I'm better now. In fact I'm going to London tomorrow.'

Joan and her son looked at each other with something close to dismay. Clearly Mona had not mentioned this. Maybe she was worried that they'd want to know why.

'How long for?' asked Joan.

'Er, I'm not sure yet,' said Lloyd. He felt as if he were betraying them somehow. He didn't know whether to explain the decision, and if so, how, without giving his mother away.

'There are one or two things I need to do,' he said. 'Then we'll see.'

'Well, it was very nice to meet you,' said Rhys, holding out his hand rather formally. Lloyd shook it.

'And thanks for the advice,' said Rhys, and then he disappeared upstairs.

'He'll miss you,' said Joan.

'I'll miss him,' said Lloyd.

'And I will too.' She came a little closer.

'I'm sorry. Our drink will have to wait.' He put his hand on her shoulder.

126

'This is all a bit sudden,' she said, ushering him to the table and pouring him out a mug of tea.

The phrase that came to Lloyd's mind was, 'I need to get away.' But that would sound somewhat mysterious and even send the wrong signals, just when they'd been getting on so well. He could see her owed her some explanation, though. He worked out the words carefully in his head.

'Those letters we found in that place beneath the attic,' he began, 'they were letters of my mother's. It sort of brought it all back. I just need to get away for a while, that's all.'

It was the truth and nothing but the truth, but not of course the whole truth. He felt a little bad at the omission, but he couldn't tell her the whole story. Not now, anyway. He was watching her face but it revealed no further knowledge of, or indeed any curiosity about the letters. She took his statement at face value. She couldn't have heard any talk, any rumours.

'I can see it must be very hard for you,' she said. 'Do you think you'll be coming back?'

'I just don't know yet, Joan.'

'I was looking forward to our evening out,' she said.

'So was I. Maybe you could come to London for a visit.'

'Well.......I don't know. It's difficult for me to get away, what with one thing and another.'

'Well, we can keep in touch. Once I've sorted myself out a little, I'll let you know. I'd hate to lose contact with you again.'

He finished his tea and stood up. Joan stood up too, and wrapped her arms around him. His mouth sought hers and he turned it into a proper kiss. She pushed him away and looked into his eyes, searching for something it seemed. Then she smiled and took up where they'd left off. There were tears in her eyes.

He was weary as he set off back up the lane, and full of woe. It was an old-fashioned word, but one that seemed apt. Forlorn was another word that came to him; he knew not from where. He

127

wasn't even entirely clear what it meant. The thick low cloud was oppressive. He could hear the rooks in the wood. He felt he had to do something to try to shake off his melancholy mood. He must stop feeling so sorry for himself. So on the spur of the moment, he paid one more visit that afternoon, to Mrs Evans of The Holding.

When he first started thinking about his return to London, he saw it as making a clean break as it were, a loosening of his ties with The Noddfa, at least for a while. But it was proving more difficult than he thought it would be. He'd spent his day so far promising to keep in touch, and part of him wanted to, especially with Joan.

So he surprised himself when he was climbing the hilly part of The Noddfa lane, and he suddenly veered off to the left up the narrow lane towards The Holding. Something told him to take it, the narrow lane up to the cottage, even though it would be to renew acquaintance and then quickly to say another goodbye, maybe to make yet another promise to keep in touch.

It was a dark, un-tarmacked track, with a grass ridge running between the two ruts. Even darker and narrower than he remembered it. On the right hand side were the woods, on the left a hillock with the funny old barn on its breast. It had a semi-circular roof made of corrugated iron, which went right down to ground level. It had always reminded him of something you'd see in an airfield in a World War II film. It was spooky to be walking up it again after all this time.

The lane approached the cottage on the side, and then ran on under the edge of the wood to another old house further on. The Holding was an old farm-worker's tenement, he supposed, as the name suggested. There was the narrow wicket at an angle between the side of the house and the garage, just as it had always been. He unlatched it and it squeaked open. It led into the small front garden, with sweeping views of Pantycelyn and the valley beyond. It had always been immaculate, the box hedges as sharply-edged as a diagram in a school maths book. They were a little less so now, still clearly sculpted, but with the odd wayward sprig sprouting out here and there. The lawn was not quite the laundered napkin it had once been, and its edges were untrimmed. Ivy was cascading down over the front porch, as if it was rarely disturbed by people coming or going underneath it. The house itself seemed a little bigger than he remembered it, which surprised him, because usually things were smaller than in recollection. It was tiny, but not as tiny as he expected. Maybe his memory had shrunk it.

He knocked at the door, as he had so many times before, and, as if by time travel, it was opened slowly just an inch or two to reveal an eye an half a mouth.

'Hello, Mrs Evans? It's me, Lloyd. From The Noddfa.'

The door opened another couple of inches and he saw a face that was completely unaltered by time. He could have been twelve again. It was just what he needed to dispel the mood that had swept down upon him.

'Well, bless my soul,' said the face, a little smile creeping over it. The voice was just as quiet and measured as it had always been, and Lloyd wondered if there wasn't now just the merest tint of a Welsh accent about it. It was hard to tell. But it seemed to him to be the biggest difference between now and then. Then it had been a distinct, and to him exotic, Caribbean accent. Now, as then, he didn't know whether the door would be opened any wider. He half expected to hear her say, 'Not tonight. He has his homework to do.'

'Come in for five minutes,' said Mrs Evans.

He noted the time limit. Mrs Evans had always had a knack of putting you in your place. And as he stepped into the living room, he felt like a little boy again, only bigger and clumsier. It was the same cosy style, with chintzy covers and gleaming brass. It was spotless.

She insisted on making him a cup of tea – it seemed impossible not to be a tea drinker here – and brought with it a couple of slices of buttered bara brudd, home-made no doubt, on a little plate. He wondered who would have eaten it if he hadn't, on no more than a whim, turned up the lane.

He asked after Mr Evans.

'Oh, he passed a few years ago now.'

Lloyd said he was sorry, and indeed he was. He knew that Mr Evans had died. Mona had told him. He'd died out of the blue of a heart attack, in his early forties. He'd forgotten. But he should have known not to ask.

He moved on to Ifor, and he was rewarded with a smile.

'He's doing very well. He went to Oxford, you know. He read philosophy. He's a professor now.'

They chatted a little more. She asked him about his life and work. She seemed impressed by the Foreign Office.

'I'm so glad you've done well. I always knew you would. And you were such a good friend to Ifor.'

Lloyd had always thought Mrs Evans had considered him rather a bad influence on her son, trying to take him away from his homework.

She clearly hadn't heard about his illness. He had the impression that she didn't get out much, didn't talk to many people, if indeed anyone. It must be a lonely existence here for her at The Holding – she had never had any friends as far as Lloyd could make out – with only the weekly phone calls and holiday visits from Ifor to look forward to. Maybe she liked it that way.

Mrs Evans got up out of her chair and fetched a photograph from the polished mantle shelf. Ifor in his graduation robes. He'd turned into a handsome young man. But there was something even more striking about the face: a kind of serenity, peace, with not a hint of smugness. It was a face Lloyd wanted to see again.

When he'd drunk his tea, Lloyd stood up and took his leave, as he knew he was expected to do. There was no protest. It had been an easy meeting again after all these years, and it was an easy parting. Yet a part of him was uneasy about leaving this solitary, dignified woman. He asked for Ifor's mobile number. She found it on a piece of paper in a little book and he entered it into his phone. They shook hands.

It was getting dark. He could hardly see his way down the lane, under the tunnel of trees. He had to feel the ruts with his feet. This came naturally, as of old. It came to him now why his feet had taken him up this lane in the first place. If there was one person he could talk to about the discovery in The Missing Room, it was Ifor.

Eleven

On the train to London, Lloyd sat back in his seat, tried to clear his head, and work out what he made of it all. He considered if his hasty departure from The Noddfa had been inconsiderate. While he was packing, Alex had mooched around in his room like a beaten dog. Even Turk had thrown him a reproachful glance as he put on his coat and picked up his suitcase.

When Mona dropped him off at the little station well before the noon train was due, she'd said a quick goodbye through the Land Rover window and then, with a squeal of the wheels as she turned around, was gone. He'd been surprised by this and, although he knew he had only himself to blame, a little hurt.

But no, he was right to leave. He had to escape. Escape the past, try to look forward. The Noddfa had begun to stultify him.

The trolley clattered by, and Lloyd bought a can of lager to go with the cheese and onion sandwiches that Mona had wrapped in foil for him. He found himself beginning to relax after a couple of sips. He consciously asked himself what he felt about seeing his father again, going so far as to articulate the question in his head with metronomic precision: 'Do – you – want – to – see – your – fa - ther?'

He tried to start with a clean slate, ignoring the inner voice which told him of course he did. At the time of the crash, he had been a bit of a tearaway, a rebel. Both his parents were teachers and he was expected to go on to university. It was taken as read. He had breezed through school with an easy ability, doing the minimum amount of work to get through. Maybe, he thought now, he had sensed unhappiness at home, although he couldn't remember being aware of it.

In the year or so before the crash – the year of his mother's affair he realised now – he had begun mitching off school with his friend Alan Sweeney, a Scouser whose Mum ran the Red Lion pub in the town. Sometimes they would steal booze from the pub, or take his brother's old dirt bike up the field above.

After the crash, all that changed. He started working hard at school, wanted to achieve something that would have made his parents proud, turned his back on Sweeney. He had always regretted that at each milestone of his education and career – graduation, first job, first posting overseas - his parents were not there to see him. That his father was alive, and would probably have heard about these feats from Mona, in no way made up for it. In fact it was as if he had done it all for nothing, as if it were all a sham.

He tried to visualise a meeting. It would be early evening, in a smart cafe-bar in North London. For some reason, it would be raining stair-rods. They would be sitting opposite each other in a booth by the window, the thrum of the rain on the glass filling in the silences.

Oddly enough, he couldn't picture his father's face very clearly. Or at least he could for an instant, but then it would go out of focus. He would be in his late fifties now, he supposed. Probably remarried. Maybe with a new family. He'd have stepbrothers or stepsisters. The thought came as something of yet another shock. He wondered if he'd changed his name.

He'd asked Mona none of these things. She probably didn't know anyway. But he badly wanted to know, so maybe curiosity if nothing else would in the end push him towards his father. But what if his father didn't want to see him? What if he were happy with his new life and family, and didn't want it disrupted? It was likely he'd never told them he had a son. There was a thought. Lloyd knew he couldn't go through life without answers, as painful as they might be.

To some extent he bought Mona's claim that everything his father had done had been to protect him, even keeping him out of his life. He certainly believed that Mona had been acting in his own best interest. She had never done anything that wasn't. But his cynical self told him that love always found a way, that the bond between father and son was strong enough to climb mountains, ford streams, and overcome every other clichéd obstacle in the book.

He would have to know the truth. But for the time being at least, the matter was out of his hands. He would have to wait until his father rang Mona again. And even then.......? Unless he hired a private detective? No, surely that would be going too far. He would let fate play a part, even though up till now it had played a pretty bad one. At any rate, it would be wise to wait a while, to see if the anger subsided so he could meet his father without hostility, at least with an open mind. On the other hand, he felt like nursing his anger.

The train had crossed into England and was nearing Shrewsbury. He looked out for that brick bus shelter like a little house that he had for some reason loved as a child. He'd noticed it when his parents took him to the pantomime in Shrewsbury. For him it marked the beginning of a different world of buses, suburbs, and the orange glow of the metropolis on the horizon, for that was how he viewed it then. He used to think the next city down the road was London. It was at the bus shelter that his excitement used to mount. How different it was now. The shelter looked forlorn, stuck in the middle of nowhere.

Soon after that he fell asleep, and woke up at Euston feeling groggy. He got the Northern Line to Waterloo and the train to East Dulwich. South East London looked grim and grimy after the hills of Mid-Wales, especially viewed through the drizzle from the railway tracks. He kept telling himself he was glad to be back, although he wasn't quite convinced.

Jill had said on the phone that, of course, he'd be more than welcome and could stay as long as he liked. She also said they had some news for him – they'd tell him when he got there. He'd already decided he'd say nothing to them about his father.

Their large, airy flat, with stripped floors, original features and white walls, was homely and familiar, but Lloyd knew as soon as they welcomed him back that he would soon want a place of his own. He was tiring of questions, expectations, of his own inadequate explanations.

Jack had cooked Osso Bucco with a Risotto alla Milanese, which he and Jack washed down with a couple of bottles of good Chianti. Jill stuck to water.

'It's by way of a celebration,' said Jill. 'Of course we're glad to have you back, but we're expecting another happy event in about six months' time. We're hoping it will be a baby.'

Lloyd was feeling mellow with the food and wine, his friends and their happiness. But the announcement strengthened his resolve to move out into a little place of his own. With a baby on the way they wouldn't want him moping around, however much they protested. They'd want to be making plans to turn the spare bedroom into a nursery.

Besides, he wanted to be on his own. When other people were around you had to put on a kind of show, continually reassuring them you were alright. He didn't feel up to it. He wanted, if not exactly to wallow in his misery, then at least to be free to follow his own rhythms, to fester in bed for a few days if he felt like it. He knew this ran counter to Keith's advice and everyone else's for that matter, including his own to Rhys. But he didn't feel strong enough for a healthy routine just now.

He gave it another couple of weeks, then told Jack and Jill that he wanted a little place of his own. He thought they'd be secretly pleased, but they seemed genuinely put out. Jill in particular wanted him to stay, so they could look after him. But he stayed firm.

With their help he found a kind of studio at the top of a large semi-detached house over in Forest Hill, on Lordship Lane. Jack and Jill insisted on him getting something fairly near to them so they could be on hand if he needed them. The three of them went over to see it together. The house was immaculate outside and in. It stood out among its neighbours climbing the hill – shone, almost. It was on the very top of the hill.

They were greeted by a tiny elderly woman called Mrs Wozniak, who had a pronounced Polish accent and a helmet of snow-white hair. The house was a bit of a throwback, like a Bed and Breakfast from the Seventies. It had white Anaglypta on the walls, thick swirling red and gold carpets, brass candlesticks and porcelain figurines on a glass shelf in the hallway, mounted on white wrought iron supports.

Mrs Wozniak took them to the top of the house, into what must have been a loft conversion. It had a large bed-sitting room, with a galley kitchen at one end and a bathroom at the other. A dormer window to the front gave spectacular views over the City skyline, and the one to the rear a panorama of suburban rooftops and chimneystacks stretching to a pale, smoky horizon. Well, it probably wasn't smoky in reality, but it looked it. Lloyd tried to imagine the days when smoke would have been pouring from houses and factories. That would have been smoky.

Linen and kitchenware were provided. Mrs Wozniak would wash the bedclothes every two weeks. She wanted two weeks' rent upfront and a deposit, but there was no need to sign any kind of lease. He could pay weekly. It seemed ideal. The other boarders in the house were students, she said. She asked him what he did for a living and he said he worked for the Foreign Office but was off sick for a couple of months. She must have taken a liking to him, because she said he could move in whenever he liked. He looked at Jack and Jill. They nodded their approval with a shrug of resignation. He took it there and then, and they shook on it.

A week later Jack drove Lloyd and his case, backpack and laptop and a few extra things they'd got to the house on Lordship Lane and carried them to the studio at the top. He helped Lloyd get straightened out – there was really not much to do – and, after many promises demanded and received that Lloyd would ring them if he needed the slightest thing, took his leave.

It was with quite a sense of relief that Lloyd closed the door on his new domain, glad to be alone at last. He managed to limit his contact with the other boarders to a nod on the stairs. He hadn't bargained for Mrs Wozniak. She was the busiest person he'd ever met, surpassing even Mona. After he'd been there a week he came home one afternoon to find her up a ladder painting the front of the house. Later that evening he went down to the kitchen to pay the rent. The table was covered with freshly baked loaves, tarts and cakes.

Her husband by contrast rarely left his armchair in front of the TV. They seemed to live in the extended kitchen at the back of the house, which included a comfortable lounge area with a dining table, separated from the kitchen proper by a counter. There were two other rooms opening out of the front hall, but Lloyd never once saw either of these doors open.

While he was in the kitchen, two very attractive Italian students came down to pay their rent at the same time. Mr Wozniak couldn't take his eyes off the two girls. Mrs Wozniak, smoking a cigarette at her regular spot, leaning over the sink by the open kitchen window, caught Lloyd's eye and said in a low voice, 'Silly boogerr.' She didn't seem to care whether her husband heard or not.

That was the moment they sort of clicked. She'd come up to his room on some pretext or other and sit in one of the armchairs, smoking and chatting away.

She was a fifteen-year-old in Krakow when the Nazis invaded. Her family had come from a town near the border so she spoke German pretty well. She fled by making her way through Germany and ended up in the South of France. From there she lied about her age and joined the British Army – Lloyd was never quite clear how – and somehow came to be driving an ambulance in Scotland, even though she'd never so much as clasped a steering wheel before. Lloyd got the impression that she was lonely.

She bitterly resented growing old.

'I'm a vrreck,' she said one Saturday afternoon when she came up for his sheets.

'A what?'

'A vrreck. Things keep drropping. Hairr drrops off. Teeth drrop out. Tits drrop down.'

She believed in speaking her mind. When she spotted the empty wine bottles on the floor in the kitchen next to the bin, she said, 'You drrink too much.'

Lloyd hadn't given it much thought, but it was true that he drank most evenings now, usually a bottle of wine and, increasingly a couple of large brandies afterwards. He'd always liked a drink. When he was working he tried to be disciplined about it, not drinking if he was on duty the next day, although there was quite a lot of boozy socialising in his job – receptions, media events, informal drinks with journalists. There'd been times before when his drinking had begun to get out of hand, and it had been quite an effort to bring it under control again.

When he first became ill, and whenever he was bedbound, he didn't even think about alcohol. Now he did come to think about it, a few drinks did dull his aches and pains, took his mind of the illness for a few hours. He felt terrible in the mornings anyway, and in a weird kind of way he felt he might as well have a hangover, something familiar and concrete to cope with, something that had a reason.

139

'I've noticed a lot of bottles going into the dustbin,' she was saying.

He resented her poking her nose in, as he saw it, but felt he had to defend himself.

'I've got this illness called ME. I get a lot of pain. Wine helps me sleep. That's all.'

'Be careful. I've seen what drrink can do if you let it get the better of you.'

'Is it any of your business?'

'Yes, it is. You live in my house. And I'm just trrying to give you some frriendly advice.'

'And I pay for my room, so it's my space. What I do in it is up to me.'

She stubbed out her cigarette, took the sheets and left. After she'd gone he had pangs of regret that he'd been so defensive, although he somehow thought she liked people to be frank with her. She probably was just trying to help.

But he began to unclick with her. She was intruding into his space too much. One Sunday, she told him she'd been for a walk in the park.

'Did you enjoy it?' he asked.

'Ach, no, too many bloody forreigners,' she said.

He suspected she meant foreigners of the non-white variety, otherwise how would she know? It had been at the back of his mind to get in touch with Ifor, although he'd done nothing about it. What kind of reception would he get from Mrs Wozniak if he invited him around?

Perhaps he was being unfair, but he decided he would be better off on his own, so he gave Mrs Wozniak a month's notice. He told her he was moving in with some friends. She was offhand with him after that. He didn't even tell Jack and Jill. They would be bound to object, give him a hard time, and they had enough on their plate with approaching parenthood.

He found a small studio flat in a new block further down the road in the centre of Forest Hill. He was the first tenant. It had plastic pine floors, ivory walls and stainless steel handles throughout. It was bland and anonymous. It suited him perfectly.

When he came to hand the keys back to Mrs Wozniak, before climbing into the waiting taxi with his few belongings, she gave him a reproachful look and again he felt a stab of regret – or was it guilt? Maybe he'd been wrong about her. She could have made that remark about foreigners in a knowing, self-deprecating way. She did after all have a dry sense of humour, often cracking a joke without cracking a smile. And she was lonely. But she did interfere too much.

When he took on the flat, it had crossed his mind that he wasn't moving very far away, that he would probably run into her sooner or later. Well, it was a risk he would have to take. He didn't have the energy to look further afield. (Or was it a subconscious act?) At any rate, he was sick and tired of putting up a front. And now, at last, he would be left to his own devices.

Twelve

Mona rang every couple of weeks or so to see how he was. They kept to small talk, neither of them broaching the subject of his father. She would tell him the moment he rang, reasoned Lloyd. He made an effort to be civil, if not much more. He told her he was staying near friends, getting plenty of rest, and making progress. When he said this to her, he almost believed it. But the truth of it was that he hardly ventured outside these days except to do some shopping at the supermarket next door.

On his birthday in March she sent him a birthday card. He was surprised to get a card and a parcel from Alex. It contained a jar of foie gras, or fwah gwaw as he spelled it in the accompanying letter. Lloyd must at some stage have mentioned that he had a weakness for it. It was amazing that Alex had remembered this and Lloyd didn't. Mona must have told Alex it was Lloyd's birthday.

Alex wrote that he'd had to search Cardiff high and low to find the one place that sold it. Lloyd was touched: it was an expensive gift and one Alex had to put in some legwork for. Alex was getting on better at school, he wrote, and with his parents. He told Lloyd off for not being in touch as he had promised, and gave him his new mobile phone number (it must have been Alex's birthday too because Lloyd remembered him saying he was going to get one).

The night before his birthday Lloyd had resolved to stay sober and do something the next day. It would be too sad to stay in the flat by himself. Maybe he'd give Jack and Jill a ring. But he couldn't get to sleep. It felt as if a clamp was being tightened around his head. He had a vivid image of it – two semi-circles of metal joined with nuts and bolts each side, the sort used to join together two pieces of piping. He feared that if the clamp got any tighter his head would crack like a walnut.

When he got out of bed the next afternoon and stood up, it was as if he was he was on the deck of a rocking boat. He felt as if he was weighed down, and would sink through the floorboards. His head gave strange lurches, like your stomach does when a plane hits an air pocket and drops down suddenly, and his vision jumped, like an old fashioned black and white film. He was losing his signal on life, tuning out.

There was no question of his leaving the flat that day. He couldn't concentrate on reading, so he just sat in front of the television, waiting for it to pass. He rallied slightly in the evening, and celebrated his birthday by eating the tortured goose liver, as Alex described it, with toast and two bottles of Brouilly. It was delectable, but he was struck by the fact that the one bright spot of his birthday was part of a dead goose.

The next day he texted Alex to tell him how much he'd enjoyed it, not mentioning the circumstances.

'I'm glad it didn't die an agonising death in vain,' replied Alex.

Lloyd resumed the pattern of his days now, except when he had a bedbound bout which could last for four or five. He'd wake at about ten or eleven, then doze until he could bring himself to stagger out of bed between one and two. He'd go down to the supermarket and get a paper and whatever drink or food he needed (and it was usually in that order). Back at the flat he'd read the paper, do the crossword, watch TV – a bit of news and the odd quiz show – and look forward to his first drink of the day with his meal around seven o'clock. He tried not to drink on an empty stomach and in fact rarely felt up to it.

Sometimes if he was going through a good patch he'd walk down to have supper at Jack and Jill's. They asked him so often that he had to accept now and again. Then he'd try to moderate his drinking while he was there, and he'd look forward to a few slugs of brandy when he got home. It would help him sleep.

Disturbed sleep patterns had been getting him down. Sometimes he'd sleep all day and all night. At other times even though he was exhausted he'd spend the night tossing and turning, often in quite a bit of pain. The last time he'd gone to bed without a drink had been such a night. His head felt so bad that whichever way he put it on the pillow, it was as if he'd landed awkwardly and cricked his neck. He had an image of his brain floating in his head like a spiked mine, and if it touched his skull it would set off an explosion of pain. It was an image that would continue in his half-awake dreams, until the sound of his own snoring jerked him awake. It sounded like a tractor with a hole in its exhaust. He was dying to sleep, but it somehow felt that he'd die if he did. Having a few drinks in the evening would help him avoid all that.

He was aware that he was regressing. His words of advice to Rhys about getting out and doing things came back to haunt him. He tried to reason with his inner self that giving into the illness completely would do him good – he'd tried everything else. But he didn't really believe it. And he didn't really care.

He went for a routine check-up at St Mary's in Paddington. He was looking forward to seeing the nice Sikh, but it was a new doctor, a guy in his thirties who seemed to do everything against the clock, in the fastest time possible - even introduce himself, so Lloyd didn't catch his name.

The speedy doctor more or less said there was nothing they could do for him, but if he wanted to he could come and see them every six months 'so you're on someone's books.' Lloyd didn't really feel like bothering but said yes. Even a chat was nice, although there was no chance with this guy. Maybe he'd get the Sikh next time. He didn't have a clue what his next step would be. He wondered if he could take any more. Sometimes he thought he was getting better, sometimes worse. He knew he was in a rut but couldn't see a way out of it.

Then out of the blue there came a call from Ifor. He'd keyed his name and number into his phone when Ifor's mother had given it him. When the name Ifor came up he was so surprised he answered it – otherwise he might not have done. He didn't recognise the voice because of course, it was that of a man, not a boy. It was gentle and lilting, like his mother's.

'I've heard you haven't been doing so well,' said Ifor, 'so I'm just ringing to see how you are.'

Lloyd tried to put his situation in the best possible light, saying he had good times and bad times, but was making progress.

'I'm coming down to London next week for a conference,' said Ifor. 'Can I come to see you?'

Lloyd had no ready excuse, so said, 'Of course. It would be great to see you.'

They made the arrangements – Ifor would come down to Forest Hill at half past two on the Saturday afternoon after the conference - and rang off.

There was no going back now. Or was there? Lloyd could always say he was sick. When he came to think about it, he was sure he hadn't left his number when he took Ifor's from his mother. Perhaps it was all one of Mona's little schemes. He could see her ringing Ifor's mother and asking if Ifor would get in touch with him.

For some reason he couldn't quite fathom, he did want to talk it over with Ifor. Yet twice that week he thought about calling him and putting him off. On the Thursday, he decided he definitely would. He was looking around his room after he'd come back from the shop, and saw that it was not a fit place for visitors.

Bottles, food cartons, dishes and clothes had piled up. He didn't have the energy to clean it up. It would mean he'd have to break his routine to do it the next day – drinking less that night, getting up earlier – and also break his routine on Saturday, the day of the visit. It seemed a Herculean task.

And then suddenly he saw his own state more clearly too. It would take quite a bit of willpower to break his miserable cycle, even for a day or two. He didn't think he had that willpower, or even if he wanted to try. His routine though was a way of coping, with the pain, with the confusion, with this limited life he felt forced to lead, with the dwindling hope that things could ever be good again. He knew it wasn't a good way, but it was a way.

Then he thought he'd ring Ifor and suggest they meet somewhere else, in Central London. But the effort required to get on a train seemed beyond him. And he could hardly expect Ifor to come all the way to Forest Hill to meet up in a cafe or a pub.

In the end, he did nothing. So on the Friday he set his alarm for nine and managed to get up by eleven. He slowly set about gathering all the bottles and food cartons in black bin bags and took them to the recycling bins by the station. He bought a paper, a baguette, some ham, cheese and salad stuff from the supermarket and read the paper while eating his lunch and gathering his forces for the next onslaught.

He washed and dried the dishes that had piled up in the sink and put them away. He put all the dirty clothes in the linen basket in the bathroom, changed his bed sheets and swept the floor. He even found some polish and a duster and cleaned the dusty, greasy surfaces.

When he finished he sat back to admire the fruits of his efforts. It gave him immense satisfaction and he wondered, not for the first time, why this was never anticipated when a chore was hanging over you, when you kept putting it off. The place looked quite respectable, and it hadn't taken him as long as he'd feared. He lay back in the chair and did as much of The Times crossword as he could – all but five clues. He had expected to feel exhausted with all the exertion but oddly enough he felt quite energetic, almost invigorated.

It was late March, and the evenings were drawing out. For the first time in ages he thought about going for a walk. There was a little park at the top of the hill, with stunning views of the city, the same as he had from his room at Mrs Wozniak's. It beckoned him somehow, although it alarmed him to think he might see her there – that was where she took her walk. It was the last thing he wanted. But he was restless, and needed to get out of the flat. He also wanted to see if he could go for an evening without a drink, so he'd at least stand a chance of feeling and looking half decent when Ifor came.

He put on his coat and climbed slowly up the hill, feeling nervous and dizzy as if he were embarking on some daunting challenge.

In the park the daffodils were out in force. He loved them, and thought of The Nodfda lane, which would be ablaze with them now. It gave him a pang of anguish to do so, and he tried to put The Noddfa out of his mind.

He sat on a park bench by the bandstand, as an old person or an invalid would do. But that's what he was – an invalid. The old-fashioned word comforted him, removed some of the turmoil from him, allowed him to accept what he was. He took in – almost breathed in – the view of the sun setting over the city. The sky to his right was a greenish blue, and to his left, peach and orange with a couple of streaks of purple cloud. He kept half an eye out for a certain elderly woman with a shock of white hair, although he felt foolish for doing so. He didn't want anything to break the spell of his mood. It was only then that he had a sense that this long, hard, winter might finally be over, and it seemed little short of a miracle. He let out a long breath and an unaccustomed sense of well-being surged over him. It was peaceful here above the hum and hustle of the sprawling metropolis. He lingered there until the warden came along to tell him they would be closing in ten minutes.

Back at the flat he watched TV, trying to resist his craving for a drink. He was tired, but almost pleasantly so, in stark contrast to his virtual semi-comatose state of late. He made it to ten o'clock without a drink, then poured himself a glass of wine as a reward, promising himself he'd only have one or two more glasses to help him sleep. He polished off the bottle of course, but was so tired that for the first time in a long time he was in bed before midnight.

He woke early the next morning – early for him – at eight-thirty and managed to be up by ten. He had four and a half hours before Ifor was due. Lloyd was on a roll with the cleaning operation and for the first time since he'd moved in took a load of washing to the laundrette down the street.

He wondered if Ifor would have had lunch, so to be on the safe side he bought salami and saucisson, pate and salad, mineral water, juice, rolls and biscuits. That could cover all eventualities.

He had everything ready by one o'clock, so he read the paper, checking the five clues which escaped him the day before. Two of them still didn't make sense, but he told himself he should have got the others. Maybe he would have done had he gone back to it.

At two-thirty on the dot the buzzer went. Lloyd gave a start, and exclaimed out loud, thinking he probably wouldn't have reacted like this had he not been expecting anyone.

He buzzed Ifor up. 'Third floor and left as you come out of the lift. It's the door facing you.'

He opened the door and heard the lift start up from the ground floor. He wondered if he'd recognise him, recognise his old friend in this stranger he was about to meet. The lift whirred to a halt, the doors opened, and out stepped a tall, good-looking man. Lloyd wasn't sure.

He looked the part of an academic, wearing a corduroy jacket and an open-necked check shirt, and carrying a briefcase. He spotted Lloyd and walked towards the door, holding out his hand.

'Hello,' he said, in that quiet voice of his mother's, and they shook hands formally. Ifor held his head slightly to one side, as if he was wary of looking at Lloyd square in the face. It was a shyness that Lloyd now well remembered, yet Ifor seemed at ease. Lloyd himself felt awkward, at a loss for words. Small steps first, he decided.

'Come in, come in,' he said.

'Nice place,' said Ifor, obeying and looking around the small flat with its view of the supermarket car park. Social convention could produce ridiculous statements in this best of us. Lloyd looked at him surreptitiously, while he was looking away, trying to find his old friend. He could see him at odd moments, but they were fleeting and ungraspable, like something on the tip of your tongue. He sensed that Ifor was doing the same to him.

'Not really,' said Lloyd, 'but it suits me to be going on with.'

Ifor smiled, as if he knew what he meant.

'Ah, what can I get you? Have you eaten? I wasn't sure. I've got some stuff in.'

'Yes, I have thanks. Sandwich lunch at the conference.'

'Tea?'

'Tea would be good. No sugar.'

Lloyd felt like a drink. But maybe it was just as well not to. Not start too early. Keep a clear head.

'So your mum tells me you're a professor now,' said Lloyd. He put a mug of tea and a plate of custard creams on the coffee table in front of Ifor and poured himself a glass of fizzy water.

'Well, a senior lecturer,' said Ifor. 'She bigs me up a little, you know.'

'You know, I went to see her when I was at The Noddfa. She's just like I remember her.'

'Oh, she's well enough. She leads a quiet life. But I get back there quite often. I'm lucky with the holidays.'

'Doesn't she mind being on her own?' asked Lloyd.

'Well, I think she was always quite a solitary soul. Kept herself to herself. It must have been very hard for her at first.'

'When she first came to Mid-Wales?'

'Yes. She was a nurse in Birmingham, you know, when she met my Dad. He was in hospital for a while. When they married and she came there, she was the first black woman most people had seen.'

'I suppose she would have been,' said Lloyd. From the first time he'd met him, he'd known that Ifor was unusual, but he'd never actually stopped to consider his mother very much.

'But people treated her OK, didn't they?' asked Lloyd.

'Oh, the vast majority were pleasant enough,' said Ifor, 'but there was always the odd one who'd spit at her in the street.'

'Good God,' said Lloyd, appalled. 'I had no idea.' He was also amazed that Ifor had confided something so big, so soon.

'Well neither did I, until recently,' said Ifor. 'It was only when I told her it happened to a friend of mine that she admitted it had happened to her. It's unbelievable what they'll do to protect you.'

'I suppose it is.' Lloyd thought of his father.

'It's remarkable how things can change', said Ifor. 'Look at me, a lecturer at Oxford. A black boy from Wales. It could barely have been imagined ten years ago. Thirty years ago in London they still had signs up saying No Blacks. Sixty years ago, in another place, we were being strung up by our necks from trees if we so much as flirted with a white woman. Things do change. And yet, we still get spat at. *Plus ca change*, as the French would say. But it's some kind of progress, I suppose. Aren't you glad you're witnessing progress?'

'You know,' said Lloyd, in the spirit of reciprocating a confidence, 'I always felt secretly sorry for you, being the only black kid around. But it's not a good feeling to admit to, is it?'

'I always felt the same about you,' said Ifor.

'Sorry for me? Why?'

'Well, because your mum and dad had died.'

Lloyd had never for one moment considered that Ifor might feel like this. It broke the ice and was as if any awkwardness drained away. He wanted to tell Ifor everything.

'But tell me about yourself. What's been the matter?' asked Ifor on cue.

It all came tumbling out. Lloyd outlined the illness, falling back on the shorthand of flu with muscle pain and exhaustion.

'You look OK,' said Ifor, as many people did. Lloyd heard the unspoken rider, 'so there can't be that much wrong with you.' But he knew that people were trying to find something positive to say, that he was wrong to project his own judgements onto them.

'That's something I suppose,' he said.

'How do you spend your days?' asked Ifor.

It was a question Lloyd dreaded and tried to avoid, which wasn't too hard as he hardly saw anyone anymore. But with lfor he came clean and described his rut as accurately as he could.

'I know I've got to get out of my rut,' he said. 'But sometimes I wonder what's the point of rallying only to collapse again. It's such a bloody effort every time.'

'I suppose you could say that about getting up in the morning,' said Ifor. 'What's the point if you're only going to get tired and have to go back to bed again? Life is cycles. You have to find your own point.'

Where had Lloyd heard that before? It was what he'd told Alex. Easy words.

'Mmm,' was all Lloyd could say.

'But you probably won't find it in bed or at the bottom of a bottle,' went on Ifor.

'I know,' said Lloyd. 'But there's something else.'

He recounted what they found in The Missing Room, and Mona's story. It was Ifor's turn to be astounded.

'You didn't have a clue, never heard any gossip?' asked Lloyd.

'After your parents were killed, well, your Mum at any rate, there was some talk that she'd been having an affair, that she and your Dad been going away to try to patch it up. Of course I only heard that years later. I was too young at the time. Although kids do sense things, don't they? Even if they can't make out the whispers, they know when there's more to something than meets the eye. They have a nose for tragedy.'

Again Lloyd had that feeling of being left out, as if he were the only one not to know.

'So, when are you going to see him?' asked ifor.

'I don't know,' said Lloyd. 'It depends when he rings Mona. And I'm not sure I even believe that he was trying to do the right thing for me. If so, why did he run off like that? What if it wasn't my mother who threw the letters down there? What if it was him? He'd found them and discovered she was having an affair. Then he went after her......."

Lloyd came to a halt, open-mouthed, shocked at what he'd just said. He'd put into words something that had been niggling him somewhere in the darker recesses of his mind.

'You're in a bit of a state,' said Ifor. 'And when you're this low, you've got to hold on to your strengths. You were always a considerate person, Lloyd. I can understand you're angry but don't let the anger and bitterness get a hold of you. My advice would be to see him as soon as you can. If you don't, it'll hang over you, eat you. You're probably not going to get better before you do.'

In his heart of hearts, Lloyd knew Ifor was right. He'd been thinking along these lines himself. But he feared he was not strong enough, not yet anyway. Underneath the anger there was the anxiety. He didn't want his father to see him as he was – useless, aimless. He came from good farming stock which considered illness to be a weakness, especially an illness as vague as the one he was suffering from.

It was getting dark now. Lloyd put on the light and persuaded Ifor to stay for a light supper – he'd promised his girlfriend he'd get back to Oxford that night. He brought out the cold meats and cheeses and laid two places on the kitchen counter.

'I'm going to have some wine,' he said to Ifor. 'Fancy some?'

He thought he detected the slightest of pauses before Ifor said, 'That would be great, thanks.'

After they finished the meal Ifor said he must go. They became awkward again, giving each other a sort of hug that missed on the threshold.

'You must come up to Oxford soon,' said Ifor.

'I'd like that,' lied Lloyd.

Lloyd offered to walk him down to the station, but Ifor wouldn't hear of it, and Lloyd didn't insist. He was looking forward to the next few drinks on his own, waiting for that mellow and painless moment. It was like flicking a switch.

Ifor's visit had been a tonic, and it was good to get everything off his chest. But his thoughts about meeting his father were still a jumble. And after a few more glasses a new doubt came creeping into his mind and lodged there. It was now more than two months since he left The Noddfa. Mona had told him at the time that his father called her every two or three months, and that it had been a while since his last call. Surely a call was now long overdue. But what if he had called Mona? What if, after all, he didn't want to see his son?

Thirteen

Mona rang two days later. It was half past six. She would have just cleared up after tea. She had some bad news, she said. Lloyd suddenly felt hollow inside.

'Spit it out,' he managed to say.

'Turk died this morning,' she said. 'It was peaceful. I think he died in his sleep.'

She sounded heartbroken. It was so unlike her to be sentimental about animals. Or humans for that matter.

'I'm very sorry,' said Lloyd, and indeed he was. Turk had been a puppy when Lloyd first went to The Noddfa. They'd grown up together. To Lloyd his death was another sign that the old order was changing, that his familiar world was, if not turning upside down, then at least leaning at odd new angles which unsettled him.

When he'd digested this news, he realised why the words 'bad news' had given him such a turn. He automatically thought it was something to do with his father. It even crossed his mind that Mona had done it on purpose, somehow. But no, he mustn't project his own dark thoughts on to her. Why would she do something like that? To make him see that things could be a lot worse? She couldn't be that calculating. It did make him think though, that it might well have been bad news about his father. It jolted him into action.

'Have you heard from my father?' he asked, his heart in his mouth.

'Well, no,' said Mona, a note of surprise in her voice. 'No, I haven't.'

'How long has it been now since he last phoned you?'

'Well, let me see. I suppose it's getting on for four or five months.' She sounded eager to talk about this, relieved that the taboo had finally been broken.

'Isn't that unusual?' asked Lloyd.

'Well, yes it is in a way.' Her tone was conversational, almost conspiratorial. 'He usually rings every two or three months. But it has been longer than that in the past. Don't worry. I'll let you know the minute he rings.'

She must have thought she'd press her advantage, now that he'd opened up a little.

'Joan has been asking after you,' she said.

Since he'd left The Noddfa, he and Joan had exchanged a couple of cards. Neither of them had said very much, just the customary enquiries after health, little snippets of news (Lloyd had struggled in this regard). Rhys, wrote Joan, was doing quite well – no miracles, but he'd been getting out a little more and seemed more willing to take on life again.

'Tell her I'm doing OK,' he said, not wanting to give too much away.

'But are you?' asked Mona. 'Are you getting any better?'

'Yes, yes, I think so,' said Lloyd, choosing his words carefully. 'I'm resting a lot so I don't spend so many days in bed at a time.'

'How do you spend your days?' asked Mona.

Lloyd took a deep breath.

'Getting through them, Mona. I can only do what I can do.'

'Yes, I know that, Lloyd. I'm not being critical.'

'Ifor Evans came to see me the other day,' said Lloyd, to change the subject.

Mona seemed very interested in this news, and wanted to know all about him. The diversion had worked. Lloyd toyed with the idea of telling Mona about Mrs Evans being spat at. And he was curious to know if Mona had played a part in bringing Lloyd and Ifor together. He was glad Ifor had made the effort to get in touch – even though he wanted to see him he probably wouldn't have got round to giving him a call. But he resented being pushed into things.

'Do you ever see Mrs Evans?' asked Lloyd.

'Not very often. Keeps herself to herself.' Mona sounded as if she disapproved.

'Have you seen her lately?'

'Well, I did happen to see her in town the other day.' It was Mona's turn to be guarded.

'You didn't happen to give her my number and tell her to get Ifor to ring me, did you?'

'Ooh, yes,' said Mona, as if searching in the further reaches of her memory, 'I think she did take your number, seeing as you're in London and all.'

'And he's in Oxford.'

'Well, it's not very far is it?'

'He's very good to her, I think,' said Lloyd. 'He was telling me about the hard time she had when she first came to live at The Holding. She had to put up with some pretty nasty behaviour from time to time.'

'Aye,' said Mona, 'I often wondered about that. I've always tried to be nice to her, but she's a private woman at the best of times. You don't want to push yourself forward when it's not welcome. It's hard to reach out to people at times. But I can see it can't have helped if people treated her badly.'

Lloyd thought he'd leave it at that.

'How's Great Uncle Stanley?'

'Oh, he's alright. He just seems to go on and on.'

The both gave a little chuckle.

'Sorry,' said Mona. 'That came out wrong. It sounds as if I want him to stop. But you know what I mean.'

The mood of the conversation lightened somewhat.

'So when are you coming to see us?'

Don't push it, thought Lloyd.

'Well, I've got some business to finish in London first,' he said. 'Or at least I hope I will have.' He hoped she get his meaning.

'But have you got enough money? Flats in London don't come cheap, even I know that much.'

Once again Mona demonstrated her knack of hitting the nail on the head. He still had some savings, but they wouldn't last indefinitely. His sick pay from the Foreign Office and gone down from full to half and was now just a fraction. They'd told him they'd keep his job open for another year – they'd have to fill it temporarily until then. Then he'd have to decide. They'd been quite reasonable about it, he thought, and he could understand their position. But he found it hard to face the future when it was hard enough to deal with the present. He assured Mona he was OK, and they said their goodbyes. As usual, he felt unsettled after the phone call from Mona, a feeling he could only shake off after the first cork of the evening had been popped.

A week later, she rang again. It was nine o'clock in the evening. He'd had enough wine to make him mellow, spilling over into hazy. When he saw her name come up on his phone, he leapt on it, as if it would stop ringing if he delayed. He took it over to the open kitchen window and took in a deep breath, hoping to sober up a little.

'Your father's just rung,' said Mona, straight off.

Lloyd lit a cigarette and looked out over the supermarket car park in the gathering gloom. He felt numb.

'Oh?'

'I won't pretend it didn't come as a bit of a shock to him, your knowing everything.'

'I don't know everything.'

'Well, he asked exactly what you did know,' said Mona. 'I had to go through it all with him, every word I could remember saying to you.'

'Was he angry at you?' asked Lloyd.

A portly, middle-aged man walked out of the back door of the supermarket, locked it, and walked towards the only car left in the car park. It must be the manager locking up for the night.

Lloyd wondered why he'd asked that question, dodging the one he really wanted to ask, the one about meeting up with his father.

'No, he just wanted to know about you,' said Mona. 'I told him you were angry.'

'What did he say?'

'He said he wasn't surprised. Anyway, I gave him your number and address.'

Was that it? Would he just have to sit there and wait? Down below, the car roared off at a lick. He was surprised he was paying such close attention to this stranger leaving work. He seemed to register irrelevant details – the make, the model, the number plate.

'I'm sure he'll be in touch soon,' Mona was saying. She probably knew this wouldn't be good enough for him.

'Didn't he give any idea when?'

'No, he didn't. I guess he's got a bit of thinking to do himself.'

Lloyd felt dispirited after the call, but on tenterhooks at the same time. He stayed by the window, peering into the gloom of the twilight, and breathed in the evening air. The sky was still a pale luminous turquoise highlighting the blue-black skyline of the buildings below. He thought back to the weeks and months after the crash. He would go to the back door of The Noddfa and look up towards the hilltop, feeling a deep melancholy as darkness descended, alone against the elements.

He waited all next day, a Saturday, for a call. He kept checking his phone – to see if it was charged, to see if he'd somehow missed a call or text. He hadn't. In the evening he went for a walk up to the bandstand in the park, checking all the time that his phone was still getting a signal. Still the call didn't come.

He was desperately tired when he got back home and went straight to bed without a drink, the first time he'd done that in weeks. He wouldn't ring now – surely it was too late. Maybe tomorrow...... He'd get some sleep and wake up early. Tomorrow he would ring.

Tomorrow came. He woke up early. After some toast and juice he found himself pacing up and down the living room. He couldn't carry on like this, he decided. He'd keep busy, turn over a new leaf. He summoned his courage and took the train up to Charing Cross and walked up to the National Portrait Gallery, a favourite. He put his phone on vibrate and carried it around with him in his hand. He lingered at each portrait for as long as he could stand it, willing the phone to vibrate, willing away the time until it did.

A week went by. Two weeks. Three. He began to lose heart and hope. He barely noticed that he was, in fact, feeling a little better physically, less exhausted and achey. He was drinking less, trying to confine himself to three or four glasses an evening so he'd be sober for the call. He managed to get into the habit of getting up at ten on most mornings, and making some plan for the day, even if it was just a long walk or a trip to the library to change his books.

Then, three weeks to a day after Mona's call he found a small packet - a jiffy envelope – on the mat underneath the letterbox of the front door as he was going out. He picked it up. It was addressed to him. He stared at the handwriting. It had been so long. But there was no mistaking it. It was his father's elegant hand, firm and clear. He turned on his heels and ran upstairs to his flat. He ripped the packet open. Out dropped a cassette and a page from a spiral notebook. He picked up the cassette and put it with the envelope on the table, while he read the note.

'Dear Lloyd,' it began – no date or address – 'I've been trying to write you a letter. I've begun so many times, but it never seemed to come out right. So I've made you a tape instead. Love Dad.'

With hands that were trembling slightly, Lloyd put the tape into the deck on the kitchen counter and pressed the play button. There was a click, a hiss, a breath.

'When your Mum told me she was leaving me,' said his Dad, as if they were just picking up on an interrupted conversation, *'it was like an explosion which shattered my world.'*

And me, thought Lloyd. She was leaving me as well.

'I'd had my suspicions for while,' continued the voice. It was eerie hearing it. It hadn't changed at all. It really was as if he'd come back from the dead.

'I always wondered if you did too. But nothing had prepared me for that day, that moment, when she told me. I can't remember what I said now. It was probably something about you. She couldn't do this to you, or something like that. She couldn't do this to us. I have to admit at that stage I was thinking mainly of me. But she could do it. The next morning she got into the car and drove away, up towards Aber. As Mona told you, I think, I rang her up and asked her to bring the Land Rover down. She did, bless her. Didn't ask any questions. Not then, anyway. My only thought was to go after her. Probably not the most rational thing to do, I'm sure you'll agree. But I wasn't being rational. So I took the Land Rover and chased her. Nothing much else was on my mind then – what I'd do if I caught her and so on. Well, as far as I can recall, I'm sure there wasn't. She had a bit of a head start but I put my foot down. In fact I didn't think I'd catch up on her so soon. She always drove like the devil. I didn't know then that she'd stopped off to pick up...... pick up that man. Must have picked him up at the railway station. Never knew his name. Anyway, when I got to that bend going into Devil's Elbow – remember, you were always a bit frightened going up there – I

161

caught sight of the car just coming off the little bridge at the far end. I could just make her out at the wheel, and someone, a man, sitting beside her. It had to be him, the man she told me she was leaving me for. I could see her give it all she'd got as she went up the slope to the top. She must have seen me. And she...... well, she kind of flew off the top bend. Like a plane taking off. The car just seemed to carry on going up after it left road, in a straight line towards the sky. And then it was suddenly gone, like a shot bird, below the horizon.'

At this point there was a pause, a slurp, and a smack of the lips.

'Sorry, Lloyd, I had to have another sip of wine. I had to have a couple of glasses before I started doing this.'

Lloyd remembered his father did always like his tipple, his wine. Not that he registered it then. It was just how it was. But it seemed so familiar. That was clearly where he got if from.

'By the time I got to the upper bend – it must have been just a couple of minutes but it felt like, I dunno, several laps of Silverstone or something – and I looked down, the car was already a ball of flame on that outcrop with a tree on top. I couldn't believe the flames. I'd filled the tank myself when I thought we were going away together, but even so.... By the time I'd scrambled down, the flames were dying down a little. But I knew it was all over. All over for me and her. For me and your Mum. Then something changed it me. I'll be honest. From the time I left the house till that moment, I hadn't given you a thought. I was on autopilot. But then I thought – what now? What's the future for me and Lloyd? I must have panicked. If I was in a bit of a state when she left, your Mum, God knows what I was like then, when I watched the car burn. Between you and me I was probably thinking how can we – the both of us, that is - how can we get out of this mess the best we can? I sat down on a rock for a minute and thought. I thought back to when she left. We were meant to leave together. Go away to Aberdovey. Only Mona knew that we hadn't. What if it was me in the car beside

her after all? Who was to know the difference? Only Mona, and I knew she'd go along with whatever I decided. If I could bring it off, that way you'd be spared..... well, everything. Your mother going off with another man. Your father chasing her. To her death. Your Dad going mad, or being arrested, or both. That's all I kept thinking – how can I spare him all that? I thought if I disappeared, they'd think it was me there in the wreckage. But how could I be sure? I tried to think of something I had that would identify the body as me. The only thing I could think of was the watch, the one with an inscription from your mother on the back. It had a leather strap, so if I threw it in the wreck on the passenger side, it could have burnt off my wrist in the flames. I didn't know whether it was a brainwave or hare-brained, but it was the only chance I had. It was only after I'd thrown in the watch that it occurred to me that he'd probably be wearing his own watch. But of course it was too late to do anything about it. I'd just have to risk it. It sounds a bit incredible now, now I'm telling it for the first time. I suppose I didn't even think I'd get away with it. It was just gut reaction. I had to get away. Out of your life. Forever if necessary.'

There was another pause and a slurp, where Lloyd could only hear the whirr of the cassette player. There was something else too – a very faint background noise on the tape: a radio or TV in another room. Lloyd tried to picture his father as he was making his tape. In a study perhaps.

'Anyway, you probably know the rest. I got back in the Land Rover and drove back to Llanfair, working things out as I went along. I'd drawn out quite a large sum of money from the bank for the holiday I was to have with your mother. Cash machines and credit cards weren't so common then. I had a suitcase already packed. I drove to The Noddfa on the back roads, over Cefn Coch, so no-one would see me driving through town. On the country roads there was more of a chance that if anyone recognised the Land Rover they'd think it was Mona. When I got

to The Noddfa, I told Mona what had happened and that I had to get away, needed time to think. She begged me not to go. Said I should stay to face the music, that no good could come of it. But I was like something possessed, I suppose, and could only see one way out. She eventually saw that I wouldn't be changed from my course. She drove me back down to Llanfair, with me crouching in the back of the Land Rover, and drew out a lot of her savings for me. She went into our house and got my case and a few other things I'd need. We didn't dare take too much in case it looked suspicious. Then she drove me to Shrewsbury to get the train to London – I thought it would be safer than getting the train from Llanfair. Or maybe it was her suggestion. I can't remember now. She dropped me outside Shrewsbury Station and we said goodbye quickly. Even then I didn't have a sense of how absurd it all was. But I think she did. Mona did. She thought she could somehow fix it so it would be alright for the three of us. You know how she is. I got the train to London with one suitcase, a bit of cash and a lost identity. Bit by bit I built a new life. Every day I thought my past would catch up with me. Yet somehow I went on day by day. But please believe this Lloyd, if you believe nothing else, that not a day has gone by without me wondering how you are, where you are, and regretting what we did to you. Your mother and me. No, me. Regretting what I did to you. Once I'd drawn breath, realised that I was going to get away with it, I wanted to come back to you. For you. I didn't really know which. But I couldn't, somehow. It was as if I was locked into my own lie. In a cell of deception. When I used to ring up Mona, she'd say you were going on OK. I knew she'd look after you...... well, far better than I could've myself.'

There was another slurp, and the voice was beginning to slur now and again.

'I'm sorry, Lloyd. I know it's such a useless word. It's the only one I can think of. I've been trying to find others. But I'm sorry this seems to be all about me. It was meant to be about you.

How much I loved you. Love. How much I love you. Words. Sorry. Love. How can they possibly convey what you really mean? But what others do we have? Anyway, I supposed you had questions, and I've tried to answer them. What I supposed they'd be. It wasn't meant to be an excuse, or even an explanation. It was just meant to be how it was. Finally. Probably too late. Too little. You'll have other questions, I know. But you haven't even asked any yet, have you? I want you to know that you can ask them. I'd be happy to answer them, or try to answer them. Maybe happy's not the right word. I would like to see you, if you'd like to see me. Like you must have, I've got a lot of complex things going on in my mind about it all. It's probably better if we take it slowly, one step at a time. But I don't know what those steps would be. I suppose it's over to you now. I'll write my mobile on the back of the envelope. Whatever you decide to do, I'll try to understand. Cheers. Dad'.

Click. The mic was switched off. The tape went on whirring for quite some time. Ran on to the end, in fact. When it stopped, Lloyd roused himself and grabbed the package from the table where he'd flung it, to make sure that the number was there, and that it was readable. He found he had ripped through it, but it was a clean tear and he could still make the number out - just. He poured himself a stiff brandy, even though it was only ten thirty in the morning. What do you want your father to say to you from beyond the grave? What do you want to say to him?

Fourteen

Lloyd had hated his father for taking so long to get in touch with him after getting his number from Mona. Yet he spent many hours anguishing about his reply, or even whether he was going to make one, so at least he had an inkling of what his father had gone through. Or did he? He could never be sure. He'd probably never be quite sure of anything ever again.

He'd been tempted to pick up the phone straight after hearing the tape, of course. But he'd had those brandies...... He couldn't rely on himself. Around noon he went for a lie down, and woke up again at three. He bounded out of bed, for the first time in a year, and tried to rehearse what he'd say when he finally found the courage to dial the number on the back of the packet. This went on for the rest of the afternoon. And evening. He'd do it tomorrow. He'd have a few drinks. But tomorrow was the same.

After four days of this, exasperated with himself, he sent a text to the number:
>Whn & Whr shall we meet?
An hour later he got a reply:
>Gordons Wine Bar. U know? Charing X. Fri 7pm?
LLoyd texted back:
>C u there & then
He was quite impressed with that U. He did know Gordons. He went there in his student days – it was one of the haunts of his

crowd. Reputedly the first wine bar in London, it was down a rickety staircase which led from an unassuming brown door on Villiers Street to a cellar with low vaulted bricks ceilings. It was an odd place to choose, he thought, for such a reunion. It was noisy and smoky, and you'd often struggle to get a seat. It wouldn't have been his choice.

In the intervening days, he ran the gamut of emotions about the meeting, as if he were trying each out for size to see which suited him best. His initial thrill soon gave way to anger again. Then he'd try to reason with himself, to convince himself that his father deserved a chance. He'd write down questions, rehearse what he wanted to say. And then resentment would build up again, and then regret for the lost years.

He tried to moderate his drinking, which had been creeping up again, so he'd be reasonably clear-headed and presentable when Friday came. This met with mixed results. He managed to confine himself to three or four glasses of wine for a couple of evenings after the text, but on the Thursday evening he overdid it somewhat. Nerves, he put it down to. But he just couldn't seem to stop. He didn't get to bed until half past three, and stayed there until one o'clock the next afternoon. When he finally felt up to squinting at himself in the mirror, his worst fears were confirmed. There was excess baggage under his bloodshot eyes. He ran a hot bath and soaked in it for as long as he could stand it. He drank a whole carton of grapefruit juice and went out for a walk.

It was a sunny, breezy day and he hoped it would blow away his cobwebs. At least he'd being going out a little more, so the journey into town no longer held the terror it once did. It would be the rush hour so he could get a direct train to Charing Cross, then go straight down the sidesteps from the station into Villiers Street, and he'd be there.

When he got back to the flat the walk had done the trick and he didn't look quite so ravaged. Then there was the matter of what to wear, a question he hadn't had to consider for months. After some thought he settled on casual, unobtrusive: jeans, T-shirt and leather jacket. He could not remember his father being particularly smart or fussy about clothes, but then he didn't suppose boys paid much attention to that sort of thing.

He made himself something to eat and got ready. His hair was long – he should have got it cut. He got the five thirty-five train. It would get him there an hour early, but he didn't want to leave anything to chance. The train was on time and he went for a walk along the Embankment, trying to steady himself. It was a beautiful evening. It couldn't have been more different from the how he'd imagined the meeting – in a modern cafe-bar in the rain.

He got down to the wine bar at about a quarter to seven. It was more or less as he remembered it, except he didn't think it had a food counter in his day. It was full of a young, suited, after-work crowd, a little different from the bohemian students it once attracted. He briefly entertained the idea that he should wait for his father before ordering a drink, but he needed one so he got himself a large Merlot. He managed to find a table for two in one of the archways that led to the old, vaulted part of the cellar. It was a small, round wooden-topped table with a wrought-iron pedestal. He sat down and noticed his hand was shaking slightly. Nerves or booze or both?

By seven o'clock he'd finished his glass and went up for another. It would have been cheaper to get a bottle but he didn't want to be sitting there on his own with one when his father walked in. He still couldn't quite believe that his father was going to do that, any minute now.

In fact it was another ten minutes before his father came round the bottom steps of the staircase. He'd begun to get quite anxious. He recognised him immediately. He was stockier, greyer and was wearing a suit and tie, but Lloyd would have recognised him anywhere. It didn't feel strange at all. In fact it

169

felt like a bit of an anti-climax. His father was looking around the crowded cellar. Lloyd half rose from his seat and lifted his arm in the air in a sort of discrete wave. His father spotted him and came over to him, smiling.

'Hello Lloyd,' he said, and put down his briefcase.

'Hello,' said Lloyd. He was standing up now and wondering what to do. He held out his hand and his father shook it, cupping Lloyd's forearm with his other hand as if to upgrade the handshake.

'Ah, would you like another drink?' said his father, nodding at Lloyd's empty glass.

'Ah, yes please,' said Lloyd. 'Red wine.'

'I'll get a bottle, shall I?' said his father, and turned towards the bar without waiting for an answer.

Lloyd sat back down, feeling awkward. He tried to sort out for the last time what he wanted to know and say, but he found it hard to concentrate. He'd made up his mind to be calm and patient, listen to what his father had to say. He was a long time at the bar, and came back with a bottle of the Merlot that Lloyd had ordered and two glasses. Their tastes in wine were similar, noted Lloyd. His father poured it out.

'I've come straight from work,' he said, looking down at his suit.

'What do you do?' asked Lloyd.

'I'm a headmaster.'

'Where's that?'

'At a high school in Morden. It's near Wimbledon. That's where we live.'

Lloyd clocked that 'we'. But before he had the chance to explore further, his father said, 'Anyway tell me about you. I hear you haven't been too well. How are you doing?

'Well, just about the same really. It's this ME thing. You know, Chronic Fatigue. It's like flu symptoms that come and go.'

170

He was grateful that his father was showing an interest, but didn't want to be distracted from what he had come to find out.

'I know something about it,' his father was saying. 'I've been reading up on it. Do you think there's any progress?'

'I don't get quite the bad bouts I used to when I'd be in bed for days on end,' said Lloyd cautiously. 'I think it's just going to take time.'

'Weren't you better off at The Noddfa? Why did you want to come to London?'

Lloyd was surprised at the question about returning to London. That's where his father was. But then again, he'd only just then expressed it to himself in so many words, so maybe it was not so surprising after all that his father couldn't understand.

'I was confused and angry,' said Lloyd. 'Angry with Mona about the deception.'

'Well, there's no reason to be angry with Mona at all,' said his father. 'Quite the opposite. She was caught in the middle, poor thing. She was trying to be loyal to both of us. Be angry with me by all means.'

'I *am* angry with you,' said Lloyd.

'As I say, you have every right to be. I've thought a lot about it over the years, as you might imagine. It does all sound so bizarre I can see. I don't want to make excuses, but I do want to explain things. As much as I can, anyway. There are things I can't even explain to myself.'

'Yes, I would like you to explain why you just walked out of my life,' said Lloyd.

'As I think I said on the tape, I don't think I was in my right mind. I'd been growing suspicious for a while that your mother had been having an affair. That stressed me out and I got pretty low. I'd been worrying about your future too. It's probably hard for you to appreciate what a stigma it was back then for a married woman, a mother, to be having an affair. In rural places like that the whole community would have judged her. When I

171

saw the burning car and knew she wouldn't survive I had this mad idea to fake my death. I can't tell you much more than that, as improbable as it sounds. I felt I was going a bit mad, and that you would be safe with Mona. You'd be free from all the scandal.'

Lloyd looked his father in the face. He looked sincere and sorrowful. His father was looking at him for some kind of reaction, and for some reason Lloyd didn't think it was exoneration he was seeking. Just acceptance of his story.

'Maybe I can understand that,' said Lloyd. 'But what I can't understand is that you just wiped me out of your life forever, see the years go by without once making an effort to reach out to me.'

Lloyd could feel himself getting emotional, tears fighting to get out. It was unlike him. He'd kept them under control for all these years. The last thing he wanted to do was break down in front of his father.

'When I got to London I was still in a bit of a state,' said his father. 'It took me a while to get myself sorted out. And then I was taking it a day at a time. I really didn't think I would make it, one way or another. I thought I'd get caught out, or have a breakdown or something. As time went by it sort of became part of my survival, to live my new identity and not look back. There were so many times, Lloyd, when I wanted to come back and get you. But it was always going to be sometime in the future, when I'd totally sorted out my new life. Of course, you never do totally sort out your life. Deep down I knew you were better off where you were. And I think now that as time went by, I couldn't face you finding out about it all, couldn't face your disappointment and anger.'

It all sounded pretty reasonable, thought Lloyd. But somehow it wasn't enough. There was something else he didn't understand, but he couldn't quite put his finger on it. Another question occurred to him.

'One thing I've been wondering about,' he said, 'is why was Mum heading for Aberdovey? You'd think if she was running away from you, she want to go to Cardiff or London or somewhere, not towards a small seaside resort where it would be easy to find her.'

His father shot him a sharp, enquiring look, as if he'd stumbled on something.

'Yes, I've always wondered about that myself,' said his father. 'I suppose she could have gone up north and caught a ferry to Ireland or something. But I'm much in the dark as you are.'

There was a pause. It was a long and awkward one, such as Lloyd had feared would mar the reunion. It had all gone pretty well up to now, he thought, but neither seemed to know what to say next.

'Have you eaten?' asked his father.

Lloyd wasn't interested in food.

'No,' he said.

'They do some good cold pies here now. And unusual cheeses. Why don't I get a plate of pie and pickles and cheese that we can share?'

'That sounds good,' said Lloyd, not wanting to refuse.

His father got up and went over to the food counter. Lloyd looked around the cellar at the gaggles of smug men and loud women. Office workers celebrating their release for the weekend. Civil servants, journalists, bankers, lawyers – at one time this would have been his habitat too. Just over a year ago he'd have been doing this, drinking with colleagues, contacts and friends on a Friday night. In his work though it would have been more likely to be on a terrace overlooking the sea, than in a dank cellar. People asked him if he missed all that. He didn't, or at any rate he could not in his present state contemplate being back in that world again. But what he did miss was the sense of purpose and status that such a career bestowed. Living without these things was much harder than he thought.

The sweep of his gaze found his father at the glass food cabinet, pointing at things within. He too looked as if he were on an ordinary Friday night out. He could have been out with his mates, rather than with a son he hadn't seen for twenty years or so.

He told himself not to be too critical, not to expect too much, as he'd promised himself beforehand. His father was taking a long time. Lloyd wondered if he was enjoying this respite away from him, hoping it would all soon be over. Yet he'd seemed genuine, guileless. He came back with the food, and Lloyd looked up at him and smiled, rousing himself from his reverie.

There was large plate of chicken and ham pie with pickled onions, gherkins and chutney, and another with wedges of cheese.

'Stinking Bishop, Maroilles and St Paulin,' said his father, manoeuvring the plates onto the small table top. He disappeared again and came back with a basket full of French bread, cut on the diagonal, and foil-wrapped pats of butter, cutlery wrapped in white paper napkins, and another bottle of Merlot.

For a while they concentrated on the food. His father urged him to try all three cheeses after they'd finished the pie. It was good, and Lloyd found that he was hungry after all. After they'd cleared it all up, they sat back and washed it down with wine with hums of appreciation.

'So have you changed your name?' asked Lloyd.

His father gave a small wry smile.

'Slightly,' he said. He held out his hand again.

'Hugh Davey,' he said, when Lloyd shook it. 'Hugh with a GH. Not so different from Huw Davies. I thought I'd keep it fairly similar, so it wouldn't look as if I was trying to hide if anyone questioned me about it. But different enough to be someone else. I was surprised how easy it was - to be someone else. Of course in those days you were less surrounded by pieces of identity like credit cards, picture driving licences, and so on.'

He was now looking pretty pleased with himself, Lloyd was dismayed to note. Or was Lloyd just reading too much into things again, assigning him faults and weaknesses that just weren't there.

'And did you marry again?'

It seemed to be a question his father had been expecting, and not with any relish.

'Yes. About fifteen years ago. To Vicky.'

'Children?'

'Emma, twelve, and Ben, eight.'

'Do they know about me?'

'Well, Vicky does now. I told her the other night, after I texted you.' He was playing around with some cheese rind on his plate, and glancing up a little guiltily at Lloyd. 'I may as well tell you, it came as a bit of a shock to her.'

'And what about your children? Are you going to tell them?'

'Well, I talked it over with Vicky, and we think it's best not to, at least for the time being.'

So. He wasn't going to be introduced to the family then. He wouldn't be entering his father's new life anytime soon. It angered him to know that he had a step-brother and sister (or was it half? Half-brother?) who didn't know he existed. The brother annoyed him more than the sister. He'd always quite liked the idea of a little sister. Whereas Ben had usurped him. Taken his place.

'Will you ever go back, do you think?'

'To Mid-Wales? No,' said his father, 'I can't see that happening.'

That last answer told Lloyd all he needed to know. He wouldn't be part of his father's new life, and his father would never return to his old one. Lloyd had come to the end of his most pressing questions, and still couldn't think of that one at the back of his mind that had been nagging him. His father was looking at his watch.

175

'Look, I'm sure you've got other questions, Lloyd, but I'd better be going now. You've got my number.'

It was as if the allotted time for the interview was up.

'Yes, me too,' said Lloyd.

His father was getting the Northern Line from Embankment. Lloyd walked with him to the tube station at the end of Villiers Street. Lloyd said he was going to walk over Hungerford Bridge and get the train from Waterloo East.

As they got to the station, to the parting of their ways, Lloyd said, 'So will I see you again, sometime?'

'Oh, of course,' said Hugh Davey. They were both awkward again now, unsure how to play their parts. 'But I do have to say that we shouldn't rush things. One step at a time. I think that'll be best for all concerned. But it's been wonderful to see you. I can't tell you........'

Lloyd wondered how to leave him. Part of him wanted to hug his father. The other part thought a casual goodbye to Hugh Davey would be better. In the end, Lloyd half-raised his hand in farewell, and Hugh Davey did the same.

As he crossed the bridge, the necklace of floodlit sights along the river sparkling in its reflection, he considered that the evening had gone as well as it could have done. What did he expect? An invitation to Sunday dinner? A bedroom in the family home? His father, he had to admit, had been reasonable. Yet the encounter had left him restless, dissatisfied. He couldn't help feeling his father was holding something back. His answers to Lloyd's questions had seemed plausible and had helped to clarify a few things that had been nagging him, but there was something missing from the overall picture, something that prevented it from making complete sense.

Perhaps there wouldn't be another chance. He was the outsider in his father's life now, possibly to be allowed in a little more when Vicky had recovered from the shock and the children were judged mature enough to be told about him. No, he didn't want that. It was what he'd been dreading, in fact, and maybe why he'd been ambiguous about meeting his father all along. He'd dreaded a second rejection. And that, in his view, was what he'd just got. No, he wouldn't be seeing his father again.

Fifteen

Lloyd went rapidly downhill again after the meeting. All bids to clean up his act were off. He'd got a text from his father a couple of days later, saying he'd loved seeing him, and asking how he was. No mention of another meeting. Lloyd's reply was courteous but concise.

Mona rang him early on the Sunday evening – it had become her regular time – and asked him how it had gone. Lloyd said he supposed it had gone as well as could be expected. Mona was full of questions. What had they said? How did they get on? What did he look like? What was he doing? Lloyd answered as fully as he could. His father hadn't sworn him to secrecy, after all. Surely there was no need for secrecy now, apart from Lloyd being kept a secret from the children? Could his father still be afraid of being implicated in his mother's death somehow? Failing to report an accident or something like that? It didn't seem plausible. It was a question Lloyd had failed to pursue, apart from asking if he would ever go to The Noddfa again, and the answer had been a resounding No. He had not asked why not.

Mona asked when they were going to see each other again. Lloyd told her about the new family, about the children who were ignorant of his existence.

'Maybe he's right, Lloyd,' said Mona. 'Maybe it's better to take small steps, let it grow a bit.'

Lloyd didn't want to take any more steps, didn't want to see his father again, didn't want to be something that anyone would have to get used to. And he didn't want to hear Mona list all the reasons why he should. But he did tell her that one of the first things his father had said was that she was not to be blamed.

'I can see that now, Mona,' he said. 'I was very wrong to take it out on you. I was just hitting out.'

'Well, it was only natural in a way,' she said. He could hear the relief in his voice.

'So when are you coming to see us?' she asked again before ringing off. 'Joan keeps asking me.'

Lloyd promised he'd think about it. He had been thinking about it, in fact, in a vague kind of way. But he'd postponed any decision until after the meeting. His savings were trickling away. The rent took out a big chunk, and so, increasingly, did drink. In a few months now, he'd have to return to work or give up his job. He couldn't imagine himself to be well enough to go back. One or two people had mentioned sickness benefit. But he didn't want to go down that route. It just didn't seem right. The future was hard to think about. When it forced its way into his thoughts, he'd have another drink. And without putting it into so many words, he was aware that there was a new barrier to his going back to Wales. He could hardly contemplate a day without a drink now. Not that he admitted to himself that his drinking was out of control. On the contrary, he thought he was controlling it rather well. He could still make it through to the evening sober, till the sun was over the yard arm, whenever that was. He'd never been clear. But it was his own yardstick. The fact that he had slipped back into his old habit of lying in bed until well after noon did not trouble him; he was ill, after all. There was the odd moment when he wondered if his symptoms now owed more to the drinking than to the ME. But it was easy to dismiss these thoughts. He always felt far better after a few drinks. The aches and pains seemed to disappear, and he actually felt more clear-headed. And if he felt terrible in the morning, well, he always did anyway.

Ifor rang to say he was coming down to London with his girlfriend in a couple of weekends, and he'd like him to meet Betty. Could they treat him to lunch in town? Lloyd would like to meet her too, he said – and indeed he was curious – but he'd have to let them know nearer the time. Nearer the time he was not feeling up to it, he texted Ifor. Maybe next time. Sorry. Jack rang to ask him over to supper. A couple of other old university friends would be there. Sorry, he wasn't up to it right now. Going through a rough patch. He'd probably be better in a month or two. Yes, of course he'd be in touch.

Lloyd occasionally asked himself if it was the ME that was destroying his social life, or his daily drinking routine, which he was loathe to interrupt. He didn't really care. His next drink was almost all he had to look forward to now, but it was enough. Enough to keep him going, and to keep the pain at bay. It was like his own cocoon, where he felt safe if not happy, away from the cold world outside. If he kept to the pattern, kept on automatic pilot, then he didn't have to think too much, or ask himself what was the point of it all? When the question did occasionally force itself into his consciousness, he sometimes worried that he would be driven to end it all at some point in the future.

During one sleepless night when the pain was particularly bad, he got up and phoned the Samaritans. It felt as if his head was gripped in a vice, which was getting very gradually tighter. He spoke to an older guy with and Irish accent. He told him he didn't know whether his life was worth living with this illness.

As Lloyd expected, the Samaritan didn't voice his own opinions.

'Only you yourself can decide that,' he said.

It still felt a little unsympathetic, but after the call Lloyd did feel better, just for having got things off his chest.

He got a couple more texts from his father in similar vein to the first, asking after his health, giving no further clue as to the small steps they were supposed to be taking. He no longer felt anything when he saw DAD come up on his phone. He was past caring. Or so he told himself. He even thought of changing DAD to HUGH, but he didn't get round to it, or couldn't bring himself to do it.

He got a short letter from Joan and that at least touched his heart a little. She gave her usual titbits of news and said that Rhys was continuing to make slow but steady progress and beginning to do some light farm work. She asked if he was also feeling a little better and was he thinking of coming home at all? He liked that 'home', he couldn't have said why. But how could he possibly let her see him in this mess, let her see that he'd failed, had failed her and Rhys, despite all his fine words.

His low point came late one Saturday afternoon. Lloyd had only been out of bed a couple of hours, and was standing at the kitchen counter opening a bottle of wine. He heard a noise that he did not at first recognise, so unused was he to hearing it. Then he realised it was the entryphone buzzer. He put the corkscrew gently down on the counter and stood stock still, feeling foolish. It rang again. He didn't move. His phone rang, and he jumped. He stared at it on the counter in panic, as if it were some lethal weapon. It was Jack. He must be at the front door. He let it ring out. He dreaded seeing the voicemail symbol come up, so he crept into the bathroom, locked the door and sat on the loo with his head in his hands to stop them shaking.

He could suddenly see himself as if he were in a film or TV drama. It was the image of someone who was in deep trouble, in need of help. He wondered if he really was losing his mind. There were many people, he knew, who still thought that ME was psychological rather than physiological, a result of clinical depression. He'd always been certain in his own mind that this was not the case, at least not his case. Now even that certainty seemed to dissolve, and he heard himself give a few almost silent sobs.

Late that evening he ran out of wine. There was an old bottle of sherry on the counter, so he drank that. Then he staggered down to Sainsbury's to get some more. Shit. It was closed. Past eleven. He felt desperate. He could break the window. No, he'd get arrested. He finally would go mad in a cell without booze. But there'd be drugs. But no, even with drugs he couldn't cope with being cooped up. He'd have to hang himself. But what with? They took your bootlaces and belt away from you, didn't they? He could tear strips from his stripy uniform and make a rope with that. No, surely they thought of that. They'd watch you or make untearable material. He'd have to hide a razor blade somewhere – in the sole of his shoe. Yes, he could get one now, a razor blade. No, shit, the shop's shut. He'd have to break in. No, wait, that's what had got him in prison in the first place. He heard laughter across the street. Girls giggling. Giggling at him? Or were they? Or were they just a drunken gaggle who'd giggle at anything? He couldn't know. He had to get indoors quickly. But he had to have booze. There was no way out, was there? What could he do? Just to get those last few glasses to send him to sleep. Jack! He could ring Jack. He looked at his watch. Eleven-thirty. Jack would still be up. Jack wouldn't mind. Jack would have wine. Jack would come and get him. He looked for his phone. He couldn't find it. Anyway, of course he couldn't ring Jack. Not in this state. What was he thinking?

He staggered back to his front door and wiggled the key in the lock. He wobbled up the stairs, bouncing from side to side, and when he got inside the flat he looked for his phone. He couldn't find it. He couldn't remember what he'd done with it. He thumped his bed, hoping to feel it under the bedclothes. Then he collapsed on top of it, completely exhausted.

He slept soundly that night for the first time in weeks. When he woke he felt oddly calm, as if the worst was over. He knew he'd felt like this before, but maybe this latest dismal episode would in fact help bring him to his senses. He found his phone on the bathroom floor. Thank God he didn't have it last night. It had saved him from a huge embarrassment.

Now that summer was approaching, he made a determined effort to get out for a walk sometimes, to lighten his mood. He'd wander up to the park at the top of the hill and sit in his seat by the bandstand, like an old man. There, with the birdsong and flowers and panoramic views, he'd feel some kind or relief for a while. But it was not the relief he was seeking and he'd return with a certain sense of defeat, a loss of nerve until he got inside and heard the comforting gurgle of the first glass.

He was sitting on the bench one Friday afternoon, bracing himself for such a return, when he spotted a familiar figure walking up the hill towards him. It was small, with a mop of white hair. It was Mrs Wozniak.

His first thought was, 'Oh, no.' It was too late to make a dignified getaway. She must have seen him before he saw her. There was nothing to do but sit and wait.

'Hello,' she said, as she approached the bench, a little out of breath. She looked done in. She seemed to have lost some of that sense of purpose, that alertness in her eyes.

'Hello, Mrs Wozniak.'

'May I?' she said, motioning to the space on the bench beside him.

'Of course,' he said, shifting up a little, unnecessarily.

'How arre you?' she asked.

'Well, could be better. You?'

She lit a cigarette.

'You look a vrreck,' she said, ignoring his enquiry.

'You don't look too hot yourself, sweetheart,' thought Lloyd, but all he said was, 'I'm still ill.'

'And still drrinking too much?'

Lloyd had in some ways always appreciated her direct approach, her frankness and even now he couldn't quite suppress a little smile. No-one else could have got away with it. It encouraged a similar openness in him.

'Oh yes, probably,' he said. 'But it's my way of coping with this illness I've got.'

'Not a verry good vay of coping. It's so easy to just give up on life. You have to take the drrinking in hand, now, beforre it takes hold of you. I don't vant to come up herre one day and find you on this bench vith a bottle in a brrown paper bag.'

'So, you haven't given up on life? You certainly haven't given up smoking.'

'Ach, Lloyd, I'm borred. I can't do all the things I used to. And therre arre fewer people to do them forr now, anyvay.'

She had two sons, he knew. They'd both done well and moved away. One lived in America, in New York he thought. The other worked in the City, and she complained about not seeing enough of him. It was its skyscrapers ahead of them that she was looking at now.

'I miss you, you know. I miss our chats. You'rre a good listener.' She was still looking straight ahead.

'Vhy did you move out so soon?'

Lloyd didn't know what to say.

'Vas it because I complained about all your bottles?'

'That and....... ' He hesitated.

'That and vhat?'

'Well, as we're sitting here with our hair down, you made a remark one day after a walk in this park, about too many bloody foreigners. It's just that I can't stand racism.'

'Ach, vas joke,' said Mrs Wozniak. 'I've seen enough of life to know that people arre people, good and bad. It doesn't matter vherre you come frrom. You think I vould be serrious about

185

something like that? Vith *my* accent? You can alvays see the good in people. Don't give up on that. You might need it.'

Lloyd's heart lifted a little. She was right. It was so easy to be wrong about people. He'd been wrong about her. He had judged her, as he had wrongly accused her of judging other people. His life might be different now if he hadn't moved out, isolated himself from everyone. He'd just wanted to be free from interference, free to live how he wanted. But freedom is sweetest when it's lacking, he reflected. Its limitations are soon reached. That was another thing about this bloody illness. It gave you too much time to brood, made you so introspective.

'Anyway, what about you?' said Lloyd. 'There must be something you always wanted to do. You're comfortably off. Now's the time to take up something new.'

'Vell, vhen I was little girl in Poland, beforre Nazis came, I vas verry good at drrawing and painting. I alvays vanted to be painter. But, vell, things got in the vay. Life got in the vay.'

'That's it,' said Lloyd. 'Paint. Go to evening classes.'

'Ach, too old.'

'You're not too old, Mrs Wozniak.'

They were both silent for a while, looking down over the lawns, roses and laurels which framed the view of the city. She seemed to be turning the idea over in her mind.

'Yes, maybe you'rre rright. Maybe I could paint.' He turned to look at her. A little smile was playing on her lips. And he was sure he could see a little sparkle return to her eyes.

After that they said their goodbyes, and Mrs Wozniak extracted a promise from him that he'd call and see her. For once Lloyd meant it, and hoped he could keep it – he no longer trusted himself.

That evening he walked back down Lordship Lane without the customary sense of defeat or loss of nerve. Although it had been sad to see such a strong person weakened, there was still hope there too. And maybe he was buoyed by the fact that he'd been more honest with her than he had with anyone in a long time – including himself. It was also the first time he'd been able to go out in just a T—shirt, after the long cold winter. It gave him a sense of liberation. He even wondered if his own hibernation was beginning to end.

He made himself some sausages and pasta with a tomato and basil sauce. He poured himself some wine but somehow, tonight, his heart wasn't in it. The image of the bench and the brown paper bag kept coming back to him. He was probably closer to it than he would ever have admitted to himself. He poured himself small glasses and sipped rather than slurped. By midnight he was ready for bed.

But he didn't sleep well. He had one of those deeply disturbing dreams. The details were hard to pin down, but he was chasing somebody. Somebody in a car. At least some of the time it seemed he was chasing it, at other times he seemed to be viewing the car from the air, as if it was being chased by someone from above. It started in rugged, hilly terrain which he thought to be Poland. Then it was on water, in wide channels through reeds like the Everglades. He was on one of those flat rafts with a huge fan-like propeller on the back like you see in movies, and he was chasing a speed boat. Then it was back on a hilly road, and this time he was way above the car. It took ages to dawn on him that it was his mother in the car. He kept trying to get lower down, closer to the car so he could see inside. No sooner did it seem that he was making progress, getting down closer to it, than he was back up where he'd started off. After many ups and downs, he got close enough to look inside the back window of the car. It was his mother, but she was alone. This came as something of a shock. And then he was aware of something behind him. Something terrifying. He was afraid to look, but he had to. Something was forcing him. And when he did, it was the most frightening thing he had ever seen. It was a black spot. A black spot moving ever closer to his mother's speeding car.

He woke himself up with a shout, and he sat up in bed, sweating. The implications of the dream were terribly clear to him. His father had murdered his mother. He'd run her off the road.

Eventually he got back to sleep. When he woke up late in the morning, he could hardly remember the dream at all. But he did remember its meaning, all too clearly. His father had gone after his mother to run her off the road, to kill her. As he'd said to Ifor, his father could have found his mother's love letters in the drawer at The Noddfa. He could have made up his mind there and then. And thrown the letters down through the floorboards in the attic where no-one would ever find them.

And then Lloyd saw with a new clarity what had been nagging him all this time, the thing that hadn't quite made sense to him. It was his father's desperation to disappear for good after the accident. If he hadn't done anything wrong, what was there to run away and hide from? Surely it had to be more than failing to report an accident, or even dangerous driving.

For an hour or more, Lloyd thought the dream had given him an insight into what really happened. He thought he'd got it at last, that thing that had been bothering him. Then, of course, he spotted the fatal flaw. Even if his father had run his mother off the road, there was no way he could have planned for the outcome. But an image came to Lloyd, a clip from an old black and white film from the 1940s or 1950s. It was one of those Hollywood actors with and English accent, like James Mason. He was dressed in the kind of silk dressing gowns that you only ever see in films of that era. Lloyd thought he was planning to murder his wife. He'd just had a revelation. He was whispering to himself, 'No man can commit the perfect murder, but chance can.'

For the rest of the day he couldn't shake off that feeling that his father had gone after his mother that day to kill her. It was a chance murder.

When Mona rang the next evening, he decided to come clean. Mrs Wozniak was right, it was time for action.

'I'd like to come back for a while,' he said. 'But there's something I have to tell you.'

'Shoot,' she said.

He told her about the drinking, how he'd come to rely on it, but was trying to cut down.

'Oh, come home, love,' she said, 'come home. It'll be easier for you once your here. I can help, and you can't just pop to the off-licence. You'll be much better here. We'd be all pleased to see you. Alex says he might come up for a few days in the summer holidays, after his exams.'

Lloyd was pleased about that, but he warned her that he didn't think he'd be able to cut out drinking completely, and neither did he want to. She said they could work out a plan together. He was apprehensive about that, but felt there was no going back. The next day he gave the required one month's notice on his flat, but didn't want to wait that long, and booked a train ticket for Llanfair for the next Saturday.

Sixteen

It was with a spirit of adventure, but not without some anxiety, that Lloyd set out for Wales a few days later. The early start was a novelty, and even though he'd had more wine than he intended the night before, he didn't feel as bad as he feared he would. He put it down to having things to do, an agenda, although there had been many times when this wouldn't have stirred him from his stupor. He wondered now, as he went through the flat making sure he hadn't forgotten anything, whether his nocturnal habits, his swapping day for night to a large extent, could be explained in part by the worry of how to fill the daylight hours.

He'd certainly been busy these past few days. On Tuesday evening he'd strolled over to Dulwich to see Jack and Jill. This was his first hurdle, one which filled him with apprehension after his pathetic reaction to Jack's calls the other day. But they greeted him like a long-lost brother, and at first made no mention of it. They sat in the large kitchen overlooking the garden eating pasta and drinking Chianti, or rather Lloyd and Jack drank it. Jill was several months pregnant and glowing. But when Lloyd told them he was going back to Wales for a while, Jack and Jill exchanged frowns and looked put out, as if this marked some kind of defeat for him and them.

'But why?' asked Jack. 'Won't you be bored out of your mind?'

'Well, you'd be surprised how busy farm life is,' said Lloyd. 'And I haven't exactly been leading an active social life in London.'

'We noticed,' said Jack, exchanging another significant look with Jill. 'Sometimes we thought you were actively ignoring us.'

'The truth is, I've been actively ignoring everyone,' said Lloyd. 'I haven't been doing too well. And putting away too much of this.' He raised his glass.

'But why didn't you let us in? Let us help?' asked Jack.

Lloyd could tell that under his controlled calm there was real anger.

'It's not that easy. You get caught in a downward spiral. Anyway,' said Lloyd, beginning to tire of this train of conversation, 'I hope that's behind me.'

'We hope so too,' said Jill. 'It's not good to cut off your friends.'

They ran him home, Jill driving. As Lloyd was getting out of the car, Jack said he'd drive him to Euston on Saturday. Lloyd began a protest, but Jack waved it aside, and insisted. Lloyd gave in gracefully, thinking it was probably the least he could do, given their yearning to help.

The next night he went up to see Mrs Wozniak. She made coffee and took him to sit out in the garden on folding picnic chairs, the kind you used to see outside caravans and tents, and smoked cigarettes. She looked tired, as she often did, but some of the old sparkle was back. She'd rung up the local college, she told him, to ask about art courses. They were going to send her some information. The courses were quite cheap, she said, as if that clinched it. Lloyd always thought of her and her husband as well off: they must have very little mortgage, if any, left on the house, and they packed the place with boarders. Yet Mrs Wozniak's nose for a bargain was as keen as ever.

'I'm looking forrward to it,' she said. 'It was a good idea of yourrs, Lloyd. Perrhaps meeting on that parrk bench was fate.'

Lloyd agreed that perhaps it was. He'd noticed that he no longer enjoyed his wine as much as he had done: the image of himself on that bench with a bottle-shaped brown paper bag seemed to intervene. It hadn't weaned him off it completely – far from it – but it had imposed limits.

He told her he was going back to Wales for a while.

'Vales? Never been. They say it's verry prretty. It's prrobably for the best. At least for a little while. You need someone to look after you, despite vat you think.'

They parted with a quick peck on the cheek and promises to keep in touch.

Lloyd was ready long before Jack came round to pick him up. He had no sense of regret at leaving the flat. It had never been home, more like a cell, and he had had no life there. It had been a sort of waiting room, a waiting space. He hadn't heard from his father for a couple of weeks. He was ready for a new life.

Jack carried his large suitcase and backpack down to the car, leaving Lloyd with only his laptop: he had accumulated virtually no new belongings since leaving Uruguay. He shut the flat door without looking back, without wanting to capture a last, lingering image. He dropped the envelope containing the keys in the mail basket in the entrance as arranged.

The day was glorious, the first time Lloyd had had a sense of real summer. It was hot, blue-skied and lush green, with an air of stillness and ease. Even the streets of South London were transformed, and the journey into town which was usually so tedious had the aura of a school outing. On the way, Jack gave Lloyd a couple of sidelong glances.

'Are you sure you're doing the right thing?' he asked eventually.

'No,' said Lloyd, realising the truth of it as he spoke, 'but it was about time I did something.'

Jack saw him on to the train.

'Well, don't forget us. You know where we are.'

193

'Yes,' said Lloyd. 'And it's good to know you're there, even if I don't make use of you.'

Jack waited on the platform until the train pulled out, and they both gave self-conscious half waves. They were indeed good friends to him, Lloyd reflected, and a great comfort. But these days he could hardly be described as a proper friend to them.

His earlier impression of an escapade, a jaunt, evaporated rapidly. As the train crossed into Wales and began to snake along the contours of the hillside, he tried his best to appreciate the beauty, to rekindle the morning's sense of hope. But cloud had come in from the West to meet the train, and the sunlight had been reduced to a pallid glimmer behind him. His mood was now melancholic, reminiscent of those twilights when he first went to The Noddfa.

Mona was there at the little stone station to greet him. It had barely changed since he was a boy. She was breezy, almost offhand with him, as if his return was no big deal. They exchanged the customary words of greeting, of health enquiries.

'Did you have a good journey?' asked Mona, as she always did, as if he had just travelled across the Sahara Desert, or somewhere where safe passage was equally as uncertain.

He felt guilty for treating her so badly, being so childish as he now saw it, and he spent the ten or fifteen minutes it took them to get to The Noddfa trying to think of ways to make it up to her. He found it hard to come up with anything concrete that wouldn't look too obvious. He'd have to keep on thinking.

In the kitchen at The Noddfa, Mona made them a cup of tea and they sat down in the armchairs either side of the range. Lloyd noticed a certain stillness about the place, or not stillness exactly, but emptiness, absence. Alex would be coming up in a couple of weeks, Mona had told him on the way up. He was looking forward to seeing him again. But it wasn't Alex. He had, after all, known him only for those couple of weeks in January. No, it was Turk whose absence made such a difference. He

194

would have been lying on the mat between them. Mona must have seen him staring at the space, for she said, 'It's quiet, without him, isn't it? Even though he was old and didn't do very much.'

Lloyd agreed that it was.

The evening was difficult. Lloyd wanted a drink but didn't want to ask for one. Mona didn't offer, as she often did, and of course he could understand that. They watched one of Mona's beloved detective series on the TV. Lloyd couldn't get into it. It seemed far-fetched and implausible. He was bored and listless. He remembered once hearing the journalist and well-known bon viveur Jeffrey Bernard on Desert Island Discs being asked why he drank so much. He'd replied that a drunk is never bored – he's always looking forward to his next drink. At the time he'd wondered if that could be true. Now he knew that it was.

He went to bed to read, and didn't sleep till the early hours. But he'd set his phone alarm for ten. Physically, he'd felt better yesterday after the early start. He resolved to try to carry on with this routine, however badly he slept. It was what Keith had advised him months ago, but of course he had to find it out for himself. Since he first began to feel ill, he'd got into his head that the only way he'd ever get better was to stay in bed until he felt like getting up. It was a hard conviction to shake off.

His desperation for sleep no doubt contributed to his deprivation of it. When the alarm went off, he wanted more than anything else to roll over and go back to sleep. But with a supreme effort of will, and stumbling slightly in his wooziness, he managed to get up and shower.

He went downstairs and forced himself to have some juice and toast. He wanted to start his new routine as he meant to go on. Mona had a cup of coffee with him. Ifor was coming home next week, she said, and bringing his girlfriend for the first time. Had Lloyd met her? No? Well, he'd have to ask them up to tea. Mrs Evans as well, if he liked. She'd seen one or two of his old friends in town, and they'd been asking after him. They said he should give them a ring sometime and they could go for a drink.

She paused in her chatter, taking a long drink of her coffee, and Lloyd guessed she was telling herself she shouldn't have said that last part, that she had said too much. He didn't mind in the least. He'd have to let her know when he had the chance that she needn't worry about mentioning anything to do with alcohol.

Lloyd was never at his chattiest in the morning, and had been confining his responses to nods and mmms. But to show her he was relaxed about what she'd said, and maybe to start atoning for his past behaviour, he asked about a couple of cousins and other relations with whom he'd never been that close. The family was one of Mona's favourite topics of conversation, and she was soon off again: So-and-so was having a baby, another getting married, someone else had been concussed playing rugby and had had to be airlifted to hospital.

After this light breakfast, which made him feel slightly sick, the day stretched before him in a way to which he had become totally unaccustomed. He decided to go for a walk, and went along the lane that led from the back of the house to the far fields which sloped down towards the woods. He passed the apple orchard on his right, where his Dad had rigged up a swing for their visits to The Noddfa when he was a young child. It had gone long ago, but he remembered the precise tree from which it hung, and he could almost see it. In fact the stillness of the summer's day summoned all kinds of memories of the vanished world of his childhood, as if parallel universes had suddenly aligned. It was looking through a telescope of time through both ends at once, where the near and far became one.

When he got to the farthest field, Cae Cwm, which was divided by a small stream in a dingle and meant Valley Field, he suddenly remembered a night when he'd been allowed to take a tent out and spend the night. It was an old-fashioned white canvas tent, such as you might see in old black and white

196

pictures of scout camps, with high sides and a pitched roof like a little house. He had no idea where the tent had come from – maybe Mona had found it in the attic or bought it from a house clearance sale. He must have been eleven or twelve. It was not long before he lost his parents.

He looked around for the exact spot where he'd pitched it, and there it was, he was pretty sure, on a flat-topped mound in the middle of the field. He sat down on it, looking over the valley that stretched away below the woods towards Llanfair, and remembered sitting there that night and looking up at the stars. He'd been feeling a little lonely, he recalled, as it was getting time to go to bed, when his father paid a surprise visit, bringing some cocoa in a thermos. The two of them sat there for a while drinking it, not saying very much. To Lloyd then, it had seemed almost like a cowboy film, when they sat around the campfire. The fact that he and his father were sitting round a gas camping lamp drinking cocoa did nothing to spoil the illusion. And this place, unlike their old house in town which was now someone else's, would forever belong to them alone. It was, realised Lloyd now, one of the happiest times of his life.

After dinner, Lloyd went up to see Great Uncle Stanley.

'I've been worried about you,' said Great Uncle Stanley, as if Lloyd had been missing for a day or two. Lloyd asked why he'd been worried, but he started talking about the fireworks that were keeping him awake at night.

'Where are the fireworks coming from?' asked Lloyd.

'Over there,' said Great Uncle Stanley, nodding out past the orchard towards Cae Cwm.

It was impossible that anyone was letting off fireworks there. Lloyd asked him how often they went off, but Great Uncle Stanley had now drifted on to the subject of the French trenches, which were still moving closer to the house. They chatted for a while. Sometimes Great Uncle Stanley made sense and seemed to know that Lloyd had been away for a few months, but most of the time he aired his familiar themes. Lloyd would have liked to have talked about his parents, and even tell him about his father, but he thought it would be pointless, and very likely upsetting. He didn't know if Mona had said anything to Great Uncle Stanley, but he thought it highly unlikely that she would have done.

As Lloyd got up to go, Great Uncle Stanley said, 'At least you've survived.'

'Yes, at least I've survived,' said Lloyd.

It was another trying evening in front of the TV. Lloyd tried to concentrate on his book. There seemed to be a gulf between him and Mona now, as if each were waiting for the other to say something. He had another early night, at eleven, and set his alarm for nine-thirty, determined to break his nocturnal cycle.

As he lay there tossing and turning, it suddenly came to him that Mona had not once mentioned Joan – almost everyone else of their mutual acquaintance, but not Joan. He was in fact dying to see her. He wondered why Mona had dropped her matchmaking, as he saw it. Maybe she'd changed tactics, thinking that if she tried to push them together, Lloyd's natural inclination would be to resist. In this she would be right, although it had clearly never occurred to her in the past. But it did make Lloyd want to see her all the more, and added a new element of curiosity. Was Joan alright? Was there a reason why Mona had not mentioned her name? He'd find out tomorrow, he decided. He'd walk down to Pantycelyn.

When he got there just before three the next afternoon, he went to the back door as usual and knocked. Unusually, there was no cheery invitation to enter. A distant tractor's engine rumbled nearer and farther as it went up and down a field. Lloyd knocked again, hard. Still nothing. He looked up at the bedroom windows – one was open – and then walked around the side of the house to the front, which faced away from the yard he'd just walked through.

198

There she was, on her knees among the rose bushes. She heard his footsteps and looked up. She got up and came towards him with a look of delight, he hoped it was, on her face.

'Lloyd,' she said. 'I didn't know you were back.'

They hugged and it turned into a kiss, a passionate kiss. But it wasn't a long passionate kiss. Joan pulled away. They looked at each other for a moment.

'I'm sorry,' said Lloyd, 'I thought......'

'No, no,' said Joan, shaking her head and frowning a little, 'don't apologize. It's wonderful to see you. It's just......,' she trailed off.

'Just what?'

'Well, I've been seeing someone. Nothing serious. Walking out with him, as they used to say. That describes it better. Although we drove.'

It came as something of a shock to Lloyd, although he could see there was no good reason why it should. She was an attractive woman.

'That explains why Mona hasn't mentioned you, for once,' he said.

'And she didn't tell me you were coming,' said Joan. She appeared flustered – very unlike her.

'Look,' she said, 'I've got soil all over your shoulders with my muddy hands,' and she brushed him off with the back of them.

'Been doing a spot of weeding,' she said, somewhat unnecessarily. 'Let's sit down.'

She led him to a flimsy metal bench on the edge of the lawn. Its white paint was peeling, and it looked as if no-one had sat on it for years.

'Who is it?' asked Lloyd.

'No-one you'd know,' she said. 'I'm not being evasive – he's a farmer from down near Welshpool. As I say, it's quite casual. He takes me for a meal or drink now and again. If I'd known you were coming I might have.......would have.......'

'Don't worry on my account,' said Lloyd, stepping in to fill the pause.

'But I want to, you see,' she said. 'I want to worry on your account. It's just I don't know...........How long are you back for?'

So it seemed she was looking for some kind of commitment, something for which he felt distinctly unready, given his present state.

'I really don't know, Joan,' he said. 'A while maybe. I'm sorry to be vague, but the truth is I haven't been doing so well recently. Coming back is meant to be, well, a sort of fresh start. I sort of feel as if I've let you down somehow.'

'Oh, that's just ridiculous.'

This brought them to the subject of Rhys. On the whole, she thought he was making progress......he was out on the tractor now. But it was frustratingly slow, and sometimes hard to tell if there was any at all.

'It seems to be two steps forward and one back, and sometimes one step forward and two back,' she said.

'That sounds familiar. That's why, well it's difficult for me to be certain about anything right now. I do like you Joan, I like you a lot, but you're probably better off with the farmer at the moment.'

'No, I'm not. He's just a bit of company for me. He doesn't really mean much to me, Lloyd, but you do. Look, I'm not expecting marriage, or anything like it. I know you're not going to be here forever, but let's enjoy it while you are.'

Lloyd hadn't actually used the word love to himself yet, but he felt his heart surge when he heard those words. He suggested they go out for a meal on the coming Saturday.

'Let me cook one for you here,' she said. 'Rhys won't be here – he's going to stay with a friend for the weekend. It'll be more intimate.'

They looked at each other and smiled. She said she'd let the farmer down gently.

Back at The Noddfa, he told Mona where he'd been. She looked taken aback.

'She's asked me down for a meal on Saturday.'

Mona's face brightened.

'Very nice too,' she said, opening her eyes wide and nodding slowly.

He'd toyed with the idea of going the whole hog and telling her about the farmer as well, so that everything would be clear and in the open. But now he saw there was no need – Mona knew the score. It helped ease the tension that had built up between them.

Mona had made one of her shepherd's pies for tea. She mashed parsnips in with the potatoes and it gave an extra tang.

'Do you fancy some wine with it?' she asked, in a celebratory mood. 'I've got a nice bottle of red tucked away.'

Then he saw her actually bite her lip. He laughed.

'That would be lovely, Mona'.

He was sure now he could enjoy a glass or two with a meal without relapsing back into his old ways.

Seventeen

Lloyd picked Alex up at the station a couple of weeks later.

'Whose car is this?' asked Alex, jumping in.

'Just an old one I got second-hand in Llanfair,' said Lloyd. 'Gives me a bit of independence.'

Alex had changed considerably in six months, as people that age can, even more mentally than physically. He was very chatty on the way back, asking questions and making observations about life, the universe and everything. In response to Lloyd's question when he could get one in, he said he thought his exams had gone quite well and was going on to do history, geography and economics at six form college.

Mona had tea waiting for them. She'd boiled a ham and served it with mashed potatoes and beetroot from the garden. She and Alex seemed pleased to see each other.

'Have you found out any more about The Missing Room?' he asked her. 'You were going to ask that historian friend of yours.'

'Ooh, so I was,' she said. 'No, I haven't got round to it.'

'Could you give him a ring?'

'Well, I suppose I could now that you two are here. He might fancy a drive over if the weather stays fine.'

The historian in question, Merfyn, lectured at Aberystwyth University and used to stay at The Noddfa when Mona was doing B&B and he did courses at the nearby Gregynog Hall which was now part of the University of Wales. They'd kept in touch.

'I've brought the webcam,' Alex informed them, and enquired if Lloyd had brought his laptop. 'I've been reading up on it a bit. There were quite a few hiding holes built by chimneys and fireplaces. So when are you going to ring him, Auntie Mona?'

'Give me a bloody chance, will you?' She liked to do things in her own good time.

As it turned out, she rang Merfyn the next day, and told them he'd come over on Saturday afternoon. This gave Lloyd something of a problem, as he'd arranged to take Joan out then. He didn't want to put it off, as it was difficult enough for them to get time alone together in the first place, and there was always the question mark hanging over his health. In fact the only night they'd spent together was that first date, when Joan invited him down for a meal and Lloyd had been able to stay at Pantycelyn because Rhys was away for the weekend. Lloyd could understand why she didn't want him to spend the night when Rhys was there, not yet anyway. It was bad enough when he wasn't there. It had turned out well in the end – wonderfully well – but Lloyd had been very nervous and so, he discovered had Joan. For two people in their thirties, it was a ridiculous state of affairs. Opportunities to enjoy the physical side of their relationship would be few and far between, they realised. Joan spending the night at The Noddfa was out of the question and a hotel just plain sordid. They had discussed going away for the weekend, though, up to the coast. Joan wasn't sure. She was nervous about leaving Rhys alone for even a couple of days. So they'd settled on going out on Saturday up to Lake Bala, where Lloyd used to go with his parents sometimes on a Sunday. There were some secluded spots on the lakeside: they would get some semblance of privacy.

Later that evening Lloyd managed to get Mona on her own for a moment in the kitchen. It wasn't that easy, with Alex around. He claimed a lot of attention.

'I don't mean to be a nuisance....' began Lloyd.

'Ye-es.,' said Mona.

'But it's just that I'd arranged to go out with Joan on Saturday afternoon. Do you want me to be around when Merfyn comes?'

'Oh yes, you should be. I don't know anything about those camcorder things. I'll give him another ring.'

She wiped her hands on a tea towel and folded it neatly on the rail in front of the range.

'You two getting on well then?' she asked, as casually as she could.

'Well enough,' said Lloyd.

Lloyd and Alex were spending a lot of time together. Lloyd was just about keeping to his new regime of getting up in the morning. He usually managed it by nine-thirty. Every few days though, he would feel so bad that he would stay there for another few hours. It was hard going. Sometimes in the afternoon he'd fall asleep in the kitchen armchair, and wake up to regret it as it was then that he'd feel at his worst.

Although Alex's incessant chatter and questioning sometimes grated on him, on the whole he welcomed the distraction, and helped fill in the empty hours that he would once have filled by dozing or drinking. He still had a few drinks now and again – he and Mona would have wine with their evening meal two or three times a week and sometimes there'd be a couple of whiskies afterwards. But he was pleased to find he could now go two or three days without a drink easily enough. It wasn't so much the physical craving that gnawed at him, but the pervading sense of boredom, of marking time, that he found impossible to shake off. It was wearing him down.

He took Alex for a walk down to the Fairy Glen, where a path through the woods crossed a steep stream over a rickety wooden bridge. It was somewhere round here, according to local legend, that an old miser who didn't trust banks, had buried his gold coins during the war. Lloyd had spent many of his boyhood hours searching the glen for the treasure. But on hearing all this Alex showed scant interest, beyond suggesting that they buy a metal detector.

Lloyd found himself confiding in Alex about his father, under strict injunctions not to breathe a word to a living soul. He was careful not to mention his darker thoughts about murder, which sometimes came back to niggle him despite his efforts to dismiss them. He just couldn't see his mother driving off that road. He could remember her being a fast driver, but she was a good driver, as everyone remarked. It was a sunny day, as far as he could recall, although he had not checked this with anyone since, and he knew that memory could play tricks about details such as this. It would have been about this time of year, late spring or early summer, so the road would have been dry and it was one his mother knew well. Something didn't quite add up.

Alex too had questions about the crash, mostly of a rather forensic nature. Why didn't the police compare the teeth found on the other body in the car with his father's dental records? Why wasn't the man reported missing? As they walked up the path through the woods back towards the farm, Lloyd explained that everyone took it for granted that it was his father's body in the car: no-one had any reason to believe anything else. He hadn't mentioned the business with the watch, or Mona's role in his father's flight. He'd confined himself to saying that after the crash his father had gone to London. As for the body in the car, Lloyd said he'd probably told his wife he was leaving her and it was left at that. In those days it seemed easier to vanish without a trace.

He didn't want to go into the crash in any more detail – he wondered if he'd already said too much – but he was curious as to what Alex would make of his father's disappearing act.

Underneath all the braggadocio and cynicism there was a streak of sound common sense. He'd listened to the story attentively and patiently enough but, Lloyd was interested to note, he made no comment on the father's action, let alone pass any judgement on it. He seemed to accept it at face value.

After dinner on Saturday, Lloyd went out to his car and Alex came bounding after him and opened the passenger door.

'Where are you going?'

'Out for the afternoon.'

'But that guy is coming to look at The Missing Room, isn't he?'

'No, that's tomorrow now.'

'So, where are you going?'

'Out with a friend.'

'Can I come?'

'No.'

'Is it your girlfriend?'

He was quite sneering and unpleasant. Lloyd supposed that this was how boys his age behaved to their friends when they went off with girls.

'Look, go away. Get out.'

Alex slammed the door, and stomped back to the house. The grouchy teenager had returned.

Lloyd picked up Joan and they drove on the mountain roads over to Bala. The skies were mainly blue, with just enough white fluffy cloud to train the sun's rays in fast-changing patterns on the slopes. When they came to the top of the lake, Lloyd turned down the narrow lane that ran down its eastern side, away from the town and campsites, and stopped by a stony brook. There they spread a rug on the grassy bank and spent much of the afternoon entwined in each other's arms. Lloyd tried his best to ignore an inner voice which kept asking, 'How can this work? What future is there in it?' Why couldn't he just relax and enjoy himself as Joan seemed to be? Neither of them had mentioned

207

love, and Joan had said she didn't expect a long-term relationship, yet Lloyd couldn't help feeling he was here under false pretences. Had had no intention of moving back to Wales – couldn't imagine a future here – and could see Joan nowhere other than at Pantycelyn.

They were both reluctant to leave, so precious was their time together. But it was getting chilly. Lloyd suggested somewhere on the way back for something to eat. Reluctant at first, saying she had to get back to make tea for Rhys, Joan eventually conceded he could get something for himself.

'He's old enough,' said Lloyd. 'Just because he's ill, it'll do him no good for you to mollycoddle him.' How easy it was to give advice.

Joan knew of a wayside inn that did good food, and from there she rang Rhys to say she wouldn't be back until later.

'Did he mind?' asked Lloyd when she came back from the phone.

'Not a bit,' said Joan. 'You're right. I probably fuss over him too much.'

When he dropped her off about ten, he was desperate to go in with her and spend the night. She could sense it.

'Not yet, not yet,' she whispered, as they lingered over their goodnight kiss. 'Give me time.'

Merfyn looked every inch the college historian, and that was quite a lot of inches. Tall, bulky, with long, greying hair, he wore a tweed jacket over a pullover. Underneath the pullover was a checked shirt, with one of its front flaps hanging over his trousers. He gave Lloyd and Alex a hearty handshake that almost hurt. Alex flapped his hand in a rather stagey manner.

'Right,' said Merfyn, rubbing his hands together. 'Lead the way.'

Lloyd and Alex had everything ready: laptop, cable, webcam, torches and strings. Mona handed over the key to Lloyd, and told them she'd leave them to get on with it. They went through the same drill as last time, with Lloyd and Alex lying side by side in front of the triangular hole between the beams of the gable end, manipulating the torches and webcam through to the other side and down through the gap in the floorboards into the space below. Between them was the laptop, and Merfyn sat on a trunk and watched the pictures.

As the torch beams swung around the vault, it was almost as exciting as the first time, even though they had discovered its secrets. At least, that was Lloyd's view. Alex clung to the hope that there was something they'd missed in the near left-hand corner. He maintained they'd overlooked it when they found the letters. They'd briefed Merfyn to pay particular attention to this corner, without mentioning the letters. Alex and Mona had agreed beforehand to respect Lloyd's wishes that nothing should be said about the letters; they had , after all, nothing to do with the vault itself.

'Again,' said Merfyn, as he monitored the screen as the other two manoeuvred the beams to the spot. Alex kept jerking his head back to look at the screen, to make sure they were not missing anything. It meant that at times the beams were swinging wildly, not giving them the time to focus on anything.

'Concentrate, Alex!' said Lloyd.

'Again,' said Merfyn. 'Again.'

Eventually he seemed satisfied that they'd seen everything there was to be seen.

'Well, did you see anything?' asked Alex after they'd pulled everything up and scrambled back from their low, narrow observation platform.

'Nothing in the space,' said Merfyn.

'What about the space itself,' asked Lloyd. 'Do you have any ideas?'

'Yes,' said Merfyn. 'I think I do.'

'Well?'

'Let's go down and get Mona to listen too.'

They sat around the dining room table. Merfyn had carried out a thorough examination of the fireplace and its step-like ledges. The last time he'd had a look it had not yet been fully exposed – Mona had just knocked the old wall down. The three waited eagerly for him to finish the inspection and begin the explanation.

'I think it's fairly certain that it's some kind of hiding hole,' he said when he joined them at the table. 'Given the age of the house, it's probably a priest's hole.'

'But the date on the front of the house is 1664. Weren't Puritans being persecuted then?'

'Under Charles II, yes. But there weren't Puritans' holes in the way there were priests' holes.'

'Why not?' asked Mona.

'Well, for one thing, Catholics needed a hiding place for all the accoutrements of their religion - chalices for Mass and so on. Puritans didn't have such easily identifiable paraphernalia. And the Catholic underground – recusants they were called – were hunted down far more ruthlessly by the priest-hunters, or pursuivants, as they were known, than Puritans ever were. Maybe Puritans – Nonconformists as they became – used the holes later, but that's a different thing.'

'But didn't all that happen *before* 1664?' persisted Lloyd. 'Why would anyone have need of a priest's hole when this house was built?'

'Well, the date and the inscription could have been added *after* the house was built, of course. They often were. I think the house is much older than that.'

'So even in a spot as remote as this, it could have been a priest's hole?' asked Lloyd.

'Well, especially in a spot as remote as this. They were quite common in The Midlands and in Shropshire, which is the next-door county of course. Many of them were built by one man, a carpenter called Nicholas Owen. He was very short and his nickname was Little John. They were usually built behind fireplaces, around chimneystacks or sometimes beneath floorboards in the attics. So this one has all the hallmarks.'

There was a silence while the occupants of the house digested this news. Lloyd focussed on one aspect of The Missing Room that had been troubling him.

'But if it was a hidey hole,' he said slowly, how did people get out? We've not dared even get in, but to get out would be another matter.'

'They could have used a rope-ladder,' suggested Alex.

'Or there's this bit here, look, that seems to be the beginning of a staircase,' said Mona.

'In that case,' said Lloyd, 'why is there that opening from the attic?'

'Maybe they wanted two entrances,' said Merfyn, 'so if their hunters found the stairs they could escape through the attics.'

'Still doesn't explain how they got out through the attics,' said Lloyd. 'I don't think it would be easy, even with a rope.'

'Maybe there's another way in – one that we haven't found.'

The others pondered this for a moment, then Alex raised his hand with his index finger extended, as if he were in school.

'Yes?' said Merfyn with a smile.

'The inscription says Deliver Redeemer Our Souls This Awful Night,' he said. 'If that was added in 1664, that was after the Catholics were being persecuted. Why would they write *this awful night* then?'

Good point, thought Lloyd.

'Good point,' said Merfyn. 'I've been wondering about that myself. It's perfectly possible of course that it was a priest's hole at first, and then used by others later. Puritans could be living in the house then. But there's something else. The word 'awful' didn't mean terrible in the seventeenth century. Its original meaning was awe-inspiring, wondrous. The other meaning didn't

211

come till much later. So if the inscription was added in the seventeenth century when larger part of the house was built, it would mean '*this wondrous night*', and if it was added later, it would mean '*this terrible night*.' Perhaps it was deliberately ambiguous.'

'And we worked out that the initials of the inscriptions spell out Dros Tan,' said Alex. 'Could that have been a clue to the hiding place?'

'Mmm, an intriguing thought,' said Merfyn. 'Something that Welsh Nonconformists would understand and their English persecutors wouldn't. I've never heard of anything like that before, but it's a possibility. Another possibility is that at the time of the English Civil War after 1641 there were plenty of Cavaliers who had to hide from Roundheads. It could have been written by one of them. And there's one more thing.'

'What?' said Alex and Lloyd.

'When Charles II was defeated at the Battle of Worcester in 1651, he fled from house to house, often using hidey-holes. These were well documented, because years later, after he was restored to the throne, he told Pepys all about it. One of his hiding places was of course the famous Oak Tree. That was near Boscobel House in Shropshire. That has a number of hidey-holes. One of them was near something called The Cheese Room. It was said he was saved from discovery because the pursuivants' bloodhounds were put off his scent by some particularly pungent cheeses.'

He paused.

'This used to be called The Cheese Room, didn't it?'

'Well!' said Mona. 'What a co-incidence.'

But Merfyn wasn't finished.

'About the time he was hiding in Boscobel – which looks a bit like this place, by the way, only bigger – he tried to flee into Wales, down the Severn Valley. At first he had to turn back because the river crossings were guarded by enemy troops. But this is one part of his years on the run that's shrouded in mystery. It's not clear what he did when he left Boscobel, but he resurfaced again in Bristol, which is, of course, on the Severn Estuary. So if he made his way from Boscobel to Bristol, it's logical that it would have been down the Severn Valley. But where did he stay for these missing days?'

The three looked at each other.

'You mean,' said Mona slowly, working it out, 'you mean he could have come here?' A high-pitched note of incredulity crept into her tone.

'I'm just saying it's an intriguing thought, a possibility,' said Merfyn. The Severn Valley isn't far from here. I know of no other priest's hole around here. Where else would he have stayed?'

'Just think,' said Mona. 'The Merry Monarch clutching my chimney-breast.' The comment was uncharacteristic, as was her almost girlish excitement.

'Is there any way of finding out?' asked Alex.

'That's highly unlikely,' said Merfyn. 'Historians have been trying to solve the mystery for years. So unless we stumble across some documents or he carved his initials in the brickwork up there.....'

He looked above the fireplace.

Lloyd stared at Alex, willing him to keep quiet about the bundle they'd found, but Alex appeared to have lost interest.

Maybe they'd never know. But even the possibility, indeed the likelihood of the place being used to afford someone protection centuries ago gave Lloyd some satisfaction. The Noddfa. Sanctuary.

Eighteen

St Mary's had transferred Lloyd to a consultant at Bronglais Hospital, Aberystwyth. He made an appointment with little hope of any benefit – none, in fact. He would doubtless be able to tell them more than they could tell him. He found the prospect dispiriting. Yet he didn't want to give up these routine visits. The conviction that he had some mysterious, killer disease that no-one had spotted frequently resurfaced when he was going through one of his rough patches. He still wanted to be on someone's books, as it were, as some kind of mental insurance policy.

But it was with a heavy heart that he went out to his car one Wednesday morning. At the last minute, just as he was about to set off down the lane, Alex came running out of the back door, waving wildly. Lloyd thought something must have happened. But when he wound down the passenger window, Alex said, 'Where are you going?'

'To Aberystwyth, for a hospital appointment.'

'Can I come?'

Lloyd didn't feel like company. But he didn't want to turn Alex down again.

'Hop in,' he said.

Alex seemed to sense Lloyd's mood and was himself quiet. In fact, Lloyd was at an extremely low ebb. Muscle pain had prevented him from sleeping well yet again, and he felt under par and close to panic. Before his return he had anticipated some sensation of sanctuary, of welfare even, but what little he had found on his arrival had quickly worn off. He was sick to death of being ill. Each time he began to hope he was making some progress, putting the worst behind him, he would suffer another traumatic bad spell. He could see no future in his career, and had no motivation or energy to do anything else, any meaningful activity that would fill his days. He'd just about managed to bring his drinking under control, but at what cost? He was deprived of his main source of solace, of entertainment even. It was a daily effort, and all he got in return was a growing sense of tedium.

Relationships were difficult, as his condition made him unreliable. What comfort he drew from Joan was overshadowed by the impossibility, the pointlessness of it all. And one of the few things he had hoped would bring a new meaning to his life, the reunion with his father, had hit a brick wall. There would always be the doubt his father's actions and motives.

He hated himself for wallowing in this self-pity, this introspection. Many times he had managed to shake off these moods, to be hopeful about the future, but now it was if he slumped back, exhausted by the effort of it all, with so little to show for it.

Driving over the mountains on a fine day could lift the spirits, summon a sense of freedom. But today there was low, claustrophobic cloud with no hint of sun behind it, no glimmer of hope.

Lloyd was roused from this brooding when he noticed the house on the right-hand side up ahead: the house in that image he carried around with him of a car wreck, of a mangled white car. It struck him all of a sudden that the car he was driving was white. He hadn't thought about it when he'd bought it. He put his foot down on the accelerator, and the car picked up speed along the straight road that ran alongside the river. He knew that just past the house the road would climb a little and then take a sudden turn up to the right. His foot was on the floor now and the steering wheel was juddering slightly. It was so easy to keep it there, to do nothing, to go into nothing. The house whizzed past in a blur. The road rose up before him and over its brow was a deep drop into the rocky river. Lloyd was bathed in a sense of relief, of peace that seemed entirely new to him, so long had it been since experienced anything remotely similar. Everything would be alright after all. Even though he was driving very fast, everything inside the car seemed to be in slow motion. It was as if he was trapped in two moments. One of his selves was here in the car. The other was outside, above it, watching. The outside self could see how fast the car was going, how quickly it was approaching the edge of the ravine. It wanted to tell the inside self to slow down, to get ready to take the corner. The inside wasn't listening.

Then suddenly the two moments merged. The outside and inside selves rejoined. As the car came up towards the brow, at the last minute, Lloyd took his foot off the accelerator and put it on the brake. The car screeched around the bend, and he just about managed to keep it on the road.

'Bloody hell!' said Alex. 'You scared me then.'

Lloyd had forgotten that Alex was there, beside him in the passenger seat. His heart was pounding furiously, and he was aghast at what he'd almost done. He didn't know what kept him from going over the edge. Perhaps Alex had cried out. The boy was looking at him curiously, as if he was trying to discern what had just happened. He could not know it all, because Lloyd himself had just discovered something himself.

The strange thing was that the sense of relief and peace that had come to him just seconds before stayed with him. And the thing he understood now was how his mother could have been feeling just before she went off the road. It didn't matter to him

217

that he would never, could never, know for sure. It was enough to come to this understanding. He had spent so long focussing on his father that he had not tried to work out what his mother had been going through. It was possible that she had come to the end of her tether, and could not in fact face her future, and live with what she had done. He knew now that oblivion, in a certain frame of mind can seem a valid alternative to a lifetime of imprisonment, imprisonment by circumstances. And the fact that he understood that, that he had been to the brink and survived, was a sense of immense comfort to him.

'Are they going to make you better at the hospital?' asked Alex.

'No, they can't do anything. But I can. It'll just take time.'

It was quite an effort for Lloyd to talk, to sound normal.

'So are you going to see your father again?'

It was Lloyd's turn to give Alex a curious look.

'Yes', said Lloyd, and he was surprised to hear the resolution in his own voice. 'But we'll have to take things slowly. I guess I'll have to learn to be patient. There's so much distance between us now.'

'You know, I've been thinking,' said Alex. 'About The Missing Room. There's missing room between people sometimes, isn't there?'

'How d'you mean?'

'Well, there are a lot of things that are hard to say to people, even when you want to more than anything else.'

'Like what?'

'I dunno,' said Alex, looking out of the window into the deep valley below. 'The things that are hard to say. I love you. I'm sorry. I'm scared of dying.'

'Or living,' said Lloyd, before he could stop himself.

'Yes,' said Alex.

'So what do you do to find your way across the missing room?'

'I dunno. Keep trying. Not give up. Do you think the King might have carved his initials in the missing room at The Noddfa?'

'It's a bit of a long shot, but I suppose it's not impossible.'

'Do you think Mona's going to get a builder in to open it up?'

'I don't think she wants to just yet, no.'

'But one day we might be able to get into it, mightn't we?'

'Yes, one day.'

They were climbing up to the top bend above Devil's Elbow, where his mother had crashed. Somehow, it had lost some of its macabre mystique.

'Because you know what the cure for boredom is, don't you?' asked Alex.

'What?' said Lloyd, even though he knew the answer.

'Curiosity.'

And after all, Lloyd was still curious.

Nineteen

To Lloyd's surprise, the consultant was thorough. She was a woman of about fifty, a little grey creeping into her fair hair at the temples. It suited her. She greeted him in Welsh. He responded likewise, but then explained in English that his Welsh was not up to describing his symptoms. Neither really was his English, he thought as he said it. She seemed to have read his notes carefully and knew about the various things he's tried, like the CBT. She asked him if there'd be any changes.

'Sometimes I think I'm gradually getting a bit better,' said Lloyd. 'I'm spending less time in bed. But then when I get a bad patch it's like I'm back to square one every time. And I've been drinking a lot, although I'm controlling it a bit better now.'

She nodded. She didn't waste words. She got him to take of his shirt and climb on the couch. She gave his abdomen a good prodding. She was the first one who'd done this. When she'd finished she took off her glasses and placed them carefully on her desk in front of her.

'Well, the good news is that you feel you're making some progress, even if you sometimes get frustrated that it's not enough. It's natural that when you have a bad spell it feels as if you're starting again from scratch. But it's not keeping you as bedridden as it used to. That's an improvement. And your liver seems to be bearing up.'

'It's just that, at my low ebbs I can't help feeling that I've got some fatal disease that no-one has spotted.'

She looked at her computer screen.

'I see that when you were in London you had just about every blood test known to man, and there are no new symptoms, so it's highly unlikely that we're missing something.'

She was easy to talk to, and Lloyd found himself in the unusual position of wanting to say more. He told her more about his drinking.

'It's the only time I forget about the aches and pains, when life seems normal again,' he said.

'Well you don't need me to tell you that that's not going to help. Far from it.'

She went on to recite the familiar mantra of what he needed to do: pace himself, rest, get some gentle exercise, eat healthily, give it time. She smiled as if to say, 'Anything else?'

He didn't want to leave it there. He decided on the spur of the moment to relate the strange episode on the journey there – the two selves. But he left out the bit about speeding towards the edge. She looked at him thoughtfully, sucking the arm of her glasses.

'Were you having suicidal thoughts?' she asked, getting straight to the nub of it.

'Not exactly,' said Lloyd. 'But it was as if I was in another place, and I was driving way too fast.'

'This type of illness can cause a lot of stress,' she said. 'The weird symptoms, the uncertainty, the way your life has been turned upside down. Try to be good to yourself. I'll see you again in three months. And I'm going to give you my mobile number.' She took a piece of paper from a pad and wrote it down. 'Feel free to ring me at any time.'

Lloyd already felt a lot better.

'The other thing I can do is include you in a study I'm going to conduct about ME sufferers. It would mean filling in some questionnaires about your symptoms, reactions, lifestyle – that kind of thing. Maybe take part in some interviews over the phone. Would you be interested in that?'

'Yes,' said Lloyd straightaway. 'Yes, I'd like that very much.'

'Good. I'll be in touch.'

Lloyd found Alex in the music store where he'd left him.

'How'd it go?' asked Alex.

'Still no miracle cures,' said Lloyd. 'But I'm going to be part of a study looking into it.'

'Will that make a difference?'

'Well, we'll have to see. But it feels good just to be taking part, as if someone's taking the illness seriously, that my opinions count. And already it feels as if I'm not so alone.'

Lloyd was a little nervous about the drive back. If Alex was, he didn't show it. As they approached the house by the river, Lloyd's mouth was dry and it was difficult to swallow. His head was swimming. He took long breaths and managed to keep his nerve, and when they'd passed it he began to relax.

At The Noddfa, Mona had two visitors, drinking tea in the kitchen. They were her cousins, Gwen and Enfis, or rather her second cousins as Mona was always quick to specify. That would make them Lloyd's third cousins, he supposed. They were somewhat older than Mona. He never knew them very well, and only ever saw them at the family gatherings of his childhood – weddings, funerals and so on. But his memories of them were vivid. He used to think of them as a comedy act. Even though they were sisters they were very different. Gwen, the elder, was tall, big-bosomed and stately, whereas Enfis was short, feisty and funny. As weary as Lloyd was after the day's events, he felt obliged to stay and make conversation for a while. Alex grew grumpy at the introductions and quickly disappeared.

They'd been up to see Great Uncle Stanley.

'Making even less sense than last time,' said Enfis. 'Still, he's marvellous for his age.' She related a story or two about him in

223

his younger days – he was clearly quite a character. She laughed till she cried and, wiping away a tear, said. 'Oh, we still laugh about it now.' This was one of her catchphrases. Gwen didn't look as if she'd laughed at anything for a good while.

'Mona's been telling us about your explorations in the attic,' she said to Lloyd. He looked quickly at Mona. She gave an almost imperceptible shake of her head – she hadn't said anything about the letters.

'Well, you wouldn't catch me up there,' said Enfis. 'Tell them about your shivers, Gwen.'

Gwen did so with relish.

'Well, when we were living here as girls, before Gran died, I always shivered when I was going down the corridor up the front stairs, about half way down, just where that missing space is. Of course I got used to it and didn't think much about it after a while. But a few years later, after we left and I'd met Ian, I brought him up here to show him around. I didn't say a word about the shivers because I knew he pooh-poohed that kind of thing. I let him go in front of me down the corridor. And when he got to the spot he suddenly stopped dead in his tracks. He sort of jerked and gave a little shout. I asked him what it was and he said it was as if he'd walked into a freezer. So then I told him about my shivers in exactly the same spot.'

'And then there's the sliding panel in the front room,' said Enfis. 'Tell him about that, Gwen.'

Gwen looked a little annoyed that her ghost story had been cut short.

'Well, you know more about that than I do,' she said, giving her sister a meaningful look.

So Enfis described the built-in cupboard in the front room, or what they used to call the parlour. It was a floor-to-ceiling affair in oak, covering a triangle in one corner of the room above the cellar steps which lead down from a door in the front hall. The top part of the cupboard, about two-thirds of its length, had double doors opening up into an alcove, which Mona had always kept as a sort of cocktail cabinet, if that wasn't too grand a name for it. Underneath was another set of double doors, about a foot high, and behind these there was a cupboard, where Mona used to keep photograph albums and, thought Lloyd, the family Bible.

'Well, at the back of that cupboard there used to be a sliding panel,' said Enfis. 'You could climb through on to the top of the cellar steps, and then go out of the cellar door into the attic.'

'Or in your case, Enf, from the outside, up the cellar steps and through the back of the cupboard into the parlour,' said Gwen, peering at her sister rather sternly over the top of her glasses.

Enfis gave a rather girlish giggle and coquettish wiggle of her shoulders.

'Mam used to keep the door from the cellar into the front hall locked, so she never knew how I got back in if I was late and she'd locked the back door. When I was about seventeen I started seeing Ben George from Bargoed Hall. He was a bit like the local squire's son and his parents didn't approve of us seeing each other. Neither did my mother – she didn't want them looking down on me. But I used to creep out along the lane by the orchard, and he used to come galloping over the hill on his horse, like in an old western. Then I used to sneak back in through the cellar and through the cupboard.'

Enfis was always good at telling a tale. The mention of the sliding panel had stirred some ancient memories in Lloyd.

'Did you know about the cupboard, Mona?'

'Of course. You used to want to play with it when you were small. It's amazing how kids just seem to gravitate towards places they shouldn't go. I had it nailed up.'

'They used to use the parlour for prayer meetings,' said Gwen. 'And when they heard someone coming down the front hall, they could escape through the cupboard down the cellar steps and outside.'

'What kind of prayer meetings?' asked Lloyd.

'Nonconformists,' said Gwen. 'I've got a book about it at home. The Noddfa's mentioned, but it's mainly about a man called Williams from a farm called Ysgafell near Caersws. He was one of the leading Nonconformists of the time of the Restoration, and they were persecuted with particular vigour in Mid-Wales – imprisoned without trial, transported, and sometimes their houses were burnt down.'

'No wonder they wanted to worship in secret,' said Enfis.

'Let's go and have a look,' said Lloyd.

The four of them filed down the front hall into the front room and Lloyd opened the bottom cupboard doors. It was still full of photo albums. Lloyd took them out. The cupboard was a plain rectangle. At the back were two horizontal planks.

'The upper one used to drop down behind the lower one if you pushed it in the right place,' said Enfis.

'Where?' asked Lloyd.

'The top right hand corner, if memory serves.'

Lloyd couldn't resist pressing it there, even though he knew it had been nailed up. Nothing happened.

'Let's go and see the outside,' he said.

In the front hall, there was now a heavy sideboard against the top cellar door, so they went out of the front door, down the garden into the orchard, and in through the outside cellar door which was always kept open. Lloyd climbed up the stone steps on the far wall which led up to the blocked door into the front hall. On the right hand side at the top was the outline of the cupboard in reverse – the bulb of the alcove, and below it the two planks of the bottom cupboard. Lloyd inspected it closely. He could see the grooves on either side of the planks where the upper one would slide down. Then it was an easy hop onto the top cellar step.

Here it was, then. Concrete proof that The Noddfa had a secret past. The episode had rekindled Lloyd's interest in the history of the house and The Missing Room. After the girls, as Mona called them, had left, he asked Mona if she thought the panel was connected with The Missing Room.

'Well, it's certainly an escape route,' she said. 'If the stairs from The Missing Room came down by the dining room fireplace, the dining room door is opposite the front room door, so it would have been just a short hop across the hall and then out through the cupboard.'

'Hmm, true,' said Lloyd. 'I've got an idea. Have you got an atlas?'

'An atlas?'

'Yes, a road atlas.'

'I think there's one in the Land Rover. But what do you....?'

Lloyd ran out to get it.

'Why don't we see if we can find that house with the Royal Oak,' he said, when he'd brought it back and opened it on the kitchen table. 'We could go and see it. What did Merfyn say it was called? Boscobel, wasn't it? Somewhere past Telford.'

They spent a long time looking, tracing their fingers across the area where they thought it might be. Suddenly Mona pounced.

'There it is, look,' she said. 'Boscobel House and The Royal Oak. It's got one of those little house symbols. That probably means you can visit it.'

'Let's go tomorrow,' said Lloyd. Mona readily agreed. He'd forgotten all about his tiredness. In fact he was feeling better than he had done for ages.

He was up early in the morning, in time for breakfast. Alex showed no interest in joining them on the trip to Boscobel.

'Well, don't get up to any mischief,' Mona told him, 'and pop up to see Great Uncle Stanley.'

It was a misty, humid day, the kind of weather that made Lloyd feel claustrophobic and uneasy. They took the country roads to Shrewsbury, where they joined the A5 which then led into the M54. Just past Telford there was a sign for Boscobel House. They followed it off the motorway and took the next right. After

227

a while they saw a yellow sign propped up on a grass verge, saying Boscobel House. Lloyd couldn't really tell whether the arrow was meant to be pointing straight ahead or to the right. He carried straight on – and on, and on, and on, down a straight, flat, narrow road.

'We probably should have turned right at the sign,' he said, but he carried on. In fact there was nowhere to turn around. When he thought the road could not go on much longer without them coming to some kind of drive or farm lane, the road seemed to go on just as much again. At last they came to a crossroads, and there in front of them was Boscobel House.

'Good hiding place,' said Mona. 'Seems in the middle of nowhere.'

It resembled The Noddfa in some ways, but was bigger. The timber frame part was an L-shape, and the beams in the foot of the L were a little more crooked than those in the stroke, suggesting it was the original cottage. Again like The Noddfa, the newer part was a storey higher. But then added to that was a castellated stone tower.

They bought tickets from the shop in one of the redbrick stables around the farmyard. They'd just missed a guided tour and there wasn't another for a couple of hours, but they could wonder around and guides would be on hand to answer any questions. The entrance was in the oldest part. In the first couple rooms there were displays of butter and cheese-making equipment which took Mona's fancy.

'Ooh, my grandmother used to have one like that,' she said, pointing at a cheese press.

Lloyd was impatient to get to the hiding place, and he gently but firmly ushered her down the corridor, through a small entrance hall and into the parlour in the newer wing. Here they found a guide with a badge saying David. Before Lloyd knew what was happening Mona whipped out a photo of The Noddfa and waved it under his face.

'We think we've got a hiding place,' she said.

For a moment David looked startled, as if he thought she was a little mad, but as she described it and the sliding panel he began to take an interest. Lloyd quoted the inscription on the front, and the date.

'Oh well, that more or less clinches it,' said David.

'We even thought Charles II may have hid there when he fled from Boscobel,' said Lloyd.

'Well, I can tell you for certain he didn't,' said David.

'How come?' asked Mona.

'Because he set out for Wales but he only got as far as a mill at Madeley a few miles from here. They were going to take the ferry across but enemy forces were guarding the river. We know that from his own account of the escape as he recounted to Pepys years later, but also from Thomas Blount who wrote about it at the time. Look, we've got Blount's record here.'

He indicated a small book in a glass-topped case on a table by the window.

'So he came back here,' said David.

'Were there ever Nonconformists' holes like there were priests' holes,' asked Lloyd.

'I've never heard of one being purpose-built,' said David. 'They weren't as detectable as Catholics, of course. But that doesn't mean they didn't use them. The date on your house is interesting – 1664. In that year the Government passed The Conventicle Act which forbade conventicles, or religious assemblies of more than five people outside the Church of England. That led to groups like the Nonconformists and the Coventanters. And two years before that The Quaker Act was passed, which required people to swear an oath of allegiance to the King, something Quakers refused to do. So there were plenty of people who had to hide at that time.'

'Hmmm, Quakers – I'd never thought of that,' said Lloyd.

'The founder of The Quakers, George Fox, had gone around Mid-Wales preaching in the late 1650s, before The Restoration,' said David. 'Many liked what they heard. They were turbulent times, with first Catholics and then Protestants being persecuted, so people were intrigued by the idea that they could commune directly with God, without the clergy as intermediaries, telling them what to do. The Quakers spurned churches of course. They called them steeple-houses. Back then they often met on remote hilltops.'

Lloyd and Mona looked at each other. This was quite a lot to take in. David took them upstairs to see the famous hiding holes. There were two. The first one was in the bedroom above the parlour, a cupboard behind a panel to the left of the fireplace. In the floor of the cupboard was a trapdoor which led to the floor below. This could have been a privy, or a decoy for the real priest's hole in the attic above, or both, said David. At any rate, it was not where Charles II hid. That was behind a door across the hall, up narrow stairs. They followed David up. Just at the top, in the floorboards of the attic, was another trapdoor, opened up to reveal a rectangular recess underneath. Mona and Lloyd clambered up and stood around the hole. It was about five feet deep and four by four square. The top few steps of the stairs could be pulled back to give access into it.

'It can't have been very comfortable for him,' said David. 'He was more than six feet tall.'

'It's about the same size as the one at our place,' said Mona. 'I'd have thought they'd have built them a bit more man-sized.'

'Well, they were there to hide people,' said David. 'They couldn't be too obvious.'

Lloyd was surprised. He'd always had a reservation that the space at The Noddfa was too small to hide a man. But this was indeed similar. As was the attic itself, although smaller and completely renovated and spotless. It was where they stored cheese.

'See these little grooves in the floor?' said David. 'That's where the acid from the cheese would drip.
There was a reason for that.'

He left a dramatic pause.

'What?' asked Lloyd and Mona.

'The smell,' said David. 'Pursuivants and the people hunting for the King sometimes used dogs to sniff out their man. The smell of old cheese put them off the trail.'

Lloyd and Mona exchanged nods. It confirmed what Merfyn had said.

'Were there marks like that on our Cheese Room floor?' Lloyd asked Mona.

'Oh, I can't remember,' she said. 'It used to have some old lino on it before I had it carpeted. But I kept out of the way while they did it.'

Mona ticked off on her fingers the remarkable similarities between Boscobel and The Noddfa: the hiding place itself, the Cheese Room, the sliding panel, the escape route. David thought there was little doubt that it had been used as a religious refuge.

'By the way,' said Lloyd, 'does Boscobel have a meaning?'

'It comes from the Italian *bosco bello* – beautiful wood,' said David. 'And the Noth-va?'

'Sanctuary,' they said together.

Outside, now that they were here, Lloyd wanted to see the Royal Oak where the defeated monarch had hid. Mona told him she needed to sit down – she'd wait for him on a bench in the yard. Lloyd walked out to the meadow in front of the house and there, right in the middle, surrounded by iron railings, was the regal tree. He could only suppose that at the time, it was surrounded by other trees, otherwise it would have been a pretty conspicuous hiding-place. He tried to soak in the atmosphere. It was inspiring that so much history was made here. But somehow, he was thinking more about The Missing Room.

On the way back, Mona said, 'Well, at least we know Charles II never made it as far as The Noddfa.' She sounded disappointed. She'd always had a weak spot for the monarchy. 'What do you think?'

'I think The Missing Room was probably left as a space, a hiding-place, when the new wing was added to the cottage. The new owner would have been Catholic, and it would have been easy to leave a gap between the chimney stack and the new wall. But the inscription and the date were probably added later, after The Restoration, by Quakers or Nonconformists.'

'Hmm, that would explain things,' said Mona. 'Don't get too close to the car in front.'

'I still think there's a bit missing,' said Lloyd. 'The way out. How could anyone have got up out of that hole?'

The house was silent when they got back. Lloyd went up to his room to change. On the way he passed the open door to Alex's room and popped his head round to say hello, but it was empty.

Mona was putting the kettle on.

'Ask Alex if he wants some tea,' she said.

'He's not in his room,' said Lloyd.

'Oh? Unlike him. Maybe he's with Great Uncle Stanley. I'll take him up a cup and see.'

But when she came down she shook her head.

'Says he hasn't seen the boy,' she said. 'In fact he denies all knowledge of him. I checked the bathroom too. I wonder where he's got to?'

Lloyd went outside and shouted at the top of his voice. He went round to the front of the house, down the garden and into the orchard, yelling as he went. He even looked inside the cellar. Alex seemed to have vanished.

Twenty

Lloyd strolled down to the yard, giving the odd shout. At this point he couldn't have said he was more than mildly concerned – just curious as to Alex's whereabouts. Gareth was getting the cows into the sheds for milking. He'd been out and about all afternoon, but had seen neither hide nor hair of him. He didn't think he could have left the house. Lloyd went back in and relayed this to Mona. He could feel his concern growing stronger. He and Mona looked at each other, trying to gauge maybe just how worried they should be.

'I'm going up to his room again to double-check,' he said. 'Perhaps he's having some kind of game with us.'

There was the crumpled outline of a body on his bed. A game console was on the floor by the side of it. Lloyd looked under the bed and inside the wardrobe, feeling a little foolish as he did so. Alex was nowhere to be seen. Lloyd stood in the middle of the room, scratching his head, wondering what to do next.

Suddenly he froze. He thought he'd heard a noise. He stood stock-still, his hand still only an inch or so away from his head, straining to hear. There was silence, punctuated only by the occasional farmyard sound. He crept a step or two forward, and then he heard it again – a rat-tat-tat – three faint bumps. They seemed to be coming from outside the room, round the corner from the open door. He tiptoed out of the room, and put his ear to the wall on the right of the front hall. There it was again, an unmistakable sequence: rat-tat-tat. He cupped his hands to his mouth, put them to the wall and shouted 'Alex! Alex!' Then he cupped his ear and put that to the wall. He was pretty sure he could just make out a muffled voice, but he couldn't tell what it was saying. It must be Alex, and he must somehow have got into The Missing Room.

'Wait there!' he shouted, as absurdly clichéd as it was. 'I'll go and get the key to the attic.'

There was another muffled cry, and Lloyd hoped Alex had got the message. He went back down to Mona, saying he must have found another way into The Missing Room. But when she went up to get the key, it wasn't there.

'He must have taken it,' she said. 'But how did he know it was there?' They were hurrying up to the attic.

'Don't ask me,' said Lloyd.

'You didn't tell him, did you?'

'I don't know where it is myself. You'd never let me in there unless you were there.'

'I keep it in a jewellery box on my dressing table,' said Mona. 'How did he find it there?'

'We'll soon find out,' said Lloyd

The attic door was open. They went straight to the triangular hole. There was a light shining up towards them, the beam of a torch. Lloyd got on his knees and poked his head through. The beam was coming from the bottom of The Missing Room. It caught Alex's face, which looked white and strained.

'Nice of you to drop in,' said Lloyd.

'I think I've broken my leg,' groaned Alex.

'How on earth are we going to get you out?'

'I found a way in,' said Alex. 'It's in the opposite corner of the gable, behind some boxes. It's another triangle between the beams, like this one. There are some rough steps down here, but then I fell.'

Lloyd crawled over to the other side of the gable, giving the news to Mona over his shoulder. There, behind some cardboard boxes, was an identical triangular gap between the beams at the bottom of the gable end. Lloyd peered through. There was a kind of ledge about a foot below, in the gap between the wall and the chimneystack, and then a series of rough ledges – they weren't symmetrical enough to be called steps - leading down to the secret chamber. Alex had been right, thought Lloyd, when he said that he thought there was a corner of The Missing Room they hadn't looked at properly with the torches. The ridges emerged in the bottom left-hand corner as viewed from the attic. They were covered in rubble, which would have made the descent precarious. Lloyd could see Alex's legs in the light of the torch. Neither looked broken.

'Keep him talking,' he said to Mona. 'I'm going to fetch a rope.'

'There's one in the cellar,' said Mona.

When he got back she told him she didn't think Alex had broken his leg.

'He can move it,' she said. 'It's his ankle that's hurting him.'

Lloyd crawled back to the new-found hole and tossed down one end of the rope. It fell short, and Alex couldn't reach it. Lloyd repeated the exercise a couple of times. At the fourth attempt Alex managed to grasp hold of it, and Lloyd told him to tie it securely under his arms.

'Now, look, we don't think you've broken your leg,' shouted Lloyd. 'See if you can position yourself with your back to me. I'll tug on the rope and you push with your good leg and your backside.'

Alex tucked the torch into the rope and slowly, gingerly, managed to shift himself round. Then, with many cries and groans, which Lloyd thought were somewhat theatrical, he was inched up. About half way up he sat heavily on some rubble and slipped down half of the way again.

'I can't do it,' he said.

'Let's have a rest,' said Lloyd.

Mona had gone to get him a bottle of water which they lowered down on a piece of string. Alex had a good long drink. Refreshed, he began again, inch by inch, making sure he got a firm foothold and bumhold each time. At last he was near enough for Lloyd to grab hold of him and virtually drag him the last few inches. Then it was still a struggle to get him up to the gap into the attic and through it. He lay gasping on the floor and Mona examined his ankle. It was red and swollen.

'Yes, I think it's a sprain,' she said. 'Let's get you downstairs.'

He hopped down with his arm around Lloyd's shoulder.

'How did you find the key?' asked Mona.

'Great Uncle Stanley told me where it was,' said Alex.

'The bugger!' said Mona. 'I'm surprised he remembered, or even knew in the first place, come to that. And you, you little devil, going into my bedroom. Once you're on the mend I'll have a few words to say to you. He told me he hadn't seen you at all.'

'We said it would be our secret,' said Alex with a sly grin. 'But I found the secret way in, didn't I?'

They got him down to the living room. Mona set him up on the sofa with a cushion under his ankle. She knelt down to have a closer look, twisting it this way and that, ignoring his wails and seeming in fact to be enjoying herself.

'How's it feeling now?'

'A bit better,' said Alex grudgingly.

'No, nothing broken. Sprain or bad twist. You'll just have to rest it for two or three days. I'll put some ice on it to keep the swelling down.'

'Aren't you going to get the doctor?' asked Alex.

Mona adopted her no-nonsense tone, which involved her use of the archaic second person pronoun.

'What thee talking about? It's just a little sprain.'

'How do you know?'

'I used to be a nurse.'

Alex looked impressed.

'Now, tell us what you were doing down there in the first place.'

Alex gave a sigh as if he realised he was in no position to prevaricate.

'Well, I thought there must be a way down to The Missing Room, and I wanted to explore. I went in to see Great Uncle Stanley to see if he knew anything. He told me where the key was. I'm sorry, Auntie Mona, I suppose curiosity got the better of me.'

'Well, thee just be grateful thee'st laid up, otherwise I wouldn't be half so nice about it. Go on.'

'I got a torch and had another good look down from the attic, through the first hole. I wriggled through it a bit more, so I could get a better look over the edge of the floorboards. I concentrated on that left-hand corner where I thought we hadn't looked properly before. I thought I could see some darkness, where the torch didn't light up the wall, so I thought that could be a way in. So I looked around a bit and moved some old boxes, and there was this identical hole the other side, a triangle where the plaster between the beams was missing. I stuck my head in and I could see this sort of pile of rubble leading down to where I thought The Missing Room would be. So I squeezed through and inched my way down, but when I was about a third of the way down I slid and ended up in The Missing Room, and that's when I hurt my ankle. So you see, there is a way in. Under the rubble it felt like a kind of rough stairs, or ramp with ledges.'

He looked at his audience with the air of a magician pulling something unexpected out of a hat.

'And I found something else.'

'What?'

'Some graffiti. It's in Welsh. *Ffrind y Gwir*. I know *ffrind* is friend. What's *gwir*?'

'Truth,' said Mona. 'Friend of the truth.'

Lloyd sat up straight in the armchair.

'The Friends of Truth,' he said. 'That's what the Quakers were called when they were founded, wasn't it?'

'Was it?' said Mona.

'Was it old writing?' Lloyd asked Alex.

'Yes. Squiggly. Who are The Quakers?'

Lloyd and Mona told him all they'd learnt at Boscobel.

'So it looks as if it might have been built as a priest's hole when the new wing was added,' said Lloyd. 'Then later whoever lived here converted to Quakerism, and possibly added the inscription. After all, they believe in direct communication with God. Then later still there were Nonconformist gatherings, after their meetings were outlawed. So at one time or another, people of many religions sought refuge at The Noddfa, according to the diktats of the day.'

'What about Jews and Muslims?' asked Alex.

'Who knows.....?' began Lloyd.

'And Buddhists and Taoists and...'

'Yes, alright Alex, we get the message.'

''In my Father's house there are many mansions',' quoted Mona.

Lloyd looked at her. What did she mean? Was it a simple Biblical quote, referring to all the people who'd hid there, or was she hinting that there was room in his father's life for him too? She returned his stare, inscrutable.

'What about the escape route through the cupboard?' asked Alex.

'I think that must have been put in later,' said Mona 'when the Nonconformists started worshipping here. If you think about it, the only reason for a sliding panel would be so that those already in the front room could get away without going into the front hall. Otherwise, it would be quicker to go through the cellar door in the hall, rather than go into the front room and through the cupboard.'

'I think you're right,' said Lloyd.

Later that evening, as he was sitting with Great Uncle Stanley, the phrase Friend of the Truth kept popping up in Lloyd's thoughts. He'd come up to fetch the supper things and ask him some questions, but it had not started well.

'Was that OK?' Lloyd had asked, taking the tray from his adjustable table, like the ones that go over hospital beds.

'Yes, I will have some, thanks,' said Great Uncle Stanley.

'What will you have,' asked Lloyd, confused.

'I don't know,' said Great Uncle Stanley. 'I'll think about it.'

He'd asked Great Uncle Stanley about The Missing Room, not expecting much sense, but had been surprised when he launched straight in.

'Well, we always knew there was a space that was unaccounted for. Some people thought it was just the chimney. Myself, I always wondered about a priest's hole.'

'And you knew where the key to the attic was?'

'Well, he asked for it. I was a bit curious myself as to what he might find.'

'Mona isn't best pleased.'

'It was just a bit of fun. Did he find anything?'

Lloyd told him about the *Ffrind y gwir*.

'Hmm, Quakers. Never thought about that. This has always been a house of secrets.'

Lloyd suddenly decided he'd had enough of secrets, enough of beating around the bush. He wanted to tell him about the letters, about the fake death. He reasoned it could do no harm, as he talked nonsense most of the time, so if he repeated it, no-one would take much notice. So he did.

'Well, well,' said Great Uncle Stanley. Lloyd wasn't sure at first that he'd taken it all in, but it soon became clear he had.

'I always wondered about Mona at the funeral. Poker-faced. Dry-eyed. As if she was concentrating on something, playing a part. But I'd never have guessed he was still alive. How is he?'

Lloyd said he was fine, but had a new life, and Lloyd didn't think there was enough room for him in it.

'I just can't understand why he ran away and abandoned me. Even if he thought he might be implicated in Mum's death, why couldn't he stay and face the music?'

'I think I can set your mind at rest about that,' said Great Uncle Stanley. 'He came to see me the night before the accident.'

He suddenly fell silent.

'And?'

The old man looked lost in thought.

'What did he say?' asked Lloyd.

'There's twelve of them now, look. I think they're coming nearer.'

Great Uncle Stanley was looking out of the window. Lloyd groaned out loud. Surely he wasn't going to wander off now, not when he was on the point of saying something of vital importance.

'Uncle Stanley,' said Lloyd, and then, much louder, 'Uncle Stanley!'

'Mmm?' said Great Uncle Stanley.

'What did my father say to you, the last time you saw him?'

Again the old man's gaze turned to the window. He seemed to be thinking hard. Lloyd was breathing hard.

'He suspected your mother of having an affair. He said he still loved her, but he wouldn't stand in her way. His main concern was you. He was worried sick about your future. He said it might be best if your mother left.'

'So why did he go after her?'

'Impulse, I suppose. One last try.'

Lloyd sat in silence while he digested this. Great Uncle Stanley was staring contentedly out of the window. Lloyd was struck by

240

the word 'suspected'. Ever since his dream, he'd been unable to shake off his own suspicion that his father had engineered her death. But if he still only suspected the affair the night before, he couldn't have seen the letters, because he hadn't come to The Noddfa the morning before the crash. He remembered Mona saying that his mother had confided her affair to Mona the night before her death. That same night, his father had gone to see Great Uncle Stanley, who was then living in a bungalow the other side of town. This backed up his father's story.

Lloyd was now ashamed of his suspicions. Great Uncle Stanley's story showed that Lloyd's own welfare had been uppermost in his father's mind. He'd just made a dreadful mistake on the spur of the moment. Things were beginning to make sense.

'Give yourself time,' said Great Uncle Stanley. 'And him. Sometimes people do the wrong thing for the right reason. He was probably doing what he thought was right at the time.'

Lloyd was on the point of saying that he'd given him twenty years, and enough was enough, but there was a huge bang which made them both jump.

'You see – I told you they were getting closer,' said Great Uncle Stanley. 'Fireworks.'

'It's thunder,' said Lloyd. It had seemed incredible when Great Uncle Stanley had spoken of fireworks that time. Maybe he meant thunder and lightning. Maybe there was method in his madness.

It was the storm that had been brewing all day. And when Lloyd heard the rain drumming on the windows, it was with a huge sense of relief and release.

Now that he'd begun to get things off his chest, Lloyd wanted to go on. His thoughts turned to Joan. He'd sensed lately a certain tension developing between them. Increasingly he was putting it down to the fact that he'd not told her the whole truth about his father. Secrets breed secrets, and while she was so patient about his moods, his brooding, his aimlessness, part of him knew there was a limit. She wouldn't wait forever for him to make up his mind. The thought scared him. Maybe if he told her everything, their closeness would be restored. His father after all had not sworn him to secrecy.

Joan had invited him down to Sunday dinner the next day. Rhys greeted him at the back door, with his now customary warm handshake and smile. It was good to see him so much better, yet Lloyd could not help feeling a slight twinge of jealousy when he saw him, although Lloyd himself was feeling remarkably energetic on what was turning out to be quite an eventful weekend.

Joan cooked a traditional Sunday roast – leg of lamb, mashed potato, greens from the garden, then apple crumble. After they finished, Rhys disappeared and, over the washing up, Lloyd told Joan his story. She kept putting things in the dish rack for him to wipe.

'That does explain a few things,' she said.

'Aren't you surprised?'

'I thought there was something, but not quite that, obviously.'

'It feels so much better now I can talk about him,' said Lloyd.

'I suppose you've got some unfinished business with him.'

'I suppose so.' Lloyd had begun to ask himself the question.

He and Joan had a couple of hours together, and they made the most of it. Mona had invited Ifor, his girlfriend, and Mrs Evans to tea, so Lloyd had to leave about four.

'So do you think you'll go and see your father?' asked Joan, as they hugged goodbye.

'Probably,' said Lloyd.

'And will you be coming back?'

'Yes,' said Lloyd with a smile, 'I'll be coming back.'

The visitors were in the kitchen at The Noddfa. Lloyd had been meaning to get in touch with Ifor, but of course, he hadn't. Mona had taken matters into her own hands. Ifor introduced him to

Betty, who was pretty, blond, but clearly no bimbo. She was very natural and funny, and they made a striking pair. Lloyd was surprised that Mrs Evans had come. He couldn't remember her ever being in the house before.

As they went through the living room on their way to the dining room for tea, Mona introduced them to Alex. He was still stretched out on the sofa, but his ankle was much better. He was monosyllabic.

Mona put on a good spread, with small filled rolls, various savoury pastries, Welsh cakes, and her old Sunday tea standby, tinned peaches and cream. Conversation was polite but cordial. Under questioning from Mona, Betty revealed that she was from Cardiff and doing post-grad research at Oxford into women novelists in Latin America. Mona was clearly impressed.

'We'd better be going soon,' said Ifor, after Mona had pressed more food on them than anyone wanted. 'But Lloyd, before we do, perhaps you could show us round the garden first? Mum's dying to see it, but she's too shy to ask.'

Mrs Evans nudged her son in the ribs and shook her head with a pinched smile.

'Ooh, what a good idea,' said Mona.

'Let me help you with the dishes first, Miss Davies,' said Mrs Evans.

'No, no I wouldn't hear of it. Off you go.'

Lloyd thought he discerned an exchange of looks between Ifor and Betty.

'I'll give you a hand, Mona,' she said. 'I'm not much of a one for gardens.'

Mona started to object but Betty was firm.

'I insist,' she said, getting up and stacking the plates. 'We can join them when we've finished.'

Ifor, his mother and Lloyd ambled slowly round the garden. Lloyd wasn't much of a guide, and in fact it was Mrs Evans who told them the names of all the plants and flowers.

Lloyd had the feeling that Ifor had something he wanted to get of his chest. And in due course, he did.

'Lloyd, I hope you don't mind, but I talked to Mum about your Dad.'

Lloyd stopped and looked at them both.

'And she's got something to tell you, haven't you, Mum?'

Mrs Evans looked embarrassed, as if she didn't know how to begin.

'Well, the thing is, I saw your father the day of the accident.'

Thoughts swirled around Lloyd's head. Was he here that morning after all? That meant he could have found the letters. He could only wait for more.

'I was walking towards the end of our lane and he came driving up the hill in the Land Rover,' continued Mrs Evans softly. 'He didn't see me.'

'But he didn't come here that morning,' said Lloyd.

'It was the afternoon,' said Mrs Evans. She let the words sink in.

'Are you sure it was that day?'

'Of course. I heard about the accident that evening. You don't forget something like that.'

'So all these years, you've known that he was alive after the accident?'

'Well, it seemed that way. It was confusing, when I read in the paper that the accident was sometime before twelve noon, when a passing car saw the flames and called the police. I saw him at half one. I told myself it couldn't be. But I knew what I saw.'

'And you've never said a word to anyone?' Lloyd hoped he didn't sound as if he were accusing her.

'It wasn't my place,' said Mrs Evans. 'I thought the Good Lord would provide an answer when it was time.'

'Go on, Mum,' said Ifor.

'Well, Ifor mentioned that you were finding it hard to come to terms with your father's disappearance, and you were wondering if there was something more behind it. I hope you don't mind. He did it because he wanted to help. It was meant to be, I know that now.'

'Mum, just get on with it.'

'When I saw your father coming up the hill, the sun was shining in his face, and I could see the glistening of tears streaming down it. And I saw the look on his face. It wasn't the look of hate, Lloyd. It was the look of love, the Lord knows, the look of someone who has lost the people he loves. I thought you should know that.'

Lloyd wasn't immediately sure what to make of her story, but he thanked her, and they went on their way.

He went to bed that night exhausted, but exhausted in almost a pleasant way, so different from the painful fatigue that had become his bedtime companion. It had been quite a weekend. Not that long ago it would have floored him, and maybe it still would in a day or two, but at least now he was feeling alright.

He knew he had been wrong about his father, wrong to fill the gaps with the blackest scenarios. It was he, Lloyd, who had created the gulf between them, and now he would have to see if he could he could bridge it, cross his own missing room, if it wasn't too late.

Twenty-one

Lloyd and his father sat on a bench on The Embankment, not far from Gordons Wine Bar where they'd met a few months before. It was a hot afternoon and Lloyd felt mellow. They'd been for a couple of pints in a nearby pub, where Lloyd had told his father about the discoveries in The Missing Room. Lloyd had decided to make a clean breast of everything, including his suspicions. His father had listened patiently.

'So you had me down as a murderer?'

Lloyd turned to look at him, to get a sense of how he was taking this. His face showed no sign of anger – in fact Lloyd thought he could detect a slight twitch of amusement. Lloyd was relieved.

'I think there were things I didn't understand, so I filled in the gaps with my worst imaginings. I'm sorry about that.'

His father said nothing.

'I was in a bad place myself,' he continued. 'Lost. Couldn't see things so clearly. I suppose you understand that?'

His father nodded.

'It's odd,' said Lloyd. 'When you see other people in a state, you think it'd be relatively straight forward for them to find their way back again. A bit of chivvying, jollying along. A few kind words.'

'Well, they can help,' said his father.

'I suppose they can. But it's not easy. Or quick.'

'No, it's not.'

The two sat in silence for a few moments, watching the boats go up and down the river.

'As we're laying our cards on the table,' his father said eventually, 'I suppose I should tell you that I did have some thoughts of murder that morning.'

He looked at Lloyd, as if he expected him to say something, but it was Lloyd's turn to keep quiet.

'When your mother told me she was leaving, I began to realise what it would mean for you. Whatever I said or did, it was bound to get out, and it would have been a scandal. You would have been scarred for life. Before I rang Mona, I did begin to think it would be better for you if she were dead. I found myself thinking how that could happen. But thank God I managed to pull myself together, tell myself I had to get a grip. I went after her without any kind of plan. Just to try to stop her, I suppose, get her to change her mind if I managed to catch up with her. But just before the crash I began to see it was madness. When she put her foot down at Devil's Elbow, I realised I'd never catch her. The car was faster than the Land Rover. I'd soon lose her. Then she'd be gone forever. There were no mobile phones or computers in those days, remember – it wasn't so easy to track people down. I was just on the point of giving up, turning around, when she crashed. Then I had the stupid notion of doing the disappearing act. Went into my own missing room, if you like. But once I'd thrown my watch into the car there was no going back. That one mad action locked me into a course of action. I'm very, very sorry I did. It's done neither of us any good. That's what I couldn't tell you before. But you seem to have changed your mind anyway.'

'Of course – the watch,' said Lloyd. 'I'd never really thought about that. It put you on the scene of the crime, as it were.'

'Exactly. On the way back I did have second thoughts about going away, but they'd find that watch....'

'You could still have stayed and faced the music, as Mona put it.'

'And what music would that be? Your mother running off with another man, your father a murderer – they'd have surely arrested me. No, you'd have been worse off than you are now.'

Lloyd digested this. For the first time, he began to understand why his father did what he did.

'Mrs Evans The Holding saw you that afternoon, driving up to The Noddfa. She said you were crying. And Great Uncle Stanley told me you'd gone to see him the night before, and were worried about me. So I began to see that I was wrong to blame you.'

'So they know? That I'm still alive?'

'Yes,' said Lloyd.

'I don't suppose it matters now,' said his father. 'It's wrong to think you can bury your past. It'll come back and claim you in the end.'

He adopted a more everyday tone.

'So what about you? How are you feeling now?'

'A bit better, I think. I've learnt not to expect miracles. I've cut down a lot on the drinking. I was coming to rely on it. It helped me escape from the pain, my sense of failure, but also from the past, and from the future.'

'Well, that's progress.'

'Yes. A day at a time. One of the big differences is this study into ME. It's a small thing in a way, but it means a lot. That I count for something. That someone is, sort of, well, taking an interest. It makes such a difference if someone takes an interest.'

'So does that mean you're going to be staying in this country for a while?'

'Yes,' said Lloyd firmly. 'I want to be part of this. I'll go back to The Noddfa for a while. I've been seeing Joan Hamer

Pantycelyn. She's been very good but I think she's been getting a bit fed up with all my dithering. Maybe we can make a go of it for a while, if she'll have me.'

'Sounds good. What about your career?'

'That'll have to be on hold for a while. Then we'll see what the future brings. Might you change your mind and come there one day?'

'Mmm, one day maybe. Things look a little different now, somehow. So you hanging round London for a few days?'

'Yeah, I'm staying with Jack and Jill and their new baby. And Alex is coming up for a couple of days. I'm going to take him to see the code-breaking machines in Bletchley Park.'

'Alex?'

'Molly's boy from Cardiff.'

'Oh yes,' said his father, rather wistfully, as if remembering a forgotten world. 'Well, if you're up for it, we'd love to have you over. Come for a barbecue on Sunday.'

'That'd be great,' said Lloyd. 'Are you sure?'

'Of course. Sorry it wasn't sooner, but it was bound to take Vicky a little time to get used to the idea.'

'Yes, I do realise that now.'

'But now she has, she and the children are dying to meet you.'

They went their separate ways after giving each other half hugs and pats on the back. Lloyd walked along the river to Waterloo. He'd surprised himself by stating so firmly his intention to go and live at The Noddfa. But when he'd said it, he knew it was the right thing to do. It had taken him a long time to get there, and he knew he'd miss the world of international diplomacy. What he would find to do, he didn't yet know. But his mind, now suddenly cleared and open and selfless for the first time in years, turned to the people who might have been holed up in the Missing Room over the years, preparing for and then possibly meeting death. Compared to those, his own preoccupations really didn't seem very significant at all.

Printed in Great Britain
by Amazon.co.uk, Ltd.,
Marston Gate.